MW00984670

Chamber of Bears

Avery Kloss

This is a work of fiction. Names, characters, places, and incidents either are the product of the author's imagination or are used fictitiously, and any resemblance to any persons, living or dead, business establishments, events, or locales is entirely coincidental.

CHAMBER OF BEARS

All rights reserved.

Copyright © 2017 by Avery Kloss
ISBN: 1979897530
ISBN-13: 978-1979897532

Cover art by Avery Kloss

This book is protected under the copyright laws of the United States of America. Any reproductions or other unauthorized use of the material or artwork herein is prohibited without the express written permission of the author.

First Print Edition: November 2017

"I am the bended, but not broken. I am the power of the thunderstorm. I am the beauty in the beast. I am the strength in weakness. I am the confidence in the midst of doubt. I am Her!" — Kierra C.T. Banks

CONTENTS

One

I woke with a start, realizing I had a bad dream, seeing the disjointed images of my family ... Kia, my mother, and Ara, my sister ... their voices in my ear, but it sounded as if they shouted ... someone crying. Sitting up, I brushed hair from my eyes, finding myself alone in the cave with the smell of smoke lingering from the fire the night before. An irrational panic swept through me, propelling me to my feet, where I stood upon a thick pelt.

"Ronan?" I rushed for the doorway, standing at the opening of the vast cavern, a lush valley before me. "Ronan?" Movement caught my notice, Wolf appearing a few paces away, staring at me with inquisitive eyes. "Where are they?" I knew he would not answer, the animal sniffing the air, unconcerned with whatever my troubles might be. He took a seat, resting his snout on the ground.

I hated that I feared being alone, always thinking the worst. Having been reunited with Ronan and Enwan, I struggled to accept the perfection that was my life now, my senses always alert for danger. Why could I not accept the joy the gods had given me? Why could I not surrender to what so clearly was, for the first time in my life, peace?

"They've gone hunting, Peta," I said to myself. "It's logical. It's expected, isn't it?" I glanced at Wolf. He had been my companion on the journey to this place, having followed me for days. Being orphaned and alone, we traveled together, although he still would not let me pet him. "Of course they're hunting."

Having mated most of the night, I doubted I would see the men again until later, when they returned with whatever they caught, anticipating the camp to be clean and the fire lit. I squinted into the distance, hoping to catch sight of Ronan or Enwan. I saw nothing other than the greenness of the valley, our cave carved in the side of a hill, a rocky path leading down towards a spring of heated water.

Thinking of the past, my sister, Ara, and I hunted and provided for Kia and Maggi, having lived in a forest far from here. A man of great intelligence and fortitude, Sungir, taught Ara and I how to hunt, knowing he would not always be there for us, the man living alone in the woods most of his life. He had taken us in, providing food and shelter. Those were some of the happiest times—a sanctuary—where I did not have to fear being stalked by big, hungry cats or the horrors of the white heathens, remembering their atrocities all too well.

"I shouldn't think of you so often," I muttered, but not a day went by that I did not miss my family, wondering what had happened to them, the pain of their sudden disappearance feeling like a thorn in the foot, one that could not be removed. I hated being alone, my shoulders drooping. Time could not pass fast enough, the men gone so long hunting. "I should hunt too." I would feel infinitely better if I were with them.

But, I was a woman. Women were meant to tend the fires and care for the babies, although I did not have a child of my own, not yet anyhow. I cast a glance at the wolf. "And what will you do today?" He would not answer me, sniffing the air with a blackish snout. Dark grey fur grew on his head, with white steaks upon the sides of his face, the rest of him brown and grey. "You wait for me to feed you, don't you?" I did feel safer with the animal around, his senses keen. He always alerted me to trouble, just as he had in the past.

As I glanced in the cave, the embers of the fire from the night before smoked, the wood for fuel all but gone. I needed to gather more soon and forage, looking for edibles here and there, the valley as fertile as any I had ever seen, the pickings ripe for the taking. Then I planned to beat out the pelts, leaving them in the sun for a while, although a part of me longed to hunt. My bow sat among my things, the men just learning how to use it, and craft one of their own. They often left so early, without waking me. Then, when they returned, they slept, exhausted from the hunt. I prepared the meals, keeping the fire going all evening, and submitting to their more carnal demands after supper, although that was far from a chore. I enjoyed that part of the day the most.

A smile toyed around my lips, memories of such things producing pleasing sensations. These feelings helped ease those of the pain and longing I felt for my family. "This is my life *now*." As I picked up a basket, intending on foraging, I spoke to myself. "I shouldn't dwell on the past. There's nothing to be done about it. I shall pray that my family is well." I prayed every day, typically finding a place of solitude among the trees to speak to the gods. "There's little else to do, isn't there?"

Slinging the bow around my shoulder, I carried tiny spear points affixed to firm pieces of wood in a separate leather satchel. I refused to be anywhere without the weapon, Sungir having taught me the value of it. Wolf noted my movements, getting to his feet. He always followed me, keeping watch. I left the cave then, venturing down the rocky path, passing large boulders on either side, until a field emerged. The grass grew high here, nearly to my belly. I stopped by the heated pool, leaving the bow and the bag of arrows on the ground.

Untying a leather skirt, it landed in the grass. "It smells a bit rotten, doesn't it?" I wore leather around my feet as well, removing that too. "You should come in,

Wolf." He sat at a distance, ever watchful, although he gazed at me lazily, knowing this to be our morning ritual, a quick cleaning, followed by a walk in the woods.

I adored the heated water, never having experienced such luxury before, the bottom of the pool rocky, yet slick. I floated on my back, gazing at the blueness of the sky, where clouds shielded the worst of the sun at the moment, but they would soon pass. Emerging cleaner, my hair hung wetly down my back. I grasped it, wringing it out, the water dampening the ground beneath me. Tying the leather skirt around my waist, I saw myself in the reflection of the pool, a woman with wide-set eyes and pale skin staring back at me. Wolf ambled over, sniffing the air.

"I know. You're impatient." I picked up the bow, tossing it over a shoulder with the satchel of arrows. "Where shall we go today? I'm tired of mushrooms. I'm hoping for berries and nuts." I planned to kill something small as well. I wished to maintain the hunting skills I acquired over the seasons, enjoying the challenge.

Walking on, my hair soon dried, the breeze tossing golden strands into my face. Wolf and I disappeared into a wooded area, birdcalls emanating from the branches above and tiny creatures rustling in the foliage. I climbed a tree a short while later, having chosen one that looked quite old, the bark rough against my skin. Its roots grew so large, some protruded from the earth. Wolf waited, licking his paw, as I grasped branch after branch, hoisting myself higher. I stopped when I had the best vantage point, seeing far into the valley, over the tops of all the trees to the mountains beyond.

"No sight of them." This wasn't a cause for worry though, because the men were young and strong; they could defend themselves, if need be. I stared into the distance, just as a large bird took flight, its wingspan immense. Breathing deeply, I felt fully awake now, the climb invigorating. "It's so beautiful here," I murmured, the warmth of the air like a lover's caress. "I can't imagine a more perfect place. If only my family could see it. How they'd love the hot water." I daydreamed of bathing with them, Maggi splashing around in the pool. "How I wish you were here."

The squawking of a noisy bird ended the wistful musings, my attention turning in another direction. Wolf waited, the animal ever patient, used to my odd whims. "All right. I'm coming." Reaching the ground, I took the bow over a shoulder with the arrows. "I hate foraging alone," I muttered, having always been with my mother and sisters for such tasks, the four of us often singing or engaging in discussion to help pass the time. I glanced at the wolf. "Now, all I have is you, and you won't even speak to me." I frowned. "You're hardly the best company." I felt far safer with the pet than being alone, though. He had yet to be fully grown, but his paws were quite large. He would appear fearsome as an adult, and I had to wonder if he might leave me then. "I mustn't dwell on that." I bent to examine a bush, finding several berries. "Ah, there we are." I picked whatever I could, having a bite of one. "Sour." I made a face.

Venturing forth, I found more berries and some edible greens, pulling a few from the ground, an odd-colored vegetable dangling. These tasted good raw and cooked, Kia having cut them into pieces for a tasty stew. Tired of walking, I took a rest a while later, drinking water from an animal bladder. Wolf ambled nearer, sniffing the ground by my feet.

"I wonder about game. I haven't seen anything, have you?" I gazed into the distance, trees filling my vision. "I'll take a look at the meadow. There might be stags." Picking at a fingernail, I pondered that idea, although my thoughts soon ran in other directions. It wasn't until wolf got to his feet that I realized I had wasted enough time being idle. "All right. You're right. I should get to it."

We continued on, stopping before an area of grassland, insects floating in the air, while some buzzed noisily. I observed the vista before me, noting movement, something grazing in the distance. Whatever it was, it blended in with the grass.

"Stags." Affixing an arrow to the bow, I slowly ventured forward, wolf darting ahead. "No, you silly animal! You'll scare it." A family of stags appeared then, bounding into the forest, having perceived us. Lowering the weapon, I sighed tiredly, annoyed at having lost the kill. "That was less than helpful." Wolf ignored me, scurrying into the grassland.

I went after him, wondering if Ronan and Enwan came this way, the men hunting earlier to replenish the meat supply. If I could capture a stag, then they would not have to hunt again for a few days. I wouldn't be alone at the cave, a situation I hated. Having survived on my own for a season, after my family disappeared, I never wished to experience it again. I preferred people, needing their company. I adored Ronan and Enwan, the feelings I had for them even deeper than I could imagine. I longed to touch and kiss Ronan, my heart constricting just at the thought of him, the man being my partner in this life.

I knew how it was between men and women—how it felt to be loved and cherished. I always thought the behavior of adults odd, especially when they mated, but with experience came understanding, knowing the pain Kia must have felt at the loss of Magnon. I doubted I would ever survive if something happened to Ronan. The thought alone made my belly twist uncomfortably.

Sensing something amiss, I held up the bow, drawing back on the arrow, my eyes alert for danger. Not one sound came from the prairie or the woods in the distance, yet I felt the change, my senses prickling with awareness. After many hunting seasons and lessons from Sungir, I knew when danger approached, but I waited now …

holding my breath.

A man appeared, followed by another, something burdensome upon their shoulders. I sighed with relief, seeing movement in the grass, wolf darting forward. He trotted past me, knowing we would go home now.

"You silly animal."

I gazed at Ronan, his smile bright, although he squinted with the sun in his eyes. Tall and lean, muscles rippled in his arms and torso, as well as his legs, his manhood hidden beneath a thin sheath of leather. Long, blond hair hung down his shoulders, his beard shorn. Enwan followed, a contrast to his friend, his features as dark as Ronan's were light. If I ever did conceive a baby, I would know instantly who the father was.

"I thought that was you," said Ronan.

The stag over his shoulders wasn't older than a season. "I haven't had a chance to do much other than collect a few nuts and berries." How had the day dwindled away so quickly? I still needed to gather firewood and beat the pelts, but now ... that would not happen.

Enwan's eyes drifted over me. "Good day, Peta. We didn't want to wake you." His stag wasn't older than Ronan's.

"You let me sleep too long. I wish to hunt with you. Take me tomorrow."

"It can wait a few days," said Ronan. "We've enough meat for a while."

Wolf waited at the edge of the forest, sniffing the wind. "I want to teach you how to use this weapon."

"In good time." Ronan nodded. "Shall we go? I'm tired and famished."

"Yes, of course." I fell into step beside him, matching his long strides. "Where did you hunt?"

"Further that way." He pointed behind him. "The grassland near the woods. There was a family of stags. We took two young ones."

"They always taste better," I said, smiling.

His eyes drifted over me, something warm flaring within them. "You looked so peaceful. I'm glad you slept, Peta. You need your sleep. We keep you up half the night as it is."

A hand fell to my shoulder, the touch sending a tingle of awareness through me. I marveled how one touch could produce such an intense feeling. "True. You and your brother are brutes." I teased him, hiding a smile.

He laughed, the sound melodic. "Brutes? I doubt that. You enjoy every moment. You can't deny it."

Enwan, having gone ahead, glanced at us over his shoulder, hearing every word of our conversation. "Is she complaining?" He frowned, but humor shone in his eyes.

"Yes, our woman's complaining. She says we're brutes."

"Indeed?"

I giggled, grateful not to be alone, enjoying the companionship. As I passed Enwan, he hit me lightly against the buttocks. "Ouf!"

"There. Is that brutish enough?"

I laughed, "Hardly, but it'll do for now."

"She's grown fresh," he commented.

Ronan chuckled, "Then some discipline might be in order. We've yet to come close to taming that wild streak."

Spying wolf in the distance, the animal instinctively knowing the way home, I laughed, "You may try, boys, but you'll never succeed."

Two

The day having slipped away from me, I hurried to gather wood, forming a small bundle by the entranceway of the cave, while Ronan and Enwan prepared the meat for supper, although most of it would be smoked and dried, to be eaten over many days. Wolf shadowed me, following as I ventured nearby, bending to take broken branches. From this distance, I heard the chatter of the men, a peal of laughter spilling down the side of the rocky hill. Smiling, I continued the chore, wishing I had the time to beat out a pelt or two, but I doubted that might happen now.

Something delicious cooked, the smell making my belly rumble with hunger. Returning to the cave, I gazed at the sight before me, Ronan sitting on a rock, picking his teeth with a small stick, while Enwan placed reddish pieces of meat over a flattened stone, a sizzling sound emerging, along with tendrils of greyish smoke.

"That's enough, Peta," said Ronan. "I'll finish it. Come sit down."

I approached, frowning. "I didn't forage very well today." I had been strangely distracted, my thoughts lingering on the events of the past. "I didn't help at all by any means."

Ronan's arm went around me, his eyes warm, made up of a pretty shade of blue. "I could never find fault with you. You're perfect, no matter what you say."

"Oh, that's not true," I laughed. "Hardly."

"As long as you warm my bed at night, I've no reason to complain in the least, nor will I. Even if you only lay beside me." His husky tenor resonated. "That is all I ask. I only wish to take care of you and please you. I adore you, Peta."

I believed every word, my heart swelling with sweet emotions. "I don't like when you leave."

He hadn't expected that response, blinking. "Leave?"

"To hunt."

"We don't go every day. You know we must prepare for the colder season. It'll be upon us soon enough, although it's not as harsh here as other places." He pulled me nearer, concern now drawing his brows together. "What's this about?"

I could hardly explain why I felt so … odd lately, often crying for no particular reason. "I want to hunt with you."

Enwan sat nearby, observing us. "She's traumatized, Ronan. You remember how she was when she came here. She'd been alone for a long time. She had to fend for herself."

"Is that true?"

"I don't know." I shrugged. "I … can't explain what's the matter."

"But, something is the matter?"

"I can hunt. I can do what you do. I can be useful to you."

"You are already." He considered this, saying, "We need more people."

"What do you mean?" Enwan tended the meat, removing several pieces.

"A bigger clan. Peta needs company. That wolf's no good. He's hardly adequate."

"Wolf's just fine. He tells me when people are coming. He warns me of trouble."

"Yes, but he's not the kind of companion who'll talk

to you. You need other women."

An unpleasant thought occurred to me. "Then you'd mate them, wouldn't you?"

"I have you." His arms tightened about me. "You please me like no other."

"Where will these women come from?" It felt as if I held my breath, dreading what he might say, fearing it.

"We're not going to find them. We're not leaving for that purpose. If we happen to cross paths with other people, we might invite a few to live here. Or we can offer shelter to someone stranded. People have been here before. The fire pit was here when Enwan and I came. We didn't make it."

"Do you believe those people might return?"

"I don't know. I can't predict the future. None of us could've known a great flood would destroy all the clans in the basin. We survived it. We were separated for many seasons, yet here we are again. I need no further proof that the gods wish for us to be together."

"Your faith is stronger than mine."

"You've had greater challenges. You witnessed the brutality of a heathen clan. Those you knew died before your eyes. Such are these times. The white clans are bent on destroying the darker ones. It's always been so as long as I've been alive."

"Then my family's in danger."

"They've always been in danger." His grip around me tightened. "You should have died many times over, Peta, but you didn't. You said you broke your leg, yet you walk as if nothing ever happened. I can't know what you're feeling at the moment, although I can see something's bothering you, but you have to know how lucky you are, how blessed."

Tears formed in my eyes. "I ... you're correct."

"But?"

"I don't know." I sniffed. "I just ... I just want to

hunt with you."

He smiled sadly. "It's more than that."

"Like I said, she's grieving. She's yet to recover from the ordeal, Ronan. We'll have to be patient." A piece of meat came my way. "Here, eat. Take it."

"Thank you."

Ronan continued to stare at me, his look considering.

"I'm sorry."

"You've no reason to apologize. It is I who should say sorry. You're not entirely well; I can see that now. You may hunt with us. If that's what'll make you feel better, than so be it."

"Truly?" An enormous weight lifted from my shoulders. "Do you mean that?"

"Yes, of course."

"I'd like that very much." I grinned, grateful that I would not be left to scavenge on my own. I could easily pick edibles along the way. "Thank you, Ronan."

"You may hunt until you're heavier with child. Then it's wise to stay nearer to home."

I blinked. "Heavier with child?"

He nodded.

The import of his words sunk into my mind, landing with a thud. "Th-that would mean ... I'm carrying a baby?"

"Indeed." He smiled.

"But ... h-how do you know?" Shock and confusion registered, but the disbelief lingered.

"Because you've not bled in a while, my love. Haven't you noticed?"

"No."

He chuckled, "You think on it a bit more. When you've drawn the same conclusion, we can discuss it further."

My mouth fell open. It was true. I had not bled in a while, knowing it to be the first sign of pregnancy. "You think I'm pregnant?"

"Yes."

I should have known that, remembering something Kia and Hanna said ... although that was a long time ago.

"We do need a larger clan," said Enwan. "I haven't a clue what to do about it, but she's without support. Female support. I worry we won't be enough for her when it comes time to deliver the little one." A frown appeared, the reality of the situation becoming clear. "I've almost no knowledge of childbirth."

"We've a while to sort it out." Ronan kissed my cheek. "Are you going to eat that?" He eyed the piece of meat in my hand.

"You may have it."

"Are you all right?"

"No."

"What?"

"I ... I'm so stupid. I had no idea." I was going to have a baby! "I should've known."

He kissed my cheek, his nose in my neck. I wrapped my arms around him, inhaling his slightly musky smell. They hunted all day, having perspired in the sun, hints of evergreen lingering in his hair. He had been in the woods too. They must have napped on pine needles, a few fragments caught in the strands.

"Are you happy, Peta?"

"I am."

"Are you worried?"

"I worry often, about everything."

"You needn't. You're with us now. We're taking care of you and the baby. You'll not want for anything. You're my woman."

Something pleasing pooled in my belly, the feeling most welcome. "I know."

"In time you'll come to trust this. You'll settle in, and you won't worry like you do. Remember when I told you how I longed for paradise?"

"A comfortable cave filled with thick pelts. Yes, I remember."

"And the perfect woman to share it with."

"I don't remember that, but … I remember how you wanted to shelter in a warmer place where there was plenty of game."

"I've found it."

"Yes."

"This is our paradise, Peta. This is where we shall raise our children. We'll grow old here. We'll always have this cave. It won't disappear."

"No. Rocks and stones stay where they are. It's people that disappear. They vanish in the blink of an eye. They're there one moment—one instant—then gone the next." An old fear returned, but I tried to tamp it down and make it go away, although it always bothered me. "This place will be here long after we're good and buried."

The lines between his eyes deepened. "That's not the point I was trying to make."

"We should eat." Enwan settled on a thick fur, chewing heartily on meat. "Did you bring any berries?"

I slid from Ronan's lap, although he continued to frown. "Yes, I've a few. We should eat. I long to bathe later too. Both of you could stand a good washing." Sitting next to Enwan, I took a piece of meat, eating it, while staring at Ronan, who continued to look troubled. I spoke my mind often, and I would continue to do so, but, from the look of it, it bothered him.

Three

Enwan held a sturdy branch wrapped in leather and kindling and tied with twine, having set it alight. A blanket of bright sparkles lit up the night sky, as we wound our way down the side of the hill through a path of rocks. A cool breeze caressed the nape of my neck, rustling the leaves of bushes. Having fed and satisfied my hunger, I looked forward to bathing, the heated water an indulgence. Wolf ambled ahead of us, his tail wagging behind him.

"It's peaceful tonight," murmured Ronan.

Insects resonated in the grass by the path, their incessant noise in my ear. "I disagree." At the pool, the water glistened beneath the light of the moon, the smell slightly foul, although it did not cling to the skin, thankfully. Untying a leather skirt, the garment dropped to my feet. Wading in between the rocks and stalks of foliage, some nearly as tall as a man, I sighed with pleasure. "Oh, bless the gods. I love this." Warmth enveloped me, soothing my aching bones at once.

Enwan entered, lowering to sit in a shallower part, grasping at wet dirt from the bottom and using it to clean himself. Ronan followed where I went, reaching for me.

"Come here, Peta."

Sodden hair clung to my shoulders. "Yes?" I happily went to him, wrapping my arms around his neck. "You smell."

"Not for long," he chuckled.

"Do you mean it when you say I can hunt with you?"

"Yes, of course, until you're bigger." His hand fell to my belly. "This will grow in time."

I had hardly accepted the fact that I was with child, the revelation still shocking. "I can't imagine it. I remember what Kia and Hanna were like in this condition. We had Sungir with us then. I never worried over anything with Sungir. He knew all about the healing herbs. He did his best to teach me, but I … feel like I was a poor student."

"You're too hard on yourself, my love. I've been in your company now for several full moons, and I've noted this. You blame yourself for things you've no control over."

"I do not."

"You do."

"No."

"You blame yourself for your family's disappearance. It's not your fault they were taken. You couldn't have done anything to stop it. Whoever came through would've taken you as well."

"I'm a poor hunter. If I'd been more skilled, I could've found their trail or some trace of them." That truth bothered me endlessly, an old feeling of frustration emerging. "I know Sungir would've found them."

"Possibly or not." His grip around me tightened. "It's not your fault. Life is uncertain. The gods have a plan for us, and it's often not something we can anticipate."

I eyed him soberly, adoring the sweetness of his face. The light of the torch flickered in his eyes, Enwan having wedged it between two rocks by the edge of the pool. "I can't lose you again."

"You won't." Then he amended, "And if you did, we'd find one another. I give you my word on that. I swear to you. You found me following blind faith across a great distance. We never should've met again. Don't you realize how remarkable that is?"

"My luck finally improved." I touched his face, feeling the scratchy quality of his beard. "I suppose the gods thought I'd suffered enough. They guided me to you to appease me, but they're unkind, Ronan. They might decide to toy with me again, punish me for no reason."

"Stop it!" He drew me closer, his mouth by my ear. "Don't dwell on those sorts of thoughts. You don't wish them to come true, do you?"

I pulled away, gazing at him. "Can that happen?"

"I don't know, but you always think the worst of everything. Do you notice that?"

"That's because peace never lasts long. Good things go away. It's happened over and over again. It's only a matter of time before everything changes once more."

He sighed in exasperation, shaking his head. "God's teeth, woman!"

"I'm sorry."

"Time will prove you wrong. I'll make certain of it. I can see you're going to be stubborn on this issue." He grasped my face, his mouth near mine. "I promise you we shall always be together. No matter what happens. No matter how bleak the outlook. I've yearned for you for so many seasons, always wondering what happened to you. I prayed to the gods that I might find you again, and I have. The gods are good. They're often harsh at times, and it may seem their judgment is unfair, but … there is a reckoning. There always is. There's a balance to life. We can't have perfection at every moment. It's not possible. But, when we have this … this love, this feeling of love, we mustn't waste it arguing over what might or might not happen."

I chewed on my lip, gazing at him. "You're right. I'm sorry. I don't know why I feel so odd."

His look softened. "Women in your condition tend to be emotional."

"I suppose." But I doubted that was entirely the reason. "I trust in you, Ronan. I adore you."

"I adore you, little pest." A grin appeared.

"Pest?"

"We let you sleep with us at the river camp all those seasons ago, and you had those tiny bugs in your hair. You infested us with them. Do you remember that?"

"I do. I didn't mean to."

"I think fondly of it, although I was angry at you. I can never stay angry for long."

"I think of it too. I remember all the people I once knew, but most of them are gone now."

"Let's talk of something else." He kissed me, his lips soft. "Hold them in your heart, Peta. They'll always be with you."

I fingered the stone he gave me, which hung suspended in a twine of leather. I wore it always. "I know."

"Now, let me wash, so we can go to bed. It's been a long day." He fell backwards, wetting his hair.

I glanced at Enwan. He had listened to our conversation. While Ronan bathed, I ventured over to him, feeling slightly guilty for never giving him the same level of attention I bestowed upon Ronan. "Where's Wolf?"

"Behind us." His gaze drifted over me. "Sit here, Peta."

"It's ... slick." The wet sand beneath my feet felt slightly slimy.

He drew me onto his lap. "Then sit here." I leaned my head against his shoulder, his arms going around me, although fingers strayed, stroking my breasts.

"Do you have words of love for me too?" he murmured his lips by my ear.

I shivered. "I ... adore you too, Enwan."

He chuckled, "That's generous of you, but I know you prefer him. Anyone can see it."

I turned to look at him, his features in shadow, with wet hair against his face. "You're in my heart too. I'd miss you, if you went away. I adore you."

"I adore you." A hand fell to my belly. "I wish to take you back to the cave now. Will you go?"

"Yes." I glanced at Ronan, who gargled water, spitting it out. "We're done. Come when you're finished."

"I won't be long." He scrubbed his face with his hands, a smile appearing.

Enwan stood, water pouring from his broad shoulders. We waded to the edge, climbing out among rocks and vegetation, Wolf getting to his feet. Enwan took my hand, leading me along the path, leaving the torch behind for Ronan. I spied the entrance of the cave in the hill, the flickering of light dancing off the walls from the fire slowly dying. This truly was paradise ... the most perfect place I had ever lived in.

***

The feel of someone's lips on my shoulder woke me, a soft pelt at my back. Hearing birdcalls at the entrance of the cave, I knew morning arrived, although I yearned for a little more sleep. Memories of the night returned, my body reliving every kiss and caress, hands and lips having produced pleasure.

"You said you wanted to hunt," whispered Ronan.

"I do."

"Then it's time to get up, my sweet."

Stretching arms over my head, I sighed. "Very well." Enwan stirred, his naked form partially hidden beneath a pelt. A hand traveled then, landing on my belly.

"Perhaps a day in bed is the best plan," he murmured, his fingers drifting lower to touch me intimately. "I've some ideas ... "

We smoked a great deal of meat last night, the smell

lingering. "Haven't we enough to keep us?"

"You wanted to hunt. If you wish to lie in bed all day, then I would not say no to it. I can be persuaded."

Enwan continued to stroke me, which proved entirely distracting. I shoved his hand away. "Stop that." Sitting up, I eyed Ronan, my hair falling around me. "Very well. I'm awake. I need to teach you how to use the bow anyhow. We've neglected it. I fear I've grown weak. I don't wish to lose the skills Sungir taught me."

Tossing back the pelt, Enwan coughed noisily, clearing his throat. "I say hunt half the day. We don't need more meat, in truth. We've enough for some time."

"I want to let her practice her skills. Half a day is good. I'm agreeable to that. I need to find some stones as well. We're also low on wood." Ronan glanced at the cave. "All the pelts need airing out."

"I should've done it yesterday. I'm sorry." I grinned regretfully.

"When we were without you, we managed to hunt and keep the place tidy. You've spoiled us, Peta." His eyes drifted over me. "You've more than spoiled us. You give us everything we want and then some. I don't mind if there's a little dust in the bedding."

Enwan got to his feet, a throaty laugh filling the cavern. "You'd be satisfied if all she did was spread her legs. You're besotted." He glanced at me over his shoulder, his naked buttocks on full display. "She's got us wrapped around her finger."

It wasn't all that difficult to please a man. Meat and mating, that was enough to keep them happy. Chewing on a ragged nail, I stared at Ronan, who sat before me. "I can be ready in a moment. I just need a sip of water and to gather my things." Enwan had already disappeared outside to relieve himself. "I want to be helpful."

"I want to please you."

"You do. Do I please you?"

"Very much so."

"I won't ask to hunt every day. I know my place is here, but I ... worry about losing the skill." This desire to continue to hunt played in with my fears—fears of suddenly finding myself alone again—needing to survive.

He seemed to read my mind. "I know your thoughts. I hope, in time, you'll come to feel secure in life, Peta. We're far away from anyone who might harm us. I've not seen another soul in ages, besides you. Enwan and I chose this place wisely."

"But you said someone else lived here before."

"A great many seasons ago. The fire pit hadn't been used in a very long time."

"I wonder what happened to them?"

"It could've been anything. They might've just left. There's water at our door, a pool beneath us, and game in the valley. We've a magnificent shelter that keeps us warm and dry." He touched my face. "Soon we'll have a little one. He or she will grow strong and sure. Then you'll have more babes after." He smiled. "It's exactly as I envisioned."

I wrapped my arms around his neck, hugging him. "I see it too. It's what I want, Ronan."

"Then, that's what you'll have, my love."

Four

We set out shortly after, bringing a bladder of water and a bag of dried meat, eating it as we went, when hunger struck. The warmth of the sun fell upon my shoulders, although that soon disappeared, as we stepped into the woods to reach the valley beyond. Wolf trotted ahead, stopping to sniff here and there, taking a drink at a sparkling brook, water cascading over the rocks. The strap of the bow dug into my shoulder, the arrows in a leather satchel.

"We're going on, Peta," said Ronan.

"Yes, I'm coming." I rushed to join him, the three of us meandering towards a swath of blue, the trees opening to the brilliant sky and a field of brownish green grass. "I see something." Moving silently within the prairie, I spied game, seeing a family of stags.

"Then they're yours." Enwan bent to pick something from the ground.

Ronan nodded. "Go get one."

I worried Wolf might spook them, as he had before. "Wolf! Come here, boy." The animal ignored me, sniffing the air, and perceiving our quarry. "Blast that stupid animal," I muttered. "I'll have to do this quickly, or they'll all run away." Pulling out an arrow, I affixed it to a taut, thin piece of leather, drawing it back. Stepping from the trees, I observed a stag in the distance, seeing Wolf approach stealthily through the grassland. I had to act now or the opportunity would vanish. Aiming and letting the arrow fly, it arched into the air, coming down upon one of the creatures.

"I wonder if she got it?" Enwan stretched his neck just as all the stags darted into the woods, Wolf having spooked them.

"The hunt didn't take long today," I said.

"Let's have a look." Ronan hurried ahead, while I followed, hoping I had hit my mark. "She's got it!"

I smiled, relieved to have finally killed something. "I'm glad."

Enwan eyed the bow. "I should practice with that. It's clever."

"It's not a new invention. Sungir often encountered traders from different places. It's how he learned about the weapon." We had found wood similar, planning on making our own. That project had stalled, though, the men busy every day with one chore or another. There would be time to sit idle by the fire during the colder season.

As I reached Ronan, he sliced through the belly of the stag, emptying its insides, blood soaking the ground. He glanced at me. "Good job, Peta. You killed it instantly."

If I had been alone, I would have prepared the animal myself, even carrying or dragging it home. "I'm glad I haven't forgotten how to aim."

Enwan nodded, squinting into the sun. "We'll always provide. You needn't concern yourself with hunting. Your place is better-suited in the cave, but I know how stubborn you are about that."

"I wish to maintain my skills for as long as possible." I frowned, wondering if I might have to hunt alone, as Ronan tossed the stag over his shoulder, grasping at the animals legs. The kill had been mine. I should be the one finishing this task.

"I'm ready to return. There's no reason to linger. We've enough meat for quite some time."

I had yet to forage for anything. "You go. I'll be

along. I want to look for berries."

He strode away, saying, "Watch over her."

I grasped the bow. "I'm perfectly capable of foraging on my own, but your company would be nice." Ronan disappeared into the forest, Wolf hard on his heels.

Enwan grinned. "It's fine weather. We should enjoy it."

An insect buzzed annoyingly. "Let's go this way. There might be some ripe enough now." I missed the times when I foraged with my mother and sisters, and how we often chatted about things and sang.

"That looks promising." He pointed to a bush.

"I've had my eye on it for a while. The berries were too small before." Kneeling, I saw now that they had ripened, picking as many as I could and tossing them into a leather bag. "This should do."

Enwan watched the forest. "Ronan wanted rocks. We should go to the quarry. There might be more bushes along the way."

"Very well."

The sugary odor of pine needles filled my senses, the path bathed in light, as we ventured further. Not knowing what to say, I kept my thoughts to myself, finding the walk invigorating. I stopped here and there to pick mushrooms, knowing which to avoid. Enwan waited for me, his look inscrutable, yet he kept watch, his attention far into the distance. When we emerged onto a rocky outcropping, the emerald expanse of the valley lay before us, birds gliding over the tops of trees.

"Is this not paradise?" He stared at the scenery. "The day we came, I knew we'd found our home."

"I agree. It's perfect." The wind caught my hair, the strands blowing behind me. "How long do we have before it's cold?"

"Last season was mild. The ground was never white. A few extra pelts were all that was needed."

"That sounds good." I remembered how cold it had been at Sungir's hut, the snow often reaching my knees or higher. "And the pool is always hot?"

His eyes drifted over me. "Yes."

"Even better." I grinned, a happy feeling emerging, which brought a sense of relief and gratitude. The decision to leave the hut and journey this way had been the right one, although it proved difficult.

"What are you thinking?"

"It was wise to find you. The prospect of it frightened me, but I'm glad I did it."

"I've never been more astonished at anything in my life."

"What?"

"Than the day you came upon us, although you didn't look all that well, covered in filth as you were."

"I'd been through the mud. It felt good to protect my skin from the sun." I remembered that day. "You told Ronan to kill me."

"I'm glad he never listens to a thing I say." His smile grew. "I thought you a boy, an urchin. I was only joking about … having you killed. I wouldn't treat an urchin so badly. You seemed harmless enough."

"Indeed."

"I'm glad you're here, Peta. I enjoy your company."

"I feel the same about you."

He eyed the rocks at his feet. "I have to go lower to the quarry. It's this way. Will you come, or are you tired? In your condition, you'll need to rest more often."

"I'm perfectly fine. I'll go with you."

"This way."

We descended, stepping over rocks, some feeling sharp, even beneath the leather I wore on my feet. The quarry he spoke of consisted of grey rock, the edges jutting sharply from the ground. Enwan chiseled away at one, breaking it apart easily enough and stuffing the fragments into a leather satchel. He worked quickly, the sound carrying. I sat on a flattened piece, eyeing him, admiring his strength, the muscles in his arms and shoulders rippling with each movement. Long, tangled hair hung to his back.

"This should be enough for now."

"Have others taken rock here? Do you know?"

He stood, tossing the bag over a shoulder. He had left the spear upon the ground nearby and other tools needing to be put away. "I imagine. Whoever occupied the cave must've come here. It's not too far."

"Why aren't there more people then? This is far better a place than trying to live on open grassland." I shivered at the memory, knowing how dangerous it was to be among the wild cats … the animals feasting upon humans at every opportunity.

"That should be avoided at all cost." He packed his things, reaching for the spear. "Shall we? I'm satisfied with what I got. If Ronan doesn't like the pieces, he can come and get his own."

I followed him, casting one last look around, seeing a bird flying overhead. "Sungir often traded men for such rocks. They were hard to come by where we were."

"I think I would've liked to meet this man you speak of so often. He sounds as if he was truly wise. You say he had white hair?"

"Yes, he was very old." I had never seen anyone with such hair in my life, even the healer of the clan by the river not being as old. "I've forgotten a great deal of what he taught me."

"I doubt that." We entered the forest, branches closing in around us. "When you've a need for the knowledge, it'll return."

I followed him, stepping over soft, peaty soil. "I hope that's true. It'd be a shame if all those lessons were for naught." We hadn't gone far, stopping at a brook, the water clear straight to the bottom. Enwan dropped his things, kneeling to wash his face and arms, tossing water upon his chest. I waited for him, watching the forest. "We should find a spot to fish. I miss the taste of that sort of meat. It's delicious."

"There's a river in the basin of the valley, but it's quite the walk."

"Have you ever been there?"

"A few times." He reached for my bow.

"What? Why do you want it?" He took the leather bag as well, setting it beside his things. "Are we resting again? I'm hardly tired, Enwan. I can keep walking."

He drew me into his arms, murmuring, "I want a moment alone with you. I know you prefer Ronan. He always has you to himself. I want you."

Startled by his words, I stiffened briefly, his breath near my ear.

"You've bewitched us both. I dare say, I never thought to feel this way about a woman." He grasped my face, the deep brown color of his eyes glimmering with emotion. "Peta?"

"Now I know what you're about. You mean to seduce me in the forest."

"Not a bad idea." He grinned.

My hands landed upon his shoulders, where I felt the heat and strength of him, the corded muscles working beneath my fingertips. "You know I won't deny you." A shiver of anticipation drifted through me, the thought of mating an agreeable way to spend the time, especially with a man I trusted and adored.

He crushed my lips with his own, his breath fresh and warm. We lowered to the ground, although he drew me over, where I straddled him, my fingers tangling in his hair. With the sound of the gently flowing brook at our back and the softness of moss beneath us, I let him move the skirt aside, his manhood pressing to me.

"All I think about is mating you," he whispered. His

fingers dug into my hips. "Tell me you want this, Peta."

"I do."

"Then take me."

Reaching between us, I guided him to where he desired to be. As he filled me completely, I gasped at the sensation, pleasure tingling up and down my spine, with the promise of more to come. His hands held me firmly, while I moved over him, my hair often falling in my face and upon his chest. Little noises escaped me, the sounds drifting into the woods, mingling with birdcalls and buzzing insects.

"Oh," I gasped. "Enwan!" I did enjoy this position greatly, having full control over him, my body taking what it needed. He let me have my way, an expression of pleasure softening his features.

"That's my girl ... Peta ... "

Unable to form a coherent thought, I clutched at his belly, feeling the taut planes of muscle here, along with a slight trembling. On the verge of losing myself wholly, I shuddered upon him, a moan tearing from my throat. In those precious moments, sensation flooded, producing an intense feeling of rapture. I collapsed upon him, satiated and tired, my heart hammering in my chest. He grasped me tightly, filling me with his seed, a manly oath ringing in my ears.

"There's no need to hurry," he murmured, a hand stroking my back.

I yawned. "No."

A chuckle rumbled in his chest.

Five

Inclement weather forced us inside for the day, the smell of smoke lingering from the fire the night before. I burrowed further into a soft pelt, listening to the sounds of someone chipping away at rock, the clinking and scraping noise annoying.

"Why must you be so loud?" I grumbled.

"Because he's determined to be irritating."

An arm draped over my belly. I turned, finding Ronan, his eyes sleepy. "It's too loud." The noise mingled with the sound of rain, a torrent falling from the skies, even Wolf seeking shelter with us, his furry body settled comfortably on an old pelt.

"Good morning, my love."

"How much longer is it going to rain? I'm tired of it."

"I don't know."

We had suffered the bad weather for days now, although I went out to forage despite the wet, soaked through to the bone from the cold. The heated pool replaced the cold, but I longed for blue skies again and sun, tired of the smell of damp earth and sodden pelts.

"Did it rain this badly this time last season?"

"I can't recall. I don't believe so."

Tossing back the hide, I glared at Enwan, who sat on a rock with tools in his hands. "Must you continue with that?"

"You've slept long enough."

"Ha! I do recall; you're the reason I'm so tired." He

hadn't been content to mate me once, waking me in the middle of the night to have me again. This was after Ronan had taken his pleasure as well. Keeping them satisfied could be exhausting, my level of energy lacking lately. I napped several times during the day, never having felt so tired.

"Come back to bed, Peta." Ronan reached for me. "Ignore him."

The scraping stopped, Enwan getting to his feet. He ventured to the doorway, eyeing Wolf, who slept. "We need to hunt. We've eaten most of the meat."

"Later," muttered Ronan.

I rolled into his arms, his lips on mine. Closing my eyes, I dreamed of Kia's delicious stews and all the other food she made at Sungir's hut. In times like these, I missed my mother, feeling sad that I might never see her or my sisters again.

"We'll have to hunt in the wet."

"I'm aware of that," grumbled Ronan. "I want to mate you, but I know you're tired. The growing babe is sapping your strength."

I had begun to feel an odd movement in my belly, the baby fluttering around there. "I suppose." A yawn escaped me, as Ronan's lips pressed against my cheek.

"You're even more beautiful now."

"Why do you say that?"

"Your skin's softer. Your hair's thicker, shinier. You've a glow about you. I want to kiss you every time I see you."

"That's always been, Ronan," I giggled. "You and Enwan are the same."

"We're the luckiest men under the stars to be with you. You're not only beautiful, but you work hard every day, and you always want to please. I can find no fault in anything you do. You don't scream and nag like other women. When I see you, you never fail to smile at me.

Your arms are always open. I do fear we won't get as much time with you after the babe's born, but I understand why that must be."

I remembered how Kia and Hanna's babies kept them busy, the infants demanding, day and night. "It can't be helped."

He touched my face. "You'll look even more beautiful swollen with child."

"I can't imagine that."

"It'll happen soon enough."

"We should hunt." Enwan approached, his face concerned. "The game will be harder to find, but we must try. If you want her to be swollen with babe, you're going to have to provide the food, brother."

"I'd rather be in bed all day."

I sighed, agreeing. "Yet, we must get up. I'm going to try to clean a little. We've let things go."

An irritated grumble left his lips. "Fine." He tossed the pelt aside, glaring at Enwan. "And where do you suppose we'll find game? The animals are sodden and sheltering. It'll be harder to draw them out."

He fingered my bow, having practiced with it for some time now. "I'm using this. Killing at a distance is an advantage. We've only just begun to explore all the possibilities. I've a plan."

"You boys go. I'll manage."

"Sleep." Ronan left the bed, traipsing naked over to where his clothing lay, donning a short leather skirt. After tying it around his waist, he picked up a spear. "What's the plan?"

"I know where the stags are. They're in a dense copse, but we can draw them out. You'll scare them free. Then I'll kill one. I'll tell you more as we go. I believe this'll work."

Ronan glanced at me. "Don't tax yourself, Peta. You needn't do anything. When the rain stops, you'll be busy enough. Keep the fire going. It's a miracle we still have wood. If the weather continues for much longer, we're going to run out of things to burn."

"I've mending to do. That'll keep me busy." I desired to go with them and stretch my legs, missing the excitement of the hunt. Enwan had my weapon today, leaving me with a few spears and some hand axes, but I preferred the bow.

"We won't be long," said Enwan. "If we're successful, we'll have a tasty stag well before the sun is even high, although we won't know it for all the clouds in the way."

"Yes, go." I waved at them, tossing back the pelt. "Bring back something good." I grinned. "I'll be waiting."

"We shall return," he said.

Ronan winked. "Keep the pelts warm, my love."

I smiled at that, watching as they stepped into the rain, not even Wolf desiring to join them. They would hunt, while I waited, just as I remembered it growing up. It wasn't customary for a woman to want to hunt. Sungir had ruined me in that respect, his lessons teaching me to be self-sufficient.

Glancing at the rain, the water pooling in the hollows of the rocky floor by the entrance, I knew I could successfully capture prey in these conditions. The cold would not kill me. It might prove uncomfortable, but a belly full of meat would cure that. I mulled that over, deciding it might be time to make another bow. Once they mastered the weapon, they would take it from me. The mending could wait. This was far more important.

***

Two days later, a reprieve finally came from the steady rain. While the men hunted, I cleaned the cave, beating out pelts in the sun and leaving them over the rocks. Wolf stayed to watch me, ambling over to sniff each new pelt. I beat his out as well, the older fur smelling especially rank.

When Ronan and Enwan returned, I settled before the fire to work on a bow, the wood having been taken from one of the sturdier trees in the area. I cut away the bark, filing grooves on either end for the leather twine. Sanding the edges, I used a rough stone, the sound filling the cavern. Enwan grilled meat, the smell making my belly rumble.

"I suppose you've not done any mending then?" Ronan grinned, the edges of his eyes creasing.

"I wouldn't have to make a new one, if Enwan hadn't stolen mine."

"It's a fine weapon." He nodded, turning over a thick piece of meat. It sizzled on contact. "The most efficient way I've ever hunted, to be truthful."

"We've pelts that need to be scraped."

"Perhaps you should set some traps."

Ronan eyed me. "Why? We've no need."

"To catch two-legged prey." He appeared confused. "I fell into one many seasons ago. They're rather useful."

"For woodland creatures," said Enwan.

"No, you need to set the trap for more women. I need someone to do the mending and foraging." I filed the wood, feeling smoothness. "I could use my own woman." I could hardly believe I had uttered such bold words, feeling mischievous.

"She sounds fresh again," said Ronan, although he continued to smile. "She handles that wood with skill. That'll be a fine weapon."

I enjoyed this task, the work challenging. It had taken many attempts to make the perfect bow, Ara and I wasting endless piles of wood before we had something even partially useful.

"This trap you speak of, how did he make it?" asked

Enwan. He sat on a rock, chewing a piece of meat.

"He dug a rather large hole. Then he covered it with branches to hide its existence. He had several of them around the hut."

"For protection, I assume."

"And to catch woodland creatures. We had a collection of claws around. The babies liked to play with them."

"I've heard of these," said Ronan. "We can make one, I suppose, but we've plentiful game as it is. We don't need such a thing for protection. We can see if trouble comes by standing in the doorway."

I remembered the clan of dark men, who resided in a small cave in the middle of grassland. I had seen trouble coming, having better eyesight than anyone there. Memories of that time brought back a feeling of terror, although I tried not to dwell on it.

"How long will this take you, Peta?" Ronan watched my movements attentively, as I sanded the wood.

"A while. Not too long."

"I speak of this night. I desire to sit with you in my arms by the fire, my love. I'm hungry."

The warm tenor of his tone drifted over me. "For food?"

"For you."

Sighing, I set the wood aside, gazing at Ronan through my lashes. "I see."

"When was the last time you ate?"

"A little while ago. I'm not starving."

"Come and have some meat. I don't wish to eat alone." I crawled over to him, settling in his lap, where his mouth connected with my cheek. "That's better." His fingers drifted through my hair, catching on tangles. "I long to groom you."

"What?" I hardly needed help with that.

"I desire to comb your hair." They made tonged

implements for this purpose, a basketful of them nearby. "I should braid your hair with shells. I've some with holes. You'd look like the daughter of a god. You were blessed with beauty."

I eyed him askance, perplexed by his words. "You're handsome, Ronan. You're beautiful as well." The men at the camp by the river were rougher in appearance, most of them with sharp features and lined skin. Ronan's smile made him look perpetually youthful. "I can braid your hair."

Enwan snorted, his mouth working to chew meat. "This conversation is ridiculous. It matters not how appealing she is as long as she breeds. It helps to bed a pleasing woman, but it's not always necessary. Even the ugly ones have merit."

"I won't argue that, but … " his eyes drifted over me, "you can't deny she's special. I've never seen a woman fairer than this one. Even as a child, she outshone all the others." His fingers traced the line of my shoulder, moving down my arm. "She's utterly perfect."

"Your attachment to her is far worse than I thought." A teasing glimmer shone in Enwan's eyes.

"Don't think for one moment you fool me, brother. I know you mate her whenever you get the chance. I allow it because she's the only woman, but that won't always be so. I foresee a bigger clan one of these seasons, and not because she's given birth to our brats."

I smiled at Ronan, although I now felt a tension I hadn't perceived before, his possessive nature a revelation. "Like I said, you should build a trap."

He laughed, "Don't tempt me. I'd do almost anything to have you to myself." He whispered, "Sharing never bothered me before, but it does now. I pray every day the babe in your belly's mine. If a boy with dark hair and eyes is born, I'll know his seed was stronger."

Six

An endless supply of newly acquired pelts required scraping and drying, the men finding bigger game. Ronan and Enwan hunted the greater wooly creatures, their prowess in this arena unparalleled. The carcass of such an animal provided an extraordinary amount of meat, and it seemed a waste when only a small portion could be eaten and smoked. At Sungir's hut, he dug a hole in the ground where he stored meat, allowing us to eat well all through the cold season. The same occurred at the cave where the dark men lived.

As the days shortened, the weather failed to cool, worrying me, although Ronan said this wasn't a grave concern, because they could hunt whenever they wished. I joined them often, although, as my belly grew, I began to attend to chores closer to the cave, cutting scraps of leather for the baby, just like I had done when Kia and Hanna had their babies.

On a windy day, with the fire ablaze in the pit, I sewed Ronan a new skirt, working a fine bone needle through a piece of leather. The blustery day hadn't prevented the men from hunting, Ronan and Enwan leaving well before I woke. Thick pelts littered the stone floor, providing a level of comfort I had not experienced before, but they required regular cleaning. There wasn't a day when I did not drag a few out to be beaten.

"Have some food, Wolf." I held a dried piece of meat, waiting for my pet to approach. He preferred to sit at the entranceway on his own pelt, keenly eyeing the view from this lofty perch. "Come here, you silly animal. I know you're hungry." He gazed at me lazily, having woken from a nap. "Food." I held the meat higher. "If you don't eat it, I will."

He remained where he was. "Oh, all right." I got to my feet, approaching. "Here. You've grown soft, Wolf." He typically stayed with me, while the men hunted. We foraged together yesterday. "Take it." He opened his mouth to receive the meat, biting with sharp-looking teeth.

I glanced at the view, the mountains in the distance jutting, some with whitish peaks. If people lived beyond the valley, we did not see any evidence of it. Returning to the pelt, I reached into a basket, grasping nuts to eat. Examining the skirt, I had only a few more stitches to apply to finish the garment. Humming to myself, I set about the task, satisfied with the result a while later. I planned to make a new skirt for Enwan as well, but not today.

Listening to the whistle of the wind, the breeze as robust as before, I wondered about my family, wishing Ara and Kia and Maggi were here. I longed for female companionship and conversation, missing it. I could not speak to the men the way I did with my mother and sisters, their opinions and advice important to me. Where were they? What had happened to them?

"You'd be so happy here." I glanced at the cave, the spacious cavern far too empty with just three people. "You should be here to help with the babe." Although I knew the mechanics of childbirth, such a task alone frightened me, but I had a good while to go before the event.

Having finished the chores, I settled on a pelt, drawing a blanket of leather around me. I had little to do now other than wait for the men to return, my eyes drifting shut. When I woke, I noted the shadows now, the sun having gone over the mountain. Men spoke in hushed tones, the sound of scraping filling the air. Opening an eye, I glimpsed Wolf standing over me, his look inquisitive.

"She's still alive," said Enwan. "He came to see to your welfare." Having ascertained my health, the animal darted away, standing by the entrance of the cavern again.

Flinging back the leather, I sat up, brushing hair from my eyes. "What did you catch?"

"Fish."

I gasped. "Truly?" How I missed the taste of fish! "You went a great distance to get it."

Enwan grinned. "A bit. It was worth it. I can see you're eager."

I scrambled to my feet. "I haven't had it in such a long time. What a treat!"

"I'm sorry we woke you." Ronan left the stone he worked, getting up from where he sat. "You looked so peaceful."

"I slept too long. Now I'll never sleep through the night."

He drew me into his arms. "I can think of ways to keep you occupied."

I giggled, pushing at him. "Oh, no doubt you will."

Enwan tossed the prepared fish onto a flattened rock in the fire, the meat sizzling on contact. The most delicious smell filled the air, my senses bursting with anticipation. Delighted, I squatted nearby, eyeing the flames expectantly, knowing it would not take long to cook.

"She cares nothing for me," murmured Ronan, a teasing glimmer in his eye. "She only wants the fish."

Enwan brought over another portion, placing it near the other. "This will cook fast." Using a flattened piece of wood, he scraped the meat free, holding it out to me. "Here you are."

I took it, although it felt rather hot. "Thank you. I'll forage tomorrow. I should've gone today."

Ronan sat next to me, his wrists resting upon his knees. "You need your sleep, Peta. We don't expect you to work so hard."

"I hate doing nothing." I chewed the meat, my eyes drifting shut, as I savored the taste. "It's wonderful." I felt Ronan's hand on my back. "It's delicious. What a treat." A kiss fell to my shoulder.

"It pleases me to see you happy."

I glanced at him. "I am happy. You and Enwan provide everything I could ever ask for."

A shadow passed over his handsome features. "But you miss your family. I know you do. As you grow bigger with child, you think about them. I know why. I know women bond with one another in such times. I'm sorry you don't have other women here to help you."

"I've Wolf. He's a man of few words, but he's entirely devoted to me."

He smiled slightly. "True. I need never worry about you. I know that animal would die to protect you."

"I hope it never comes to that." I gave him a portion of fish. "Have you had any?"

"Not yet." He took it, eating.

The aroma of fish filled the cavern, as flames flickered off the walls. I settled into Ronan's arms, feeling the strength of him at my back, while the fire warmed my face. He touched my hair, which hung heavily, strands brushing the pelt beneath us.

"So soft," he murmured. "You're even more beautiful like this, so much softer."

Chewing heartily, I shivered with pleasure, adoring being spoken to in sweet ways, knowing how deeply this man loved me—how desperately I loved him.

"There's more. We outdid ourselves." Enwan sat nearby, placing several freshly cut flanks of fish upon the heated rock. "We don't have enough to smoke, so eat up. It'll all go bad by morning."

"I've been considering digging a hole at the back of the cave. Perhaps, if we dig far enough, we'll find it colder. It's a shame to let meat waste."

"The earth's too packed. It's solid rock in places. It'll be nearly impossible to dig any distance."

"We haven't tried yet."

"You may, if you wish, but I doubt it'll be helpful."

Ronan shook his head, his expression slightly exasperated. "I'll look for some tools. We need a heavy stone ax. I'll try it when I can."

"You said this was the perfect home." Enwan lifted a portion of fish from the scalding rock, bringing it to his mouth, where he blew on it.

"No place is ever perfect, but this is as close as it comes." His affectionate gaze skimmed over me. "My woman is perfect."

***

The wind died down shortly after sunset, the heat of the fire warming the cavern. Ronan and I went down to the heated pool, the light of the moon illuminating the path, while insects made their presence known, being noisy in the underbrush.

"I want to speak to you."

Holding my hand, he led me around several boulders, the rocks scattered down the side of the hill. "About what?"

"Enwan needs a woman. He's agreed to take a journey north to find one."

Stunned, I stopped in my tracks. "What?"

"We've plenty of time before the baby's born. You can hunt for yourself; you've proven so time and time again. It's not going to get much colder than this, Peta. I won't worry about you freezing. You've Wolf to watch over you."

"You're leaving me?" I felt a moment of panic. "I'll go with you. We mustn't be separated. If we're separated, we'll never see one another again."

"That's not true. I know my way back to the cave. We'll mark trees on the way out. I've memorized this valley anyhow."

"Please don't do this."

"Let's get in the water. We'll speak on it some more. I have to make you understand why this must happen. You know why. You're lonely. We're gone all day hunting, and you're alone with a dog that can't speak." Dropping the leather skirt, he held out a hand to me. "Come, my love. Let's get in."

I stepped on the rocks near the edge of the glistening pool, it smelling slightly foul. "I don't like your idea at all. I fear it shall be the end of us." Deep to my knees, the heat enveloped my skin. "I thought you'd wait for someone to pass through."

He lowered into the water, bringing me with him. "We've been waiting. In all this time, I've not seen another person, not a wanderer, not a hunter or a trader. Nothing. This is truly untamed land."

"Others have been here. You said the cave belonged to someone."

"A great time ago."

I washed my face, my hair partially wet, the strands floating in the water before me. Ronan braided some of the locks, affixing pretty shells. He adored playing with my hair, but such activities always led to mating. His hands fell to my shoulders, where he gently pressed into my skin with the tips of his fingers.

"How do you feel?"

"I'm perfectly well."

"Have you had any pain?"

"None at all." I hated that he was considering leaving me. "Please don't do this. Wait at least until the baby's born. Can't you wait?"

"Yes."

I turned to look at him, his face partially illuminated by the moon, a slight smile toying around the edges of his mouth. "Truly?"

"We'll wait until the baby comes. I still think we've

plenty of time to fetch another woman or two, but if you're against it, then we'll wait."

"Thank you." Relief had me breathing easier. With any luck, someone would wander through and decide to stay, thereby not requiring the men to leave. I never wanted to be alone again. "Then I can go with you. I can make a sling and carry the baby. It's what Kia did. I helped her make it."

He touched my face. "You could persuade me to do anything."

"I doubt that. You're quite stubborn."

"So are you."

"I want to go with you. We mustn't separate. If something were to happen, we'd never see one another again."

"You're wrong. Look at us. We were apart for seasons, and now we're here. You mustn't fear everything. Nothing is forever. The gods have a way of challenging us, pushing us to our limits, but they also show remarkable mercy."

"I haven't seen a great deal of mercy."

"I have." He kissed me. "You're here with me. This isn't a dream. You're in my arms. You're going to have my baby. We're destined for one another. I know you're worried about your family. I've every hope of finding them for you."

"I'll help find them too. Once the baby comes, we can go." Wrapping my arms around his neck, I drew closer. "Is that agreeable?"

"You should be a trader. You've a skill at bargaining."

I laughed, "That was hardly bargaining. I mostly begged you not to leave me." I would do it again to assure he stayed, pride the least of my considerations at the moment. "I love you, Ronan."

His hand drifted to my belly, feeling the rounded bump. "I love you."

Seven

The feel of something licking my face made me open my eyes. Wolf scampered away when he realized he had been caught. "Oh, you pest," I grumbled, slightly astonished at his bold behavior. He had slowly begun to inch his way further into the dwelling with each passing night, so much so, I made another bed for him near the fire, where he sat after the men returned, waiting for delicious scraps. "Now you're licking me." I sat up, gazing at the empty cave, seeing the blue of the sky in the opening, the perfection of the day only just beginning. "Come back! Come sit with me." But he wouldn't, the animal having gone outside. "Oh, fine."

Feeling restless, I desired to breathe fresh air, the rain finally ceasing after inclement weather. It had been several days since Ronan and I spoke at the pool, his promise not to embark on a journey without me a relief.

"I should get up," I murmured, tossing back a pelt.

I ventured out to use the latrine around the side of the cave, having a drink of water on the way back. The brilliance of the sun forced me to squint, the sky cloudless and blue, the color breathtaking.

Wolf scurried below, sniffing at the base of the hill, although he disappeared behind one of the boulders. Wanting to scavenge, I planned to enjoy the day, vowing to find lush, ripe berries, as there seemed to be no end to them here, the landscape as fertile as I had ever encountered.

Donning leather for my feet, tied around the ankles and a leather skirt, I tidied the cave briefly, tossing tonged implements into a basket, Ronan having groomed me last night, untangling my hair. He adored this task, often kissing me in the process, the grooming leading to mating. Whenever I saw the comb in his hand, I knew what he planned for the evening. He had but to hold it up, smiling, while I ate supper, a hint of what was on his mind. The memory brought a smile to my face.

The fire having died down, the cave smelled of sweaty pelt and burnt meat, the meal last evening consisting of some sort of bird, although the creature tasted far too fatty, the cooking process messy. I would have to scrape the remnants from the stones in the fire pit later. None of that mattered now, as I needed to hurry to forage, if I were to nap later.

Tossing the bow and arrows over my shoulder, with a leather sack for incidentals, I carried a basket, setting out a short while later. Wolf, observing my exit, hurried to me, sniffing my feet.

"We must be productive today. No more lying about and sleeping. I know you've been waiting for me to forage." Passing the rocks, I stepped into the woods. "Now's your chance to stretch your legs, Wolf."

I eyed the gloomy chaos of branches over my head, the sun struggling to pierce the thick canopy. With it cool and shady, I suppressed a shiver, hurrying along a well-worn path, while the prickly ends of bushes brushed against me. The trail led to a field of flowers and insects, which I would bypass today, desiring to find berries, and they could not grow so out in the open.

Wolf, thinking I planned to cross the grass, ventured forth, although he stopped a few paces away, realizing I did not follow. The animal returned at once, his footfalls nearly silent.

"I fooled you, didn't I? I've been far too predictable." Not on a discernable path, I threaded my way through bushes and trees, bending to pull a few mushrooms. "Here's a start. We can eat these."

From here, I prodded onward, discovering a bush of

berries, and picking it clean. Satisfied with the find, I smiled at the basket, knowing the men would delight in the fruit. Continuing on, I thought of my mother and how she would smoke insects from their nest to steal their sticky nectar. As a child, I adored the treat, never having found such a nest here yet.

"Ronan would love that."

I eyed the trees, the soft fragrance of some flower lingering. Memories of the past often returned when I foraged, mostly because that was the time I spent with my mother and sisters, the three of us chatting and exploring, the forest providing nuts and fruit, along with a few surprises. I wandered among giant trees, wishing I could climb them, but in my condition, it was best not to. Lost in thought, I jumped when a bird vaulted into flight over my head, startling me.

I had not been paying attention, my mind occupied on wistful memories. "Wolf?" I had not seen my pet in a while, the animal usually nearby. "Wolf?"

An uncomfortable prickle skimmed down my spine, an inkling of something I had not felt in a long time—danger. I knew instinctively I was not alone then, my senses screaming at me, cursing me for not being more attentive. When I first arrived at Ronan and Enwan's home, I had been wary, ever watchful for the smallest hint of trouble, but that lessened over time, a sense of security clouding my judgment. I knew this now, as two men stepped before me, and another behind.

"What have we here?" asked one of the men.

Their skin burnished from the sun, they looked as if they had been traveling, carrying bedding and leather bags, their legs threaded through with muscle. Each held an ax and a spear, their eyes pinned on me. I gasped at the sight, my hand flying to my weapon, although the man behind me perceived the motion, knocking the bow from my shoulder. The bag of arrows fell, a few tumbling loose upon the leaf strewn ground.

"A girl with a weapon," the man behind me said.

I glared at him, suddenly furious with them and myself for not being faster. Living with men had made me soft and weak, having relied on them for everything. "Don't touch me!" There was no point in trying to be polite. I could see from their eyes what they wanted—what they planned. They would not touch me.

One of the men appeared slightly taller, a fur wrapped around his neck, although it must have felt unbearably hot. He possessed an air of authority, his hand grasping a spear. "Here's a fine prize, men. Wouldn't you say? Have you ever seen anything as … precious?"

Eyeing the scattered arrows, I longed to take one, but a man stood far too close, his odor noxious. He had not bathed in a long time, his skin as greasy as his hair.

"She is indeed a treasure," he said. "I don't believe I've ever seen a woman so … clean. There isn't a mark of dirt upon her."

"She'll make a fine present for our lord."

"I don't wish to give her to anyone, Zendi. She's ours."

"I don't belong to any of you. I have a mate."

"Indeed you do," said the third man, his gaze on my belly. "She's good and bred. That much is for certain."

Why did the name Zendi sound familiar? My mind searched various memories, although none of that mattered at the moment. "They'll come to me. My husband's nearby." Then I worried that perhaps these people might have killed Ronan and Enwan. I stared at each weapon, not seeing blood. "I need only scream, and they'll come." I doubted that, though. I had no knowledge of exactly where they hunted today, not having paid all that much attention to their conversation the night before. I prayed they hunted close to home … or else … this might prove disastrous.

A flash of tan caught my notice, Wolf having jumped from the foliage. The attack happened so quickly, the men did not have the chance to defend themselves, Wolf growling ferociously, latching onto the ankle of one of the men, his teeth sinking into flesh.

"Where did he come from?" shouted Zendi.

I chose that moment to flee, leaving the bow and arrows. Darting into the woods, the basket of berries flew from me, overturning.

"Get her!"

"Someone kill the animal!" shouted one of the men. "He's about to tear my leg off!"

A branch hit me in the face, followed by another and another. I sprinted, traveling at some distance, but the sound of twigs snapping behind me brought a renewed fear of capture. I could not outpace the brute in pursuit, the man gaining.

"Come here, bitch!"

"Ronan!" I shouted at the top of my lungs. "Ronan!" I felt his hands in my hair, the fingers closing around the strands, some tearing from my scalp, but I ignored the pain. "Ronan!" A firm arm went around my chest, resting just above my belly, lifting me from the ground. "Ronan!" A dirty hand pressed against my mouth, silencing me.

"Shut up!"

Kicking and struggling, I lifted my knee to bring the back of my foot into contact with his soft man parts, a pained groan escaping him. He released me, whereby I fell to my knees, but I bounded to my feet the next instant, racing into the forest, while the man bent over, gasping.

"Ronan!"

I heard the sound of Wolf then, the animal crying out in agony, yelping. Tears formed in my eyes, knowing what that meant. They had killed him; I knew this without even needing to see it. Having recovered from the kick in the groin, the greasy man stomped towards me, but I had already cleared a great distance, the breath burning in my lungs from the effort. My only thought remained on fleeing far away, far enough to take cover and hide. I had few options at the moment, having left the weapon behind.

"Get her!"

That sounded alarmingly close, the man named Zendi uttering those words. He passed his friend, bounding behind me far faster than I could ever possibly run.

"Stop! We mean you no harm, woman!"

"Ronan!" The sound of my voice sliced through the forest, a high-pitched, frantic uttering. "Ronan!" I knew I could not run like this forever, my breath nearly gone, my heart hammering in my chest. I had to think of the baby— the stress we both labored under in this quest for freedom. I might not succeed at the moment. "Ronan!"

"Blasted! Make her be quiet!" A hand grasped at my hair, the fingers gripping, pulling. "Stop!" He jerked me into his arms, an angry countenance peering at me. Deep lines dug into the weathered skin of his face, revealing his age. "You're more trouble than I thought, woman."

I could scarcely breathe, my chest burning in pain. Having screamed Ronan's name as loudly as I could, I doubted I could even speak now, my throat aching.

The greasy man doubled over, gasping for breath, while resting his hands on his knees. "God's teeth, that was unnecessary. I hope the little twit's worth it. I'm spent. The bitch kicked me in the balls."

Laughter rumbled in Zendi's chest, his smile faltering when he looked at me. He had yet to release my hair, pulling my head back painfully, while he held me firmly with an arm around my back. "This one's worth a sprint through the woods, Pondo. You'll recover from the ordeal soon enough."

The third man appeared, blood dripping from his spear. I assumed he had killed Wolf, my pet having died protecting me.

"We should leave at once," he said. "She made enough noise to wake the dead. Whoever she called for, I'm certain they'll come."

Hope flared within me, Zendi seeing this, his smile flattening. "You're my prize, woman. I shall gift you to my lord."

"We shall share her later," said Pondo. "That's the least she can do for causing so much trouble."

"She'll remain unmolested. She's not for you." Zendi frowned, releasing the grip he had on my hair, but a length of leather rope appeared then, with which he tied my hands.

"Ronan!"

He slapped me hard with the back of his hand. "Shut up! I'll have to bind her mouth as well."

"Our lord would never know about her," said the third man. "We can do what we like. She'll keep us warm at night on the journey home."

"Like I said, she's not for our pleasure."

"Then why take her? Leave her. I've a bad feeling about this." He eyed the forest warily.

A length of leather covered my mouth, being secured at the back. I struggled then, but I could hardly move, my hands bound.

"Take her weapon. Go get it, Kunchin. Enough talk. We walk." Zendi pushed me. "Walk, woman."

I stumbled, angered by the treatment, my head smarting from where he gripped my hair and where he hit me. I vowed to get revenge on them then, the trio having ruined the peace of the day, killing my animal. Glaring at Zendi, I hated him with a passion I had never felt before.

He noted this, saying, "Be careful with her. She's stronger than she looks. She's smart too. She's planning our deaths. I can see it in her eyes."

Laughter filled the air at that statement.

Eight

I would not cry at the death of my animal, not in front of these heathen men. With my hands tied before me and my mouth bound, I could not scream again, wondering if Ronan or Enwan heard the earlier calls. My throat smarted from the effort of screaming, the sound surely having reached them. Eyeing the forest, I hoped they approached, expecting an arrow to fly from nearly every angle, because they each carried a bow.

"Faster," muttered the greasy man named Pondo. He used the blunt end of his spear to propel me forward, pushing me.

I glared at him over my shoulder, while trying not to stumble upon the knotted roots and debris strewn upon the ground. With Zendi and Kunchin before me, Pondo brought up the rear, hitting my back repeatedly with the end of the spear. Hardly idle while I walked, I methodically loosened the binds around my wrists, slipping them free in short order, although I held the leather to not give this away.

When we stopped to have a drink by a sparkling brook, I waited while the men knelt, Kunchin filling a bladder with water. I mumbled something, not being able to speak because of the gag in my mouth.

"What is it?" Zendi pulled the leather free, leaving it hanging beneath my chin.

"I need to relieve myself."

He nodded. "You may go, but only a short distance."

He threw water upon his face, while Pondo did the same.

This task occupied them, while I stepped quickly away, leaving all my things behind, but it could not be helped. Dropping the binds and removing the leather from my neck, I ran with all my might, my heart hammering in my chest. The thunder of feet echoed behind me, the men in pursuit. I grasped onto a low branch, hoisting myself up. Trying to climb, the size of my belly proved a challenge, but I managed to work my way up the tree, holding my breath and praying they had not seen me. Hiding behind the thickness of the trunk, I glimpsed movement, the men approaching. They passed directly beneath me, their expressions stern, while they gripped spears. After they disappeared from sight, I remained where I was, finding a higher branch to sit on, not certain of my safety in the least. I doubted it would be that easy.

They can't possibly be that stupid, can they?

Sure enough, I heard the snap of a branch, a man appearing. Zendi stalked through the foliage, moving aside low-lying limbs and peering behind bushes. "She's here somewhere. She didn't go far. Look at the trees!"

Pondo and Kunchin come into view, the men having fanned out to search a wider area. I knew they would find me, the certainty of it sitting ill in my belly. In a bid to disguise myself, I lay upon a thick branch, careful not to crush the babe inside of me. Keeping my head down, I closed my eyes and prayed … praying I had not been seen.

"You can come down from there, woman." Zendi stood at the base of the tree, his hands on his hips. The spear rested against the trunk. "I see your hair. Come down."

Swallowing bitter disappointment, I sat up, staring stonily at the forest, and cursing my luck. "I won't. Go away. Leave me."

Pondo and Kunchin neared, Pondo saying, "She's a pest. We should mate her and leave her. She's not worth the trouble. I've a bad feeling about this."

"We can't. I plan to gift her to Greggor. It'll help atone for my misdeeds," said Zendi. "She's perfect for that end."

The name Greggor drifted over me. I knew that name! A childhood memory resurfaced, the impression not good. Having stood, I reached for a branch, nearly missing it, my fingers a fraction too far.

"Be careful!" shouted Zendi. "You're no good to me dead. Come down from there at once!"

"Ronan!" I shouted at the top of my lungs. "Ronan!"

"Damn the gods!" muttered Zendi. "Someone has to stop that!" He grasped a branch, hauling himself up, while I continued to scream.

"Ronan! Ronan!" I took a deep breath. "Ronan!"

I doubted I had ever seen a man angrier, his swarthy features burning bright red, his eyes ablaze in a murderous light. Moving from him, I clung to a limb, working my way to another, and screaming with all my might.

"Ronan!"

"I'm going to beat you within an inch of your life!"

"Ronan!"

He lunged for me, but I stepped downward, my feet nearly slipping. I quickly ventured lower, surprising him, although I knew I could not escape now. Two men waited below.

"Ronan! Ronan! Ronan! *Ronan!*" No sooner had my feet landed on the ground than Pondo reached for me, fingers closing around my arm. "Ronan!"

His other hand wound around my neck, stealing my breath. "Shut up, bitch! That's enough!" He secured my hands, only this time, behind my back, while a leather strip went into my mouth, tied roughly, tangling in my hair. Disappointed that the escape had not gone well, I remained determined to try again at another time, Zendi coming to stand before me.

"Be on the lookout. She's made enough noise." He appeared grim, his mouth a thin line. "You're going to pay for that. I haven't time to mete out the punishment now, but rest assured, you'll get what you deserve for that senseless chase." I mumbled something, not being able to speak. He moved aside the leather, where I managed to bite at one of his fingers. "Bitch!" He slapped me, although he did not use all his strength, holding back sufficiently enough, oddly not wanting to hurt me.

"Ugly brute!"

He shoved the leather between my teeth, sneering angrily. "That's enough from you." Giving me a shove, he muttered, "Keep walking."

"She's not worth it," said Kunchin. "We don't need her to appease Greggor. He'll welcome us back with open arms, no matter how sour the parting was. This one's only going to bring trouble."

"That may be, but I'm determined to see this through. Watch the woods! I don't doubt her man's out there looking for her. She made enough noise."

Pondo darted ahead, casting an angry glance at me over his shoulder. "No woman's worth this much aggravation, not even one so beautiful. Our lord hardly needs her. He has a wife."

I felt the blunt point of a spear at my back, urging me onward. Gritting my teeth upon the leather, I glanced into the trees, praying—hoping Ronan and Enwan heard my cry for help. I could not possibly have screamed any louder, my throat throbbing from the abuse.

***

We stopped infrequently, the walk brisk. I overheard Pondo grumbling about the pace, Zendi saying, "It's fast enough. She's in no condition to run. Just be vigilant.

Keep a close eye on the forest."

Marching with my hands bound behind my back proved awkward, my shoulders and neck aching. I had to be careful not to trip over anything, because I had no way to brace the fall. Annoyed and increasingly worried over the situation, I pondered how I might escape, my thoughts examining one idea after another, working through every possible scenario. I hardly had time to think about the name Greggor, knowing exactly when and where I had heard it ... so many seasons ago.

"Let's rest for a bit." Zendi stopped before a brook, the water flowing gently over smooth rocks. Grasping at the leather around my mouth, he pulled it free.

I spat, hating him. We had gone so far; screaming now would be useless.

"Your arms must be sore." His eyes drifted over my face, a wary, yet concerned look in them. He reached out to touch my breast, knowing I could not stop him. At this juncture in my pregnancy, they appeared fuller than ever before, the skin surrounding the nipples darker. "You are rather defenseless now, aren't you?"

Stepping away from him, his fingers lost contact. "I ask that you untie me."

"Ask?" A hint of a smile appeared. "I think you'd better beg, woman."

"Then leave them bound," I said tonelessly, loathing this creature beyond measure. I lied, "I don't care."

Kunchin and Pondo knelt by the water's edge, having a drink and washing themselves. I yearned to do the same, feeling parched and dizzy, but I would never beg for the privilege, my pride recoiling at such an idea.

"I'm checking the perimeter," said Pondo. "It's too quiet."

"Yes, go." Zendi observed me carefully. He untied the fur from around his neck, dropping it to the ground. "Turn around."

I did as I was told, hoping to be free. I would not run—not now, but ... a drink would do me wonders.

"I need you in good health. You'll slow us down even further if we have to carry you. Go drink." His fingers closed painfully over my shoulder. "But if you think to run again, be warned. I'll take great delight in beating you." His mouth near my ear sent a shiver through me. "I'll spank your naked arse with my bare hands. Don't doubt I wont."

I would not dignify that with a response, ignoring him. Kneeling before a rocky embankment, I cupped crystal clear water, drinking it. Then I washed my face and arms, delighting in being clean. A breeze caressed my face, the forest strangely quiet.

Are you out there, Ronan? Are you coming?

I had set aside thoughts of Wolf; my pet having been murdered by these heathen brutes. I could only imagine him lying somewhere, his eyes frozen in death. I wanted to cry, but I swallowed back the emotion, channeling it into anger, which would serve me better.

Pondo returned a while later, his look bland. "We're good. No sign of anything other than these bleedin' insects." He slapped his arm. "They're eating me alive."

I sat with my arms over my knees, my thirst satisfied. The bow stood against a tree in the distance, but, were I to jump to my feet and run, I would never reach it in time, the men preventing such a thing. When another opportunity at escape arose, I planned to make a move. Until then, I held my emotions in check, letting anger swell within me. I could only imagine how distressed Ronan and Enwan were, the men having returned from hunting by now. They would see the empty cave, the fire long extinguished, and no evidence I had returned from foraging. They would know something was amiss.

"We walk until sunset, then we make camp. That'll bring us far enough away from detection," said Zendi. "We kill game, if we see it. I'm starving."

Kunchin grasped a spear. "Then we must walk quietly. No talking." He pointed the weapon at me, the stone sharpened at the end. I held still, not wanting to show fear at this empty threat. "Don't step on any branches."

"She's been fine."

"Your memory's too short," said Pondo. "She ran earlier. Don't think for one moment she won't do so again. She might be burdened with someone's brat, but that hasn't affected her legs in the least. She's fast."

Zendi knelt before me, his dark eyes alight with warning. "You will behave."

"I will?" I could not help testing him, wondering just how far I could push.

A hint of a smile appeared. "I like how you refuse to cower. It's impressive. It won't help you in the least and might actually make things worse, but I do admire your courage. It's rare to see in a woman."

"Might I tell you what I think?"

He laughed wryly, the edges of his eyes creasing deeply. "Oh, I can imagine."

"You and your men should enjoy what's left of your pathetic lives. Breathe deep the air. Savor the feel of the sun upon your shoulders. Enjoy what's left of this day."

A bushy eyebrow lifted. "Yes?"

"It shall be your last."

Nine

Laughter filled the air, Kunchin frowning. "I thought we were to be silent? You're making enough noise to scare away game."

"She's entertaining." Zendi grinned. "What's your name? I've been remiss. I can't believe I haven't asked this yet."

"That's because you lack manners."

His smile faltered, a sigh escaping him. "All right. That'll be enough out of you. You push too far now." He grabbed my arm, bringing me up with him. "Are you ready to continue?"

It gladdened me that he asked this, his concern for my welfare a surprise. "If I must."

"Yes, you must." He gave me a push. "I'll leave you unbound for now, unless you make trouble again."

I pointed to my mouth. "What about this? Aren't you worried I'll scream?"

"You might want to cover her mouth," said Pondo. "She bellows like a wounded bull."

"Indeed," I said. "I could scream when you least expect it."

Zendi's eyes narrowed. "You goad me, woman. I don't like it." He reached out to wrap his fingers around my neck, drawing me near. I could breathe still, the touch firm, yet loose. "You try me. If you continue in this, you'll find yourself on all fours. I'll mate you first, and I won't be gentle. You'll receive the same treatment from Pondo and

Kunchin. They haven't had a woman in a great long time. I know they're more than eager."

His foul breath fanned over my face. Resisting the urge to scratch his beady black eyes out, I held my tongue, knowing better than to speak now. I prayed he did not follow through on that threat.

He seemed satisfied with my lack of response. "Good. Now we walk quietly until supper. If you make one sound—one peep—you'll not eat tonight. If you scream, you'll be mated … by all of us. I suggest you keep that pretty little mouth shut." It looked as if he remembered something. "What's your name?"

"I thought I wasn't to talk?" I whispered, swallowing with difficulty, as his fingers had yet to leave my throat.

"Speak, wench!" he ground out through his teeth. "Your name?"

"Peta." The grip around my throat loosened.

"Peta."

I nodded.

"In a way," he whispered. "I almost hope you do something stupid. I can't think of anything I'd rather do now than mate you. You've the softest skin I've ever felt. I've never seen eyes so blue—like the flowers in the wet season, at the height of their bloom."

"I'm sure there are women where you come from."

"Yes, but you're fairer than most."

How could I respond to that? I hadn't been in a clan since childhood, hardly recalling what people looked like, although I remembered my mother and sisters well, their skin dark and glossy.

A regretful flicker danced in his eyes. "But, alas, you're not meant for me. I've a desire to appease my master. I wish to atone, and you'll do fine in that respect."

"Atone for what?"

"I don't wish to rehash the past, but suffice it to say, I've angered him."

"This Greggor person?"

"Yes."

"Your brute leader."

"Hardly. He's strong. He's brave."

"I've seen him."

He blinked. "You have? When?"

"Many seasons ago at a cave far from here. He came with his men—you among them. You murdered all the men there."

"A cave on a hill in the middle of a plain?"

"Yes."

He nodded absently, his mind working. "I ... do recall something like that. We were heading home from journeying west to trade, but it hadn't been good. The cold season was at our backs."

"And do you remember how you attacked the dark clan?"

"There were white women. We liberated the captives. We brought them home with us. They found mates."

"That may be, but you killed all the men. Every last one."

"As we're wont to do. I don't see what your quarrel is in all of this."

"You wouldn't, you heartless, soulless heathen." Hatred tinged my tone. "You didn't think at all how it might affect those living there—in peace. We didn't need to be liberated. No one asked you to slaughter the men. They took care of us. They kept us warm and dry. They fed us. They were kind. Far kinder than," I poked his chest with my finger, "you."

"You've a long-standing grievance."

"I do."

"I don't recall seeing you."

"I hid in a small cavern at the back. I could see you through a gap between the wall and a rock."

"It's beginning to make some sense."

"The last thing I wish to do is meet your … leader."

"Yet that is exactly what'll happen. Not only will you meet our lord Greggor, but; I'll hand you over to him as a gift. I'll leave it to him to tame you."

You won't get the chance …

Pondo approached. "Are we leaving or do you wish to stand here for the rest of the day talking?"

"We leave."

"You trust me enough to walk unfettered?" Why did I have to goad him? I could hardly believe my gall. I should be grateful for this, as it would allow me to kill him later.

"Until you do something ill-advised. I've given you fair warning, Peta. You make one noise, you try for escape, you'll be mated—hard. Then I'll beat you soundly."

Was that an empty threat?

"I almost hope she misbehaves," said Pondo. "I wouldn't mind having a go at her or two."

"Walk!" grated Zendi. "Enough of this talk. The day wanes."

***

My belly grumbled, although I had eaten dried meat and berries earlier before falling victim to these men. Zendi allowed me to travel unbound, my hands free. I did not speak, nor make any sound, but I kept my eyes on the forest, praying for rescue.

"Wait here," commanded Zendi. "Watch her. We're going to kill a stag."

Pondo eyed me. "It'll be my pleasure."

"Do not touch her." Zendi pointed a finger in warning at him. "She's to remain unmolested."

His eager expression vanished. "I don't see why. Greggor will never know if we had a little sample. He'd be none the wiser."

"If I can't trust you to follow orders, you'll have to come with me. I'll leave Kunchin with her then." Wiping his brow with the back of his hand, he appeared irritated and weary. "I'm not in the mood for insolence. I've heard enough of it from her."

"I won't touch her," he grumbled. "I'll wait, but hurry. Light's fading fast."

"Which is another reason I shouldn't be standing here speaking to you." He grasped a spear, his look stern. "We'll return as soon as possible."

Pondo nodded. "We'll wash up in the creek."

"You do that." He sniffed. "You stink."

"I'm well aware."

Kunchin approached. "We must be quick. I spy game in the field." He pointed to the trees, where grassland could be seen between the branches. The day's travel brought us close to an open expanse.

Picking at my nail, I waited for them to leave, knowing my bow stood against a tree with a leather bag and a bladder filled with water. I held my breath—worried—excited—terrified they might take the weapon. In their haste to hunt, they strode past it, grasping spears and axes. Once out of earshot, I gasped for breath, realizing I held it. They left the bow!

"Come along," grumbled Pondo. "Let's wash up, but don't do anything stupid, woman."

"Of course not. I'm exhausted." I eyed the men, seeing their shapes move towards the grassland, in shadow now, the sun lowering. "A bath is a sound idea."

"Yes ... " He waited for me.

The creek wasn't especially deep, the water icy cold, but I relished it, feeling oddly feverish. I saw my flushed skin in the reflection of the water, wondering if I'd had too much sun, but we traveled under the protective canopy of thick, leafy branches. Kneeling, I tossed water into my face, washing my arms and chest, shivering.

Pondo waded in, sitting in the deepest part, throwing water over his shoulders. He scrubbed his face, wetting long, dark hair. "You should tend to me."

"What is it you wish me to do?"

"Clean my hair."

"If you lean back, you can wash it yourself."

"I'd rather you do it."

Annoyed, I got to my feet, removing the strips of leather and leaving them on a rock by the creek's edge. I ventured to where he sat, standing by him with my hands on my hips. "Now what?" I asked dully, not relishing this task in the least.

"Tend me." He stared dumbly at nothing in particular, his face glistening with wetness.

"Fine." I came to stand behind him, bending to splash water on his back. "How's that?"

"Wash me."

I was about to argue, but I thought better of it, using my fingertips to knead his flesh, although I found it repugnant. He seemed to like that, his head rolling forward, bobbing back and forth. The cold water chilled me thoroughly, but I continued to massage him, doubting it to be an effective cleaning technique. I enjoyed working the knots from Ronan and Enwan's shoulders, but the same could not be said now.

"You have a soft touch."

Making a face, I eyed the forest, observing the deepening shadows, the night approaching fast. "You should bring your head back so I can wash your hair." He did as I asked, gazing at me with an open mouth, which I found revolting. I grasped at the soggy tresses, squeezing them beneath the icy brook, all the while trying not to look at him. "There you are. You're suitably clean now." I forced my tone to sound as pleasant as possible, hiding the revulsion I felt. "I need to relieve myself."

He washed himself between the legs, his hands

moving beneath the water. "I've something else for you to clean."

Wading to the edge of the embankment, I prepared to implement the plan I formulated. "You've been very nice. Perhaps, I could do something for you."

"Where are you going?"

"I must do as nature intended. I won't go far."

"You should stay where I can see you."

"I will, but I'd like some privacy. You can understand that, can't you?"

He thought about that far too long.

"I'll be right back." I did not wait for him to respond, the man seated in the middle of the stream still. "I'll be right over here." I walked away as calmly as I could, although the urge to run had never been stronger. When the branches closed behind me, hiding the creek, I darted for the tree, retrieving the bow, while affixing an arrow.

The sound of a bough snapping echoed noisily, the man crashing through the forest, his look frazzled. "You've gone far enough, woman!"

He stood a few paces away, his face in line with the arrow, which I let fly. The tip ripped through his skull, embedding deeply in the middle of his forehead. His mouth worked, his eyes wide with shock, but the damage had been done. He took one step forward, falling to his knees, as a trickle of blood poured from the wound, wetting the ground. Then he stumbled, landing with a thud.

A smile of relief softened my features, the weapon feeling at home in my hands. It felt like an old friend. All I needed to do now was wait for Zendi and Kunchin to return, hopefully with a tasty stag in tow. I fully intended to eat—after I killed them.

Ten

The men took longer to return than anticipated. I made a fire near the base of a nearby tree, having dragged Pondo's body into the underbrush, kicking away at the bloodied dirt to hide a dark red smear. Satisfied with my efforts, I grasped the lower branch of a tree with my weapon slung over a shoulder, climbing several branches up. Here, I crouched and waited, listening to the sounds of animals, an owl's call echoing softly. The men would think all was well, seeing the fire to guide them home.

I pondered the situation during this time, knowing hunting in the dark presented a challenge, although the firelight would help towards that end. Luck helped me find thick, broken logs that had long dried out, the wood potentially burning brightly for a greater period of time.

A man's laughter resonated, instantly alerting me of their approach. I stood, stretching my legs for the first time, the muscles tight. Ignoring the discomfort, I stared into the darkness where I'd heard the noise, waiting. Zendi and Kunchin approached, their footfalls far from quiet, the men bantering about something, another laugh ringing out. They must have been successful in the kill, anticipating cooking whatever they had.

Now it's my turn ...

I waited until they stepped into the light of the fire, an arrow leaving the bow immediately, flying through the air with great speed. It hit Kunchin in the chest, the man speaking at the time, his eyes widening. Knowing I had to strike again as fast as possible or else Zendi might run, I affixed another arrow, pulling back on the twine made of rawhide. Zendi lifted his chin to me, his eyes wide with alarm. I released the arrow, the sturdy wood with a stone tip spiraling towards him, although he moved in that instant, the arrow catching him through the shoulder, slicing his arm from one end to the other. Suspecting something like this might happen, I positioned another arrow, preparing to shoot.

"Stop! Don't do it, Peta! Let's talk about this."

"The time for talk is over." I wasn't stupid enough to think his ploy would work in my benefit, knowing that if I put the weapon down and climbed to the ground, he would rape and kill me. I knew it with absolute certainty. "Say goodbye, Zendi."

"Blast it!"

Those would be his last words, as the arrow swiftly embedded in the space between his eyes, the man collapsing in a heap next to Kunchin. Kunchin's wound hadn't killed him yet, the man moaning, blood spreading beneath him. I climbed down carefully, my bare feet on firm ground a moment later. Coming to stand before Zendi, I pulled the arrow free from his head, wiping the blood on his leather skirt. I always retrieved my arrows, if at all possible.

"It won't be long now," I murmured, eyeing Kunchin.

Blood appeared around his lips, his eyes wide with fear. "Bitch!" he hissed.

"You had no right to kidnap me. You had no right to take me from my home—from my man."

Anger rippled through me, the sentiment so strong, it shocked me. He groaned with pain, as I placed my foot upon his chest. I clutched the arrow, pulling it free, causing him excruciating agony. His ragged, tortured cry echoed into the night. I waited a moment, seeing him still entirely, all life leaving him. Wiping the arrow clean on his skirt, I slid the weapon into the leather bag.

They had brought back a small stag, the animal already gutted. It only needed dismembering to be ready for the fire, although I suddenly did not wish to spend the night with three corpses. I doubted I had the energy to move to another camp, dragging the animal with me. Considering my options, I decided to move the bodies a distance away, leaving them to the elements.

Upon completing this task, I carved out a few chunks of meat, holding them over the fire with sticks, until they sizzled and burned, the smell making my mouth water with anticipation. I ate, sitting by the warmth of the blaze, thinking about what had just occurred, fully intending on returning home in the morning.

Being alone brought back memories of the time I spent lost in the woods after leaving Sungir's hut. I had Wolf with me then, the animal shadowing my every move. Now, I had no one. I hated the feeling of being alone, fearing the slightest noise, worrying over the sound of a cracking branch. I knew it was irrational fear, having already killed three men who posed an immediate threat. I should sleep well tonight, combining all of their bedrolls, but ... I hated being alone.

Glancing at the butchered stag, it was far too much for me to eat, the meat going to waste. I hadn't the time to smoke any of it. That would not matter anyhow, as I expected to be home by tomorrow evening.

"It's only one night," I whispered, staring into the flames. "One night."

I had gone through their things, finding dried meat and tools, combining the most useful items into a leather pouch. Several bladders filled with water would prove useful as well. I had more than enough to aid me on the trip home. I found several grooming items as well, bones to pick my teeth with and an ivory tong to run through my hair. While reclining on the thin pelts, I draped Zendi's fur over my legs, working the tangles from my hair. Allowing the fire to die down, I settled in for the night, finding the bedding comfortable. The bow remained by my side, the arrows within reach as well. One could never be too careful.

***

The squawking of noisy birds woke me, the sun streaming down through the branches of the trees. Having slept fitfully, I yawned, sitting up and glancing around warily. I would not waste another moment here, rolling up the bedding and gathering my things. I set out directly, leaving the corpses behind, birds of prey having found them already.

Stopping by a stream to wash, I threw water in my face, contemplating the journey home. I might have to climb a tree to ascertain my whereabouts, the men not having taken me that far. Excited for the reunion later, I found an old, thick-trunked tree, its branches enormous. Leaving my things on the ground, I took the bow and arrow along, climbing gingerly from limb to limb, balancing easily on the wide branches. Nearing the top, I gazed at the forest, seeing nothing other than trees. Dismayed, I hoped to spy the mountains near our cave, the peaks coated in white.

"That's not good." I carefully examined my location from all angles, seeing nothing other than trees, with a smallish prairie behind me, where the men had hunted the stag.

I knew we came in this direction, and, therefore, if I returned that way, I should eventually find familiar territory. Deciding to walk, I planned to climb another tree later, hoping to glimpse the big mountains of my home. I had broken the branches of bushes on the walk, and there had to be footprints, the men far heavier. Carefully, I climbed down, dropping to the ground a few moments later. Some of the anticipation of seeing Ronan and Enwan dimmed, a worried feeling creeping into my thoughts. What if I could not find the way back? I had never been that adept at directions and things. I had a terrible habit of getting lost.

"I'll look for signs then. I can't just walk blindly today. It's too important." With my hands on my hips, I gazed about, hating that every tree looked the same. The wind scattered leaves, threatening to hide footprints. "Damn," I muttered, feeling even more disoriented now.

Annoyed with myself, I slung the bedding over my back, along with a heavy leather bag.

"Please, gods. Don't forsake me again. Help me find my way home. Please."

With a hint of desperation, I set out, hoping to find the path or some sign of where we had been yesterday. I assumed the direction I chose to be the right one, my instincts warning me that I might not be right, though, which I hardly appreciated. It wasn't until late in the day that I stopped to climb another tree, a sense of panic drifting through me. From its higher branches, I eyed the never-ending stretch of forest, fanning out on all sides.

"Damn you, gods! What sort of help is this?" No mountains came into sight, not from any direction. "Blast and damn!" I had yet to find any sign of us passing through yesterday, and I should have. If I had gone the way we came, I should have found something.

Dismayed and tired, I descended, sitting at the base of the tree with my face in my hands. In hopes of reaching Ronan and Enwan today, I had walked fast, faster than I should have. I wanted so desperately to be home soon, to be in the valley where my heart had taken root, where my dreams had come true. I yearned to see my love's handsome face, to feel his tender embrace. I longed for my own bed, for the safety I felt there, but I wasn't truly safe, was I? I had been taken while foraging near my home by a small band of heathens.

"No place is safe," I whispered miserably. "He must be in a state now." I could only imagine Ronan's distress. I would not doubt that he and Enwan had been searching for me ... looking closely at the ground and bushes for any clue to where I had gone. "I'm here," I muttered. "Here in the blasted forest again."

Having a bite to eat and a sip of water, I got to my feet, feeling an ache in my legs and back, my bones begging for rest. I pushed onward, although I walked slowly now, the shadows of evening closing in around me. A cold breeze blew through the branches, rustling the leaves overhead. I could smell moisture in the air, worried about rain. I hurried onward, spying a ravine a short while later with enormous, moss covered boulders strewn about on either side. I passed through them, trudging on, while looking for shelter.

A gust of wind took my hair and tossed it into my face, a storm approaching. I needed to find shelter—now! Climbing around the rocks, I found a large rock with a bit of an outcropping, a sort of overhanging roof. I could sit beneath it until the rain ceased. Just as the first drops hit my shoulders, I squatted here, the ground smelling of damp earth. Bushes blew wildly before me, offering a fair amount of privacy. I had managed to not only get out of the rain, but to hide myself.

Unrolling the bedding, I sat with the fur over my legs, feeling reasonably warm despite the colder temperatures. A crack of noise rumbled, the storm arriving in earnest. Flashes of light streaked in the sky, visible through the branches of the trees. I waited for the tempest to end, chewing on dried meat and contemplating what a failure today had been. Yes, I had killed the men who had taken me, but now ... I was alone. My thoughts turned as dark as the weather, an uncomfortable feeling lodging in the pit of my belly.

"Where am I? Why does nothing look familiar?"

Resting my chin on a knee, I watched the rain dispassionately, wondering if I might have to sleep here tonight.

Eleven

Disappointed not to be reunited with Ronan, I settled in to sleep, all the while listening to the sound of rain. Finishing the rest of the dried meat, I found a few nuts at the bottom of a leather bag, eating them as well. If I did not arrive home tomorrow, I would have to hunt. That thought bothered me greatly.

"I should be at the cave now. I … I've gone in the wrong blasted direction," I grumbled irritably. "That explains why I'm still in the forest."

I slept on two thin leather blankets with the third over me, and Zendi's fur. This provided enough comfort, although I could feel something crawling on me, small black insects desiring to remain out of the rain as well. Not able to sleep like this, I shook out the bedding, spreading a layer of ash from the fire upon the ground. The insects did not like this, staying away. I settled in again listening to the rain, although tiredness brought sleep at last.

Come morning, I woke to birdcalls, something dripping near my head, water falling from the rocky outcropping. My bones aching, I licked parched lips, although I had water in a bladder nearby. I sat up, tossing messy hair over a shoulder. I had been so certain I would return home yesterday. I even primped and preened, running an ivory comb through my hair, wanting to look my best for Ronan.

"I shouldn't have bothered." Picking at a jagged toenail, I contemplated what I might do today to find my way back. "I could turn around and go the way I came."

I vaguely remembered where the sun had been on the walk, knowing where it set. I thought I had reversed that, which would bring me home, but now I questioned that decision, doubting I had been correct. I would have to go back and start again. The stench of decaying bodies would help guide me, but I did not relish the task.

Sighing wearily, I gathered my things, leaving the outcropping and finding a gurgling creek. Washing myself, I listened intently to the forest, hearing the happy singing of insects and birdcalls, the animals feasting after a night of rain, food now plentiful. I stopped to pick berries, devouring each one, stripping the bush clean. I found mushrooms as well, plucking them from the ground and eating them.

Wearing leather around my feet, I still felt the sharp edges of rocks, my feet protesting each time I stepped on one, which happened often. Towards midday, I stopped to rest, using a tree at my back, while I lifted the bladder of water to my lips, having a drink. Utterly spent, I desired to sleep, never having been this tired in a good long time, memories of when I ventured alone present in my mind—thoughts drifting to one memory and then another, a feeling of defeat sagging my shoulders.

"I should be used to being alone by now. I've done this—" The snapping of a branch caught my notice, the sound nearby.

I sat up, grasping the bow, an arrow in my hand. *Something comes!* Another twig snapped, followed by what I could only describe as a voice. A woman's voice, then another, this time, sounding younger. I knew without looking that someone from my mother's race approached, the language not spoken by Ronan or Enwan, but I knew it. I had learned it in a cave, many seasons before.

Not knowing whether they might harm me, I debated if I should lower the weapon, my hands trembling slightly.

Before yesterday, I had never killed a man. Since then, I had been forced to kill three. The last thing I wished to do was harm another, but ... if they proved threatening, I would have little choice. I listened to them speaking, discerning a woman and two younger girls, their conversation centering on some squabble they'd had earlier in the day. Hiding behind the tree, I waited until they drew nearer, stepping out before them, although they remained at a distance. The girls saw me first, a shriek resounding.

"Mamma! Look!" she uttered in a guttural, raspy voice. "White woman!"

They immediately took defensive postures, the mother holding a walking stick before her, which reminded me of my mother. The girls withdrew small, sharp-looking stakes, standing with legs wide apart, their eyes blazing with fear. Dark-skinned and short, they wore leather skirts, their feet bare. They each held a leather pouch, having been foraging.

The sight of them produced an odd yearning, the feeling slightly melancholy. They reminded me so much of my mother and sisters, yet they were different people. "I mean you no harm," I said in their language, grateful I had gotten the words out. I had not spoken it in a long time. They seemed to understand me, the older woman's expression stunned. "I'm traveling through. I'm lost."

Lowering the stick, the woman glanced at her girls. "She speaks our words. Isn't that odd?"

"Yes, Mamma." The little girl glanced at me. "How do you know our language?"

"My mother looks like you. She found me when I was very young. She raised me." I smiled, feeling the tension lessen at once. "Is your clan nearby?"

"Near enough," said the woman, a distrustful look in her eye. "You're here to find them, aren't you? If I tell you where we are, you'll send men to kill us. This is a ploy."

"No! I'm only one woman." I took a step closer. "I'm lost. Three men kidnapped me. I killed them. You needn't worry about anyone else. I come alone."

"I've never seen hair that color," said the younger of the girls.

"She's so tall," murmured the older girl.

"I've been walking for two days. I'm tired. I'm trying to find the great green valley with mountains beyond, but … I'm lost."

Something in my tone seemed to alter her opinion of me, her gaze staying to my belly. "You say you're alone."

"I am."

"Women don't travel alone."

"I told you; I was kidnapped. Three brutes took me from my home against my will. I killed them at the first opportunity. Now, I need to go back, but it's difficult." I hoped I had spoken the correct words, my skill at this language unpracticed.

She took a few steps nearer, her attention on my weapon. "What is that?"

"I use it to hunt." I grinned. "It's been a trusted friend. I'd be lost without it."

"Women don't hunt."

"I must, if I wish to eat. I've been alone a great deal. The god's hate me." I smiled brighter, hopeful at the prospect of a hot meal later, preferably before a fire with these people.

The younger girl approached. "That's a pretty necklace." She pointed to my chest, where a purple stone lay suspended in leather. Many seasons before, Ronan made this and one for my sister. "There's a woman from our clan with a necklace like it, but the stone's a different color."

My smile fell. "What?"

"Hers is grey with green, but just as pretty."

The older woman eyed me keenly. "What's your

name?"

"Peta." Still reeling from this revelation, I asked, "The woman with a necklace like mine isn't named Ara, is she?"

The little girl smiled. "Why, yes, she is."

"A-and her mother and sister are with her?" I held my breath, my heart hammering in my chest.

"Yes. They came more than a season ago to be with us." The older woman approached. "I'm Tosh. These are my daughters Veena and Clowen."

It felt like my knees might give out, and I lowered to the ground, pressing a hand to my chest. Overcome with emotion, I began to weep, unable to control myself. I never truly expected to see my family again, the loss of them being the most painful thing I had ever experienced. I swallowed with effort, my eyes blurring with tears.

"Kia spoke of losing her daughter," said Tosh. "She said the girl was of the white race."

"C-can you take me to your clan, please? I must see my mother and sisters. I must. We've been separated for more than two seasons. They disappeared one day and never returned. I ... I can't believe this. I can't ... " I shook my head, feeling light-headed and dizzy. "It's too much."

"She doesn't mean us harm, Mamma," said Veena. "I don't see why we can't take her with us. She knows our language. She's one of us, in truth, even if she looks different."

"I won't argue that fact." A smile flitted across Tosh's face. "Your mother would be pleased to see you again. She speaks of you often."

I got to my feet clutching my things, while wiping away tears. "I'm ready. I'm ready to see my family."

"Come then," said Clowen. "It's this way."

I fell into step with them, my heart feeling as if it might burst. We followed a thin path through the forest, the clan having used it often by the looks of it. Passing a stream, we emerged onto a hilly prairie, with the smoke of cooking fires drifting into the air beyond. I did not see people yet, but I could hear dogs yapping.

"It's not far," said Veena.

"I know." I had not given much thought to the fact that I was about to venture into a clan of strangers, although at this time of day most of the men would be hunting.

After crossing the field, I glimpsed various cooking fires, seeing dark-skinned people tending them. The sound of animals and babies crying filled the air, a pile of bones to my right from many hunts. I scanned the camp, seeing mostly women and babies, a small child running around naked, his hair as black as night.

"They might be away at the moment," said Tosh. "You may stay with us until they return."

"All right."

I felt a twinge of disappointment, having envisioned a happy, euphoric reunion, but now I had to wait until they returned. The camp looked messy, with bones scattered in piles and the air smelling of feces. They had not designated a proper latrine, going wherever they chose. All the clans I had lived with, including the dark-skinned people in the cave, had dug proper latrines.

"This is our fire," said Veena. "You may sit and rest, if you wish."

Several women turned their heads towards us, one of them getting to her feet. The sight of a white women aroused their curiosity, no doubt.

Tosh said loudly, "She's Kia's daughter. There's no cause for alarm."

I was about to sit, when a man approached, his short, stocky legs bowed. He reminded me of the men at the winter cave, his dark face swarthy.

He frowned. "What is the meaning of this? Who is this woman? You know this is forbidden. We can't have her sort here."

"This is our healer, Munfred." She stared at him. "This is Kia's daughter. I welcomed her here to reunite with her family."

"Palo will not be happy about this," he blustered, his angry gaze upon me. "We stay away from the whites. They're dangerous. She'll bring death, mark my words."

"I only wish to see my family. I mean no one harm."

He blinked, stunned I had spoken his language. He had to lift his chin to look at me. "We shall see about that, white woman."

"Peta. My name's Peta."

Twelve

Having been tentatively accepted, I took a spot by the fire, a dog ambling over to sniff me. "Hello." I petted his head, his tongue darting out to lick my fingers. Several children came to observe me, standing at a distance, their voices in hushed discussion. I smiled at them, saying, "Hello." Astonished that I spoke their language, they giggled. "I mean you no harm."

Clowen waved them away. "There's nothing to see here, you little troublemakers." She tossed another branch into the fire, the flames flickering around it a moment later. Several women strode past, eyeing us. "You're a curiosity."

"I can see that." This reminded me of the clan by the river, where my mother and sister were the only dark people. They had been tolerated, but just barely. The only reason they accepted them and protected them was because of me. "When do you think they'll return?" I noted the position of the sun, the day wearing long.

"Soon." She offered me some dried meat. "You must be hungry."

"Thank you."

Several men broke from the trees, approaching with a stag, the legs tied to a thick branch. Two of them carried the carcass, while the third led the way, a spear in his hand. I sucked in a breath, knowing my being here would cause a stir, one of the men spying me.

"Look!" he shouted. "A white woman!"

The trio stopped in their tracks, staring open-mouthed.

"She's Kia's daughter," said Clowen. "She's come for her family."

Munfred, having heard the commotion, got up from his comfortable pelt, facing the men. "Leave her be. Palo will deal with her."

That statement concerned me, my brows drawing together. "What does that mean?" I eyed my weapon, grateful I had it.

Tosh approached with an armful of branches, her gaze on the men. "Everyone will be naturally curious." She tossed them to the ground. "It's to be expected."

"Don't stand there looking stupid," admonished Munfred of the men. "You've meat to cook."

Their women drew near, casting a glance towards me. They motioned for the men to continue, several children ran to them as well, everyone impatient for a piece of meat. I tried to remain calm, knowing I would elicit this reaction from every man returning. As more emerged from the forest, I felt the weight of many stares, a cacophony of conversation swirling around me, one man in particular gravely concerned, his dark features glossy from perspiration.

Munfred approached him. "I gave her permission to stay for the moment. She speaks our language. She claims to be Kia's daughter."

I instinctively knew him to be the leader, his presence authoritative, people bowing to him. He wore a leather cloth around his hips, his feet encased in fur. Short and stout, his body appeared to be a thick mass of muscle, each step he took making them bulge beneath the skin of his legs. I prayed I did not have to use my weapon, desiring the meeting to be peaceful, yet I could not guess his thoughts.

Munfred and the leader neared, arriving to stand before me. I feared having to get to my feet, knowing I would tower over them. I stood slowly, noting how everyone in the camp stopped to stare at us, more people arriving from the forest, women and children emerging. My sisters and mother would be among them, the anticipation adding to my anxiety.

"She says her name's Peta." Munfred pointed to me. "This is our leader, Palo."

"Thank you for welcoming me. I mean you no harm. I only wish to be reunited with my family."

Palo had to lift his chin to look at me. "Who do you say your family is?"

"Kia, Ara, and Maggi."

"I know of whom you speak." His gaze drifted over me, noting the swell of my belly. "Are you alone?"

"I am. Heathen brutes kidnapped me, but I escaped. I'm on my way home, but I ... I'm lost. I stumbled upon you people." I dared to hope that this would continue to go smoothly. "I haven't seen my family in two seasons. I'm quite eager to see them." I smiled tentatively, hoping they would not find me a threat. People drew near to listen to the conversation, a wide circle having formed.

"You must understand our concern. We can never be too careful when dealing with the whites, even women. I fear you'll bring destruction." He eyed my belly. "You've a man, no doubt. He'll come for you. He'll kill everything in his path."

"He's far away. I'm trying to find him. The brutes that kidnapped me were white, but they're dead now. I killed them. You've nothing to fear from me. I only come to see my family."

"I shall have to consider this." He glanced at the people all around. "She's not to be harmed. She's a guest for the moment, until I decide if she stays or goes." A flurry of discussion echoed, a baby crying.

A woman pushed through the crowd, her stature short, and her hair a mass of tangles down her back. I recognized her at once, tears filling my eyes. "Kia!"

Her mouth fell open. "By the grace of the gods!"

"Mamma!" I rushed to her, hugging her, as a gasp resounded, the clan not having anticipated such a display.

"Peta!" she cried, grasping onto me tightly, her skin smelling of sweat and sun, her body trembling. She drew away, holding my face, tears streaming down her cheeks. "My girl. I never thought to see you again."

"I've been searching for you! I'm so glad you're well. I worried so!"

"Peta?"

I turned to see Ara, my sister holding a baby. "Ara!" And then Maggi appeared, the girl as tall as Ara. "Maggi!" We fell into each other's arms, the feeling so joyous I thought I might faint. I touched each of their faces, kissing Maggi on the forehead, then Ara, while they did the same to me, Ara touching my belly. "I'm so happy! I can't ever remember such happiness!"

Kia, although crying, said, "She's my daughter, Palo. There's nothing to worry about here." She glanced at the crowd. "Peta's my daughter. You needn't be concerned."

"Disburse!" shouted Palo. "Go to your fires. Let them have their peace." He considered us thoughtfully. "I shall think on it. No decision has been made yet. Having a white woman in the clan is dangerous."

"Thank you, Palo," said Kia. "You're a wise man." She bowed her head. "We shall honor your decree, whatever it might be."

Ara's baby fussed, the infant quite young. "You've a baby!" I grinned, patting my belly. "I'll have one too shortly."

Kia's hand closed around my forearm. "Come to our fire. We've a meal to prepare and stories to share. There's so much I wish to know."

***

I sat with Ara, my sister's knee touching mine, while the baby nursed from her breast. One of his tiny fists held strands of her hair, while his eyes remained closed, his small mouth working. My arm around her shoulder, I smiled at Maggi, who sat across the fire. She helped my mother carve out a portion of meat, placing it over flattened rocks to cook.

"Don't make mine too dry," said Ara. "I hate it overcooked."

Kia removed a slice of meat with a stick. "Who would like this?"

"I would," said Ara.

"Shouldn't we feed our guest first?"

"I'm not a guest. I'm family." The smile on my face stayed in place. "You all eat. I'm so full of happiness, I can't possibly take anything else in at the moment."

"Keep cooking, Maggi. I wish to speak to your sister." She scooted nearer, sitting on my other side. "Let me look at you, child." She touched my face. "You've grown into a woman. Someone's bred you. Who?"

"I found Ronan and Enwan!"

Her eyes widened. "No."

"Yes! I found them in the warm season. They're living in a beautiful valley, in a cave on a rocky hill. There's a pool of water that's hot too. Hot! It's glorious to bathe."

"You look clean." She touched my hair, seeing the braid laced with various small shells. "I'm surprised you found them, Peta. I know how fond you were of Ronan."

"It's his child I carry." I shrugged, feeling sheepish. "Or it's Enwan's. I can't be sure. If the babe comes out looking like me, then it's Ronan's." I giggled at that. "But it doesn't matter. I adore them both, but my heart belongs to Ronan."

Ara lifted the baby to her shoulder, patting his back. "We worried about you. When we were taken, we worried about you being alone in the hut."

"Your disappearance has plagued me for two seasons. I remember going to the hut, while you all remained by the creek. Then, when you didn't return, I went to find you. You'd gone. I saw your footprints and several bigger ones belonging to men. I knew they'd kidnapped you." I glanced at Kia. "Or did you go willingly?"

"It wasn't our choice." Kia sighed heavily, her eyes staring into the fire. "We were bathing when they came. Three of them. They were of my race. They … took us. They forced leather into our mouths and bonds on our hands, stealing us away. I longed to scream—to call out, but I couldn't. I've never felt such terror as that day."

"Did they harm you?" I could not count the number of horrible dreams I'd had, worried over their welfare. "Were you beaten?"

"They took us to trade," said Ara. "That's what we discovered. They bartered us off on the first clan we came across, a small group of men who needed more women."

"It's all in the past," said Kia, her expression flattening. "I don't wish to relive it."

"Then you weren't treated well."

"They bred me and mamma," said Ara. "Mamma had another baby, but the boy died. I lost a child early on. We weren't fed well. They forced us to walk. They did … beat us occasionally."

Something sharp turned in my chest, the feeling awful. "I'm so sorry." Tears formed in my eyes at the thought of their suffering. "I had hoped it wouldn't be so. I prayed you'd be taken care of."

"As luck would have it, several of the men went to hunt and never returned," said Kia. "The remaining men disappeared one by one. Two other women were with the clan. We set out on our own, finding these people. We've since settled nicely. Palo's a good man. He's fair. I can speak to him about my concerns, and he listens. They don't deride women like the white clans. We have some power here."

"I'm glad." I glanced at Ara. "Might I hold him?"

"If you wish. I'd like my hands free to eat." She gave me her baby, the boy asleep.

"What did you name him?"

"Bunder."

"Who's Bunder's father, or do you not know?"

"I assume that's him," she pointed to a nearby fire, where a younger man sat, his eyes on us. Surrounded by several men, they talked and ate. "That's Lowe." She smiled slightly. "He's ... friendly with me."

I could tell Ara was fond of him, her expression infused with affection. "You've found a partner. I'm happy for you." I glanced at my mother. "And you?"

"I'm ... well, you know me." She chewed on a piece of meat.

She would never find love like she had with Magnon, the man having died seasons ago, murdered by Greggor and his men. "You mate whoever you like, whenever you like."

"We all do," said Ara. "It's not like the white clan, although I am fond of Lowe. I prefer him." He acknowledged our appraisal, getting to his feet. Short and stocky, he ambled over, his legs bowed. A pronounced ridge lined his forehead, his eyes alight with interest.

"Ara."

"Lowe. Come meet my sister, Peta. You know, the one I've been talking about for ages. She's found us." She patted the pelt. "Come sit. You needn't stare at me from such a distance."

He lowered to the pelt, his demeanor shy, yet inquisitive. I held the sleeping baby. I adored how tiny he was, how helpless and sweet. Being with my family brought me immense joy and connectedness, the feeling euphoric.

"Do you have anything to say, Lowe?" asked Kia. "You look odd."

"Never seen a white woman before."

I laughed at that, the sound carrying.

Thirteen

The clan settled in for the night, cooking fires dying down, while sounds of mating filled the air. I slept on a pelt next to Ara and Lowe, with Maggi and the baby between us. Kia had her own pelt across the fire. Stars glinted in the sky overhead, the moon hidden behind a thick bank of clouds. With a clan full of strong men and my family, I felt blissfully safe.

At daybreak, I snuggled into the pelt, hating that a dog barked noisily. The baby woke several times during the night needing to be fed. He slept now, Ara having already gotten up. She left him with me, the boy pressed to my breast. Having walked for two days, my body craved rest, the baby in my belly kicking gently. I sat up a while later, flinging hair over my shoulder and gasping. The leader of the clan, Palo, stood at the foot of the pelt with a spear in hand.

Not knowing why he had arrived, I stared at him, Bunder beginning to fuss. I reached for him, holding him close. "What is it?"

"You cannot join our clan. It's been decided."

"I don't wish to. I'm traveling on to … where I live. I won't be here long."

"Good."

The talking woke Maggi, who grumbled something, turning away from me and burrowing further into the pelt. Kia glanced at us, having been up already.

She frowned. "This is my daughter, Palo."

"I'm aware of that."

"She means us no harm."

"Yet having anything to do with the white people always brings trouble."

"She won't."

"I worry all the same." He scowled. "Someone's looking for her. She's going to have a baby soon. Someone will want to claim that child."

"My husband. I'll be with him again shortly." A yawn escaped me, the baby crying now. "Oh, you're so noisy."

Palo grunted, displeased by the conversation. "I don't want trouble."

"I won't cause any."

"You better not." He stomped off, approaching a group of men who waited, all of them holding spears, preparing to hunt for the day.

I glanced at Kia. "Good day, Mamma." I smiled, squinting in the sun.

"Where's your sister gone? She should mind that baby."

"I don't know." I didn't see her, as haze filled the air, several cooking fires alight. The flames burned through damp wood.

"Attach him to your breast. That'll keep him quiet for a bit."

"H-how do I do that?"

"Hold him to you. He'll latch on. He's about to wake the dead."

I did as she said, the baby turning his head to my breast, his mouth closing on a nipple. The feeling surprised me, Bunder suckling aggressively. "I don't have milk yet."

"It'll keep him until your sister returns." She got to her feet, her look pensive. A grouping of men stood at a distance watching us. "None of them have seen anything like this."

"Your clan?"

"A white woman with a dark babe."

"You told me to hold him."

She eyed the forest, where Ara appeared. "There she is."

"Oh, good. It's time she feeds her child. I've some things to take care of."

Ara approached. "What are you doing, Peta?"

"He was noisy." I lifted the baby, my nipple popping out of his mouth. He began to cry immediately. "See. Noisy just like that. You should feed him."

She took him, settling in next to me. "I should thank you, I suppose."

"That would be kind of you." I teased her a little.

"Everyone's talking about you."

"I know." She held the baby to her breast. "Where were you?"

"Saying goodbye to Lowe. He's hunting." A playful smile toyed around the edges of her mouth. "He wanted to mate."

"Oh, I see."

"We forage soon." Kia chewed on a piece of dried meat, her attention on the woods. "This is familiar, isn't it?"

"Being with a clan?" I asked.

She smiled wistfully. "It reminds me of the clan by the river, although they weren't my people."

"And then the flood came." That memory wasn't a pleasant one.

"It did." She nodded. "And we spent many seasons deep in the forest. I prefer being with my people."

"I know you do."

"And you'll want to return to yours."

"I ... " She was correct about that, a feeling of yearning gripping me tightly. I worried about Ronan and Enwan. I had only been gone two days, but I knew they would be greatly concerned. "I'll have to find a way back. I lost the direction. Perhaps someone here knows where the valley is."

"You'll have to ask." She knelt before us. "I'm grateful you're well, Peta. I knew you'd survive. Sungir taught you and Ara well. You can hunt and provide. You were meant to find Ronan again. You're bonded to him in a unique way. No matter where you are, you'll find him."

"I hope so."

Maggie sat up, grumbling, "You're all so noisy! I can't sleep."

"We forage soon," said Kia. "It's time you're up anyhow."

I scrambled to the edge of the pelt, hugging my mother. "I missed you so dreadfully." Old feelings of loss and anguish appeared, my throat constricting. "I can't tell you how awful it was. For one whole season, I sat in that hut waiting for you to return. I was alone a great many days. I thought I'd go mad. It took every bit of courage I had to leave."

"You're a brave girl."

"No, I was desperate. I can't be alone. I hate it."

She touched my face, her fingers feeling rough. "You're where you should be. You're with your man. You'll have his child soon enough."

"I wish we could live together. You and Ara and Maggi should come with me. It's paradise. It's the most beautiful land I've ever seen. We live in a large cave. There's room for everyone."

A sad smile appeared on her weathered face, her black eyes glistening. "Don't you see? We belong with our own, Peta. Ara's found a mate. Maggi will too, when she's older. We're settled here now. You're where you should be."

"But ... I wish—"

"It's as it should be. The gods have decreed it such. Whatever's happened, it's been with this result in mind.

We were meant to be parted so you could find Ronan."

I understood this, but … "I miss you so dreadfully."

"You'll have your own child to manage soon enough. You'll be too busy to live in the past."

"You're saying this might be the end? We might never see each other again after I leave?"

"Possibly." She took my hand, squeezing it. "You're resourceful. You always were a strong girl, stronger than you think. We've found one another again for the moment. It's eased my mind to know you're in a good place. I won't worry anymore about where you might be or if you're well. I know you're with Ronan and Enwan. I'm very happy about that, Peta. It gladdens me."

"And you're with your people." That should have made me happy, but I could not help feeling sad. "Will you stay in this place for long?" It did not look like a permanent settlement, the clan sleeping outdoors without shelter of any kind, although a few flimsy structures stood here and there. A good wind would blow them over.

"It's our place for now. The game's plentiful. The foraging is good. I don't foresee leaving for a few seasons."

"Then, if I can find my way back to the cave, I might be able to return here to visit. It's not as if we're forever separated."

"That can be done. I'd adore seeing your child when he or she comes."

"The place I live is so beautiful. The cave is on a hill with a view of the valley below. There are mountains all around with tips of white. It's temperate too. The cold season's nearly upon us, yet it's not terribly cold. I won't even need furs."

"It's temperate here too."

"I so wish you would come with me. Come live with us, Kia. I beg you."

She sighed, a sad smile softening her features. "I see

how it has to be now. Ara and I and Maggi have found our place. We belong here. We've been accepted into the clan. I know Ronan and Enwan are good men, but they have you. You're of the same sort of people. I prefer my people, Peta. I'm sorry. I'm content here."

I tried not to cry, knowing she spoke the truth. "Perhaps I can stay a few days then. I long to hear about your adventures. You'll never believe mine. I befriended a wolf! He was my faithful companion on the journey to the valley, but he died two days ago. I was foraging near my home when three heathens took me. I waited until an opportunity presented itself, then I killed them." Her eyes widened. "I've never harmed anyone before. I sat in a tree and shot them with arrows, just like Sungir taught us. I had to."

"This confirms my thoughts. You're more than capable of protecting yourself, even this heavy with child." A flicker of pride shone in her eyes. "I never doubted it."

"I have something else to tell you. The men that took me belonged to a white clan. Their leader's name is Greggor." I watched her carefully, her features hardening. "You remember that name, don't you?"

"How could I ever forget it? He and his men came to slaughter us in the cold of the morning. I remember it all too well. You were just a child then. You and the other children hid in a small cavern at the back of the cave. You did not witness the atrocities."

"But I did. I saw everything through a gap between the wall and a rock. I saw what they did, Mamma. I saw it all."

She digested that, her eyes narrowing. "You saw the man they speak of? That man, Greggor?"

"I recall him being tall and dark."

"Yes."

"What terrifies me is that his men were near my home. They came upon me while I foraged. I chide myself for letting my guard down, for feeling too safe. Although it's an ideal place, danger can lurk, even in paradise."

She nodded. "It's best to always be vigilant. One can never be too sure."

"They were going to take me to him, like I was some sort of prize. Can you imagine?" I felt a twinge of revulsion. "That horrible man. His people murdered ours. Then, after all this time, he's still about causing trouble."

"But you saved yourself. You prevailed."

"I tell you, I swear this. If I ever see that man, I shall kill him. I will avenge the wrongs he's committed against us. I'll avenge Wolf's death too. I fear and pray I have the chance one day."

"Be careful what you wish for, Peta. Some things are better left alone. You've a husband to care for. You're going to be a mother soon. You should leave all the rest to the gods to manage. Let them be the ones to mete out justice. Your revenge is living a happy life. In that respect, you've already won." She leaned in to kiss my cheek. "I love you, Peta. Nothing makes me happier than seeing you again. I wish you every happiness, child. I do."

Tears filled my eyes. "I love you, Mamma. You're the reason I'm the way I am. Sungir taught me hunting skills, but it's because of you that I learned strength of mind and determination. I'll never give up on the ones I love."

Fourteen

We ventured into the forest together, carrying baskets. I brought my bow, while Ara slung Bunder over her back, the baby secure in a swath of thin hide. With Maggi leading the way, it brought back memories of the past, how we often ventured into the woods together to find nuts and berries. I grinned at the sight of us, walking in a line, hearing the talking of other women and children in the distance.

"I miss this," I murmured.

Ara glanced at me. "What do you do when you're home?"

"I forage with my pet." Then I remembered what happened to Wolf. "Although he's dead now. I found him after I left Sungir's hut."

"A real wolf?"

"Yes. He came upon me when I was lost. He followed me for days. He was very young, too young to be on his own. When I return, scavenging won't be the same. I won't have my companion."

"What happened to him?"

"Greggor's men killed him."

Her brows furrowed. "Where have I heard that name? It sounds familiar."

"Indeed," I said bitterly. "Many seasons ago at the cave with Magnon and his clan. Do you remember?"

"Of course I remember. They took us in and fed us. Kia found her mate only to have him slaughtered by white men."

"And their leader was named Greggor."

"And his men killed your pet?"

"They came upon me foraging and kidnapped me. I

managed to escape, but my animal … he died for me. He tried to help me."

"I'm sorry." She touched my shoulder. "How do you know they were Greggor's men?"

"They said so."

She spat. "That despicable man! He lives still? He's in these parts?"

"I don't know. His men were traveling through to other lands. They looked and smelled like they hadn't bathed in a good long time."

"If they're near here, we're in grave danger."

"I didn't see any other clans. You're the first people I've encountered."

"The past has returned to haunt us."

"Who are you speaking of?" asked Maggi.

"People from before you were born," I said. "The man who killed your father. He's a terrible, horrible white man."

A sharp pang of anger rippled through me, realizing Maggi would never know her father, the man cut down in the prime of his life. Greggor had speared him, leaving him to die on the rocks before the cave, Kia finding him there in the cold.

"I doubt you'll have trouble again," said Kia. "We mustn't dwell on the past. I've done so for too long. I yearned for Magnon all the seasons we spent at the hut. I can't think about it any longer."

"It's the first I've heard of it," said Ara. "It's unfortunate an old enemy continues to live."

"Not if I ever encounter him," I muttered.

"Berries!" Maggi darted into the foliage, squatting before a bush.

"Let's not speak of him again," said Kia. "I wish to forget it."

I gazed at the ground beneath my feet, seeing a grouping of mushrooms.

"You'd best heed my warning. I know your feelings on the matter. I know you want revenge. Such things are for the gods to take care of."

The trauma of the ordeal lingered, but I knew it would diminish in time. "Yes, Mamma."

"Let it be, girl. Go home to your husband. Go have your child."

My rounded belly pushed out the leather skirt I wore. "I do look forward to it. I can only imagine how distressed Ronan must be. He hasn't a clue where I went."

"He's smart. He knows you can look after yourself, even in your condition."

"I wonder if he's searching for me now?"

"He'll return to the cave. It's where you belong." A hint of sadness appeared on her face. "You shouldn't delay here too much longer."

"I wish to spend some time with you, a few days at the most." I frowned, watching my sisters picking berries. "I worry I might not find it again. I've somehow gotten turned around."

"I shall ask one of the elders if they've ever heard of a green valley with the type of mountains you describe. Perhaps, someone knows the direction."

"That's sensible."

"You'll recognize landmarks at some point. Your eyesight is far better than mine."

I giggled, "You never could see very far."

"No."

Maggi approached, carrying a basket. "We've picked it clean."

I kicked a mushroom. "Are these edible? They look edible."

"Yes," said Kia. "Pick them, although there are few."

"I want to wash in the creek." Ara waved to us. "There's water over here. Come."

The last time we had been to a stream together, my

family disappeared. A twinge of unease rippled through me. I eyed the forest keenly, seeing nothing other than the trees, although I heard voices in the distance, a group of women foraging.

"Lead the way," I said, feeling the weight of the bow across my shoulder. I would keep careful watch over them, never leaving their side—not for an instant.

***

Sitting by the fire, we cut a piece of meat into thin slices, Ara's man, Lowe, having brought it over. He sat with us as well, his eyes drifting over me. I chewed heartily, grateful to have such a fine meal. We dined on fruits and nuts as well, the aroma of grilling meat filling the air. A camp dog or two trotted by, sniffing around for scraps. A mangy-looking animal with only one eye lingered, the mutt hungry. I tossed him a piece of meat, which he promptly ate.

"This is an odd weapon," said Lowe, eyeing the bow. "How do you use it?"

"I can show you tomorrow, if you wish."

He picked it up. "You kill from a distance with this."

"Yes. It's quite useful."

"Women don't hunt."

"I've been alone often. I have to hunt or I starve."

He set the bow down upon the pelt, his finger feeling the smoothness of the wood. "It's finely made."

"I did it myself."

"You have a man?"

"I do."

"And where is he?"

"Looking for me, I suppose. I don't know."

"He's with the white clan."

"No. He's alone with his brother." They weren't blood related, having met many seasons ago.

"And you live with them?"

"Yes."

"But not with a clan."

"No. We're only a small clan."

"How can you survive in this way?"

"We do." I shrugged. I felt his appraisal, Ara and Kia listening to the conversation. Maggi sat between them, the baby, Bunder, sleeping in soft leather at her feet.

"And they mate you?"

I should have expected the question, knowing the only thing men cared about after a meal was ... mating. "Yes." As I stared at the other fires, I noted several instances of mating occurring at that very moment. I certainly hoped he did not think I would submit to him.

Ara, having overheard every word, scooted nearer, Lowe's attention drifting to her. She held a stick in the fire, a piece of meat sizzling. I felt a small measure of relief, my sister having offered up enough of a distraction, her man's attention fully on her. I inched closer to Kia, my mother busy weaving thin strips of leather together.

"Are you happy here?"

"I am."

"You and my sisters could come with me."

"Then where would we be?"

"We can live together again."

"I love you, child, but ... I prefer my own people. I've told you that."

I knew that would be her answer, but I had to try again. "I wish ... I wish ... we could be together. I miss the company of women. I hadn't known how much I missed it, until I found you again."

Her stark features softened. "One day your clan will be bigger. You'll bring in more women. More men will come. You'll grow."

"I don't know how. Not many travel where we live." I shivered at the memory of Greggor's men, the trio having entered our valley and brazenly stolen me away. "I'm happy now with you, but I miss Ronan."

"Of course you do."

"Watch my baby," said Ara. She got to her feet, Lowe leading her to his pelt by a nearby fire.

I eyed them with envy, wishing I had Ronan to mate with, feeling lonely this evening, despite being surrounded by my family.

Kia's hand settled over mine. "You're a grown woman now. You're capable. You have the power to create whatever life you wish."

"But I don't. I was taken away from my home. Those horrible men ripped me from my life."

"Briefly."

"True, but everything's in turmoil now. I can feel it." This odd sense that things would never be the same again niggled away at me. "I was too happy. Things were too good. The gods hate it when I'm truly at peace. They always come and ruin everything."

"You're far too young to be so bitter, Peta." She smiled sympathetically. "I know why you're like this. You've seen a great deal of tragedy in your life. You've overcome much. You've survived worse than this. You'll find your man again. I remember Ronan. He was resourceful. He survived the flood when so many perished. Strong men died when the water came."

I nodded, staring into the flames. "It's just that … I have a bad feeling. I don't know what it is, but … something's not right."

She squeezed my hand. "You can face whatever it is. I have faith in you. Despite what you think, the gods have not forsaken you. They led you to safety time and again. They've reunited us. We have this moment together. You mustn't be sad over what may or may not happen."

"You're always so wise, Mamma."

Fifteen

We slept together on a shared pelt, the crackling of the fire providing warmth for a while. I snuggled in next to my sisters, with the baby between us. He woke twice during the night wanting to be fed. I stared at the twinkling specks in the sky, listening to the sounds of mating from a nearby camp. I thought about Ronan, an aching feeling of loss bringing tears to my eyes. I prayed he was safe. I prayed to see him again. I had to find my way home.

Tired from a fitful sleep, I woke to an empty pelt, Kia cooking some meat from the night before, the smell making my belly rumble. I eyed her, wondering why she had left me sleeping. She seemed to sense the unspoken question.

"You're growing a baby. You need to rest."

Brushing hair from my eyes, I sat up. "Where is everyone?"

"Foraging."

Bunder slept beside me. "She left her baby."

"One of the other women can feed him." She handed me a piece of meat. "Here, eat." She stared at me. "You look tired."

"I didn't sleep well." I took the meat. "Thank you."

"Lowe's waiting for you."

"Who?" Then I remembered he was my sister's man. "Why?"

"He wants to learn more about that weapon. You should show him how to use it."

Chewing the meat, I yawned. "If I have to."

"It would benefit us. If you teach him, he can teach the other men. It's a useful weapon. Sungir was wise to show you how to hunt. Ara doesn't hunt all that often anymore. She's settled into more traditional ways."

"I don't hunt often either. Ronan and Enwan provide, but I don't want to lose my skills."

"Smart girl." She smiled. "Woman. You're not a little girl anymore."

I picked pieces of twigs and leaves from my hair. "I have to speak to the elders later. I'll show Lowe how to use the weapon and how to make one, but then I should go home." I frowned, realizing such a feat might take more than a few days.

"You look troubled."

"I can't help thinking I should leave at once. It feels urgent."

"You're carrying a baby. Women's emotions are heightened during this time. I cried a great deal with each pregnancy."

"I remember that."

"I was too sensitive to everything. You might be the same."

"What I'm feeling is just because of the baby?" I patted my stomach.

"Yes."

"I hadn't thought of it that way."

Lowe strode towards us, his darkly colored legs covered in black hair, as was the rest of him. The whiteness of his eyes glowed, their intensity focused on me. "We go soon, Peta. I've been waiting for you to wake."

Taking a sip of water from a bladder, I eyed him. "Your patience has been noted."

He seemed perplexed by that response. "I am patient."

"Hopefully, he's a fast learner." I glanced at my mother.

"You'll have to assess that on your own."

"Is it safe to go with him?"

"It's not safe to be with any man." She ripped off a piece of meat with her teeth, a hint of a smile emerging. "But you're hardly weak, Peta. You could easily best him."

Getting to my feet, I towered over Lowe, the man's face reaching my neck. He had to lift his chin to look at me. "This is a hunting lesson. Not a mating lesson."

Dark, bushy brows drew together. "I take no lesson from any woman."

"Then you don't wish to learn how to shoot these arrows? I thought that's why you're here."

"I ... I do. I will learn."

"And I will teach."

"I'll follow what you do."

"Which will be to teach you how to shoot."

"I'll do what you do."

I said in the white man's language, which Kia could understand, "What an annoying buffoon. Will he be like this all day?"

She laughed, "Most assuredly."

I groaned, rolling my eyes. "The gods mean to torture me." The baby began to fuss. "Are you ready?"

"I am."

I slung the bow around a shoulder, reaching for the bag of arrows. "Fine. I want to stop by the creek before we go out." I held a stone ax, which I planned to shove into my skirt.

He eyed it. "Why are you taking that?"

"For protection."

"You've the weapon. Isn't that enough?"

"Possibly. I use this to slice open game."

He held a spear. "That's what this is for."

A few men remained behind to watch over the women. They stood at a distance staring at us. "We're ready then. Let's go." I cast a glance at Kia. "Will you be safe here?"

"Yes, of course." She waved me away. "Show Lowe the weapon. He's smarter than he looks. He'll behave himself." She eyed him. "Won't you?"

He sucked in a breath, an indignant flicker dancing in his dark eyes. "I will."

***

A short while later, Lowe and I emerged from the forest, having come to an open prairie, where I spied game. The men hunted elsewhere, although several women foraged not far off, my sisters not among them. Lowe spoke little, following closely behind me, his footfalls heavy. I feared he might frighten the game away, but they had not seen us, a family of stags grazing among tall, golden grass.

The heat of the sun burned down upon my head, a trickle of perspiration falling between my breasts. I wore a leather skirt, the stone ax tucked between the leather and my belly. Sensing Lowe's interest, I withdrew an arrow, affixing it to the thin band of rawhide, drawing back on it. Knowing where to aim, I let it fly, arching through the air towards a smaller stag. It embedded a moment later, the animal falling, while the others darted into the forest.

Startled, Lowe gaped at me. "You killed it."

"Perhaps. It might just be wounded. Let's go and see." I ran towards where the stag lay, the animal terrified. "I'm sorry. We thank you for your sacrifice." I slit its throat, blood pouring forth. Then I ran the blade down the belly, disemboweling the creature, a mixture of organ and gore spilling forth, the blood seeping into the ground at my feet. "Now you see how it works." I stood with my hands on my hips, an annoying bug flying around my face. "It looks easy, but this weapon's deceptive. It takes practice." I realized I would have to make a target out of leather, just like Sungir had done. It was how I taught Ronan and Enwan.

He fingered the bow. "I want to try."

"Let's bring this back to camp. Then I'll make a target for you. We've scared all the game away, for now anyhow."

He nodded, reaching for the stag, which he slung over his shoulders. "Let's go."

I eyed the prairie, ever watchful for other predators, those golden haired beasts that like to eat human meat. It was never safe in open grassland, the dangers too numerous to count. I followed Lowe, passing several women in the woods. They eyed me, one girl reaching out to touch my hair. I smiled at her, taking my ax and cutting off a small portion.

"Here you are."

She took the hair, her eyes wide with astonishment.

"Tie it with something, or you'll lose it." The other women stared at me. "Good day." I hurried to catch up with Lowe, who hadn't bothered to wait. At camp, he tossed the animal on the ground by Kia's fire, my mother nowhere to be seen.

He turned to me. "I want to learn. Show me how to, Peta."

"Do you have some leather? I need a big piece."

Without another word, he strode off towards his campsite, digging through a pile of pelts, pulling out a thin-looking patch of rawhide. When he returned, he nodded. "Will this do?"

"Yes."

"Now we practice."

"If you insist."

I hid a smile, pleased with how the day had gone. He hadn't been too keen on taking directions from a woman, but the true test had yet to come. When he realized just how difficult it was to shoot an arrow straight, he would curse me up and down, blaming me for his lack of skill. I braced myself for this, knowing I would more than likely suffer a throbbing head before the day finished.

In the forest, I searched for four sturdy branches, tying them together to make a square shape. Then I affixed the hide, stretching it from one end to the other. Hanging the target from a tree, I stood at a distance, pulling back on an arrow and letting it fly. It struck the leather a moment later, piercing the middle.

"I'll show you how to hold the bow." I gave him the weapon, although he had been watching me closely. "You—" He held it exactly as I had. "All right. Here's an arrow." He took it, affixing it and pulling back. Releasing it, it flew wildly, spinning and embedding into the ground. "Will you let me show you how to use it now?"

He grunted, frowning.

"It's not easy. You have to practice." I turned from him, intending on retrieving the arrows, but his fingers dug into my arm. "What?"

"We mate first, then practice."

Having expected such a thing for most of the day, I reached for the ax, lifting it to the tender flesh beneath his chin. "I think not." He blinked, not having anticipated this reaction. "I don't want to mate you. I'm here to teach you how to shoot, you obnoxious, yet predictable man." I pressed the sharpened stone to his neck, making him flinch. "Shall we practice or do you wish to die?"

A growl of frustration left him. He took a step back, glaring at me. "I don't like white women."

"I don't mate dark men." Shoving the ax into the skirt, I lifted my chin. "The choice is yours. Practice or we return to camp."

A disappointed glimmer clouded his expression. "We practice."

"Then retrieve the arrow, and you'll try again." He grumbled something under his breath, stalking past me. Satisfied we now understood each other, I waited for him to return, praying he would at least have the decency to listen to my instruction. "Thank you, Lowe." I took it from him.

He continued to pout, nodding soberly. "We mate after we practice."

I sighed, shaking my head. "You can mate Ara. I've told you, I don't mate dark men."

Anger flared in his look, but he suppressed it. "Give me the weapon, woman!" he roared.

I did as bidden, hoping he would not continue to harp on about this issue. "Here you are."

"Show me how to do it. Show me how to hit it like you did."

A lesson in aiming correctly loomed. He possessed the strength to hold the bow steadily, but could he even see the target? "Where's the target?"

"Forward."

"You see it?"

"Of course I see it, woman," he grated. "Show me how to hit it."

I needed him to set aside his anger and relax his posture. "You've been very patient, Lowe. I don't doubt you'll do well at this."

He grumbled in reply.

"Let your anger go for the moment. It won't help your aim."

"Then mate with me. I can't think of anything else."

I had to focus his attention on the task at hand. "If you can successfully hit the target, then you can mate me." But I had no intention of being with him in this manner, praying he would not do well. I smiled slightly, trying to mask my worry.

He nodded, a glint of determination flaring in his eyes. "Then show me. Show me how to do it."

Sending out a silent plea, I hoped Ara would find us, so she could take care of the lust of her man. I had little intention of honoring this promise. "There is a better way of holding the bow. Let me show you."

Sixteen

I narrowly managed to escape having to mate with Lowe, but I felt distinctly uneasy with this clan, careful now not to be alone with Lowe or any of the other men. After teaching him how to use the bow, he demanded I show him how to make one, but I took Ara with me on this task, not wanting to be alone with her man. He followed me around as it was, as did a few of the others, their curiosity growing by the day. They had never seen a white woman before, even the elders expressing an interest, Palo insisting we eat with him on several occasions, his fire being the largest in camp.

Picking at my teeth, I sat with Ara watching Maggi and Kia scraping away at a recently acquired pelt. Lowe sat at a nearby fire, his eyes trained on us.

"You can mate him, if you want."

I tossed the twig I had been using into the fire. "No. I don't want to."

"He desires you."

"I'm aware of that."

"All the other men too."

I sighed, knowing my time at the camp had come to an end. I had stayed longer than I should anyhow. "I have to go home soon."

"I might never see you again." She stared at her fingers, dirt beneath the nails. "We might never cross paths … ever again."

"How long will the clan stay here?"

"I don't know. Palo makes the decision to go or stay."

"I have to speak to him. I need help deciding which direction my home is. I've never been this lost before. I'm not that far from the valley, but if I travel the wrong way, I'm even further than I should be. I need to know where the mountains are."

"Then ask him."

We would have dinner with him tonight, the aroma of grilling meat filling the air. My sister smiled tenderly, her expression revealing a hint of sadness.

"I'm happy you found us, Peta. I hope you come back one day."

Patting my belly, I felt the baby move. "I will. I know where you are now. I'll mark the trees on the way out. I can find it then again."

"You're braver than I. The thought of traveling alone terrifies me."

"You're strong, Ara. Sungir taught you everything he taught me."

"I've forgotten some things, though. You were better at remembering which herbs are best for what ailments. I know some, but … I fear making a tonic with the wrong ingredients."

"It's been ages since I've even thought about all of that. I've only just settled in the new cave."

"The cold season is upon us. It'll give you time to practice those arts, especially when the ground is covered in white."

"It's not so cold where I live. It's mild. You should come with me. There's a pool of heated water. I bathe every day. It's the most wondrous thing."

"That does sound lovely. I know you hate cold water."

"I've grown used to it. I really do wish you and Kia and Maggi would come with me."

She smiled sadly. "I want this too, but … we prefer our men. You prefer your men. When we were little, such things didn't matter in the least. But now … we want to mate with our own kind."

Kia set the pelt aside, having overheard the conversation. "This isn't goodbye, Peta. When you leave, we'll meet again. I feel it."

"I do too." It still saddened me, though. I loved my family, but we could not live together. "I shall always think of you. I'll always pray you're all well."

"We're fine. We're where we should be. You needn't worry about us. I know you'll be well too. You've grown into a capable young woman. You're smart and strong. You'll find your man again."

"I hope so."

Lowe ventured over to join us, his features even darker in the waning light. "I'll escort you to Palo's fire. He's ready to eat."

A slight chill lingered in the air, obliging me to bring a leather blanket, which I wrapped around my shoulders. Ara held Bunder, the baby asleep. Kia and Maggi followed behind, as we passed various fires, the men gazing with interest. I had spent the days teaching Lowe how to shoot arrows, the man practicing on targets in the forest. He had grown proficient enough to hunt, having killed a stag earlier today.

At the leader's fire, we sat together on one side, while Palo, his healer, Munfred, and their wives sat on the other. Lowe squatted near Ara, his feet caked with dried dirt. Everyone in the camp stank, the smell of unwashed bodies lingering. I had forgotten how it was, having lived now with Ronan and Enwan and an endless supply of hot, clean water. They did not have that convenience.

"I wish to learn how to shoot this bow," said Palo. Older than most, his black hair hung down his back. Several children ran about behind him, as he had mated with various women. "You will teach me." He stared directly at me.

I bowed my head slightly. "It would be an honor to teach you, leader, but Lowe is capable enough now. He has acquired the skill. He made his first kill today." I could not possibly stay with the clan a moment longer, desiring to leave at daybreak. "Is that acceptable?"

His gaze skimmed over Lowe. "Is this true?"

"It is. I've killed. The bow is a fine weapon. I'm learning to make one. We should all learn how to use them. We'll need them, if the white men attack again. We can best them now."

Palo sat cross-legged, with his hands on his knees. He wore a leather skirt, but it did not completely hide his manhood. "This is a good thing to have then. We've never been able to protect ourselves from the heathens. It would be good to have a weapon for such a purpose."

Munfred drank from a bladder, while the flames before him reflected in his eyes. "What if the white men have the same power?"

"Then it's an equal fight."

"We've not seen any in these parts," said Lowe. "She's the first to cross our path."

"But not the last," said Palo, frowning. "She's not alone. Someone's seed grows in her."

I took that moment to express my concerns. "I would ask for some advice. I must leave to find my man, but I'm lost. Do you know of a valley with mountains? It's not far from here, perhaps two day's walk. I must find it."

"You've work to do here, girl. You cannot leave."

"I've shown Lowe how to use the weapon. I've taught other men too. They don't need another lesson from me. They're capable all on their own." To stroke his ego further, I added, "Your men are smart. They learn fast." Although, that had not been entirely truthful. I found them incredibly hardheaded and slightly dull of mind, but after a great deal of time explaining the same thing over and over, they seemed to grasp the idea.

The leader's attention drifted to Lowe. "Do you agree?"

"I can teach the men. I know it all now."

Keeping my features bland, I stared at the fire, knowing that statement to be entirely bravado. Kia eyed the fire, where meat dangled from thick branches.

"Then you may leave."

I inhaled a sigh of relief. "Thank you."

Palo glanced at the healer. "Do you know of this valley?"

"I know where mountains are. They're west of here."

That would explain how I had missed them. I had been heading in the wrong direction entirely. "Mountains that are white?"

"Yes. Someone we've traded with has seen them. If you go west, you should find them."

"Thank you."

"Let's eat," said Palo. "Or the meat's overdone."

His wife stepped forward, the woman wearing several beaded necklaces. She slid the meat from the branches, capturing it in a basket. She offered the food to her husband first.

"Thank you, wife." He took a portion, glancing at us. "Eat. There are berries and nuts as well. We've plenty."

Kia nodded. "Thank you. You're more than generous."

He chewed heartily, his attention on me. "I wish you a safe journey."

"Thank you. Will the clan remain here long?"

"At least another season, maybe two. The game's plentiful. There's no reason to leave."

That thought made me happy, knowing I could visit again in the future, perhaps after I had the baby. "Good. I'd like to see my family more often."

The chief nodded, bellowing, "Drink! Bring me something to drink!" This effectively concluded the conversation, the man leaning in to speak to one of his men.

Having shared a meal with the elders, Kia and Maggi and I returned to our pelt, Ara joining her man on his. She left Bunder with us, the baby asleep. I stared into the flames before me, feeling the heat, my belly satisfied.

"Are you prepared to leave?" Kia sat close, her knee touching mine.

"I've some dried meat. It's only a two day walk. I can hunt along the way. I'll be fine."

"I know why you must go, but I'll miss you all the same."

My arm went around her shoulders. "I'll miss you."

"You're happy with Ronan. I'm glad you found him. He's perfect for you."

"Can't I persuade you to come with me? It's the most lovely place I've ever seen. There's fresh water at the door of the cave. You don't even need to collect it. It just falls from above. The valley is green and fertile. Berries and nuts grow in abundance in every season. It's perfect."

She sighed, her stern expression softening. "Then you've found what you were looking for. It's your paradise. I've my own paradise here, with my people."

No matter how many times I asked her, I could not persuade her. "If you ever find yourself without your people or needing a place to stay, come find me."

She touched my face. "We shall see one another again, Peta. I feel that strongly in my heart. You'll always be my daughter. I'll always wish the best for you. That's why it's imperative you return to your man and your life. Your baby will need its father."

I nodded. "I know."

"Come daybreak, we shall say goodbye for now."

"Until we meet again."

"Yes."

I hugged her, feeling the heat of her skin. "I love you, Mamma."

"I love you, my dear child."

Seventeen

I left before Maggi woke, hugging Ara goodbye. She wiped tears from her cheeks, her tone soft and pleading. "I wish you could stay a while longer."

"I've already been gone too long. Ronan must think the worst happened to me. I have to go home."

"I know, but I'll miss you."

"You've a baby and a man to take care of. You're busy with your life. I'm going to have this babe soon. I'll be busy too." I gazed at her neck, seeing the green and brown stone Ronan had given her all those seasons ago. The purple one hung from leather around my neck. "We're always going to be sisters. Nothing can change that. I'll come visit again after I give birth."

"You're terrible with direction. You'll never find us."

I gigged at that. "I will. I was turned around for some reason. I should've kept an eye out better, but being kidnapped confused me." I plan to mark trees, so if I ever came this way again I can find the camp. "I love you, Ara."

She hugged me. "I love you."

Having packed my things already, I could leave before the rest of the clan woke, the smoke from a dozen defunct campfires making the air hazy. "I wish you all the best. Bunder is the sweetest baby. I hope mine's just as easy."

"I pray you have a safe delivery. I pray I see you again."

I squeezed her hand. "You will."

Kia hugged me. "You should go before they rouse. I know the men follow after you. I don't want anything to delay your journey. You've two days of walking ahead of you."

Glancing at the various fire pits, all of the inhabitants slept, a dog barking in the distance. "I'll be off then." The sun had yet to rise, casting deep shadows, but not for long. "Tell Maggi I love her."

"I will."

Picking up the bow, I slung it over a shoulder with the arrows and another leather bag. I carried enough dried meat to see me through, but if something unexpected occurred, I would have to hunt. Kia's tearful gaze lingered on me, her mouth pressed in a thin line.

"You're strong, Peta. I know we shall meet again. Safe travels, girl."

I waved to them, trying not to cry, but tears fell down my cheeks nonetheless. If only they would have come with me. If only I did not have to make this trek alone. One of the camp dogs trotted after me, but when I failed to stop, venturing further way from the clan, he turned around and headed home.

The forest smelled of wet earth and pine needles, my feet snapping twigs here and there, the sound echoing. I vowed to be more careful, affixing hide to my feet for a softer passage. Near midday, I stopped to pick berries, eating them from the branches, my fingers discolored. Finding a brook, I washed my face and hands, admiring the clearness of the water.

Watchful for anything unusual, I stopped every so often to listen, hearing nothing other than the cadence of bugs in the underbrush and birds fluttering overhead. Before the sun drifted completely, I climbed a tree to have a look at where it set, needing to assure myself I went in the right direction. Grasping branch after branch, I hoisted myself as far as I could, staring at mountains in the distance.

"Is that you?" A twinge of excitement rippled through me. "Is that my mountain?" I spied the white peaks, seeing them layered with taller ones behind. "It is you!" I could not reach them tonight, but by tomorrow evening, I would be home safe and sound in the cave. "The elders were right. Oh, thank the gods." A feeling of relief swept through me.

Lowering, I hung from the bottom branch, dropping to the ground. Having laid out the pelt, I made a small fire, sitting close to warm my bones before sleeping. My feet ached from the day spent walking, my ankles appearing slightly swollen. Reclining with a rolled up piece of hide behind my head, I admired the glowing orb in the sky, visible between the branches of the tree. This reminded me of my time in the woods before finding Ronan, realizing I did not feel as frightened or alone as then.

The bow laid within reach, the arrows even closer. I carried a spear as well, the weapon at my feet. One more day of walking and I would be reunited with Ronan, having missed him dreadfully. I prayed he wasn't too worried over me, but I knew he felt distraught. I chided myself for spending too many days with my mother and sisters, but such a thing could not be helped.

A burning branch snapped, startling me for a moment. I gazed at the fire until it became nothing but embers, the heat having thoroughly warmed me. Lifting the edges of the pelt, I slid beneath it to sleep, closing my eyes. The creatures of the night stirred, the sounds resonating every so often, but they soon drifted, as I delved deeply into the world of dreams. A series of images occupied my mind, some sweet and some disturbing; yet, by morning, all of the dreams scattered, utterly forgotten.

Not wanting to waste a moment, I hurried to gather everything, rolling the pelt and tossing dirt into the fire pit. After affixing leather to my feet, I strode briskly, breathing deep the fresh morning air. I ate as I walked, chewing on a portion of dried meat. Needing to cross the remaining forest, I stopped a while later to drink water, marking a tree with a small X. I had done this every so often along the way, in hopes of returning one day to see my family again.

Later, I stood at the edge of a prairie, a sense of unease clinging to me. I hated open spaces like this, preferring the shelter of trees. It dawned on me that I had come this way before, when I first came to the valley. If I ventured around the edges, staying within the forest, it would take another day easily.

"There's nothing to be done about it," I murmured. "If I don't cross, I don't see Ronan."

If I stayed to debate the issue longer, I would lose my nerve. Stepping into the tall grass, I hurried, grasping the spear with one hand, while the bow swung by my side. I scanned the field from end to end, not seeing game, but I knew predators lurked, their hide the color of the grass. They could pounce without warning, killing me with ferocious teeth.

"Please, gods! Please see me to safety," I whispered.

Towering mountains loomed, their peaks brilliantly white against the blueness of the sky, although at this time of day, the sun began to descend, shadows swallowing the grassland. I gasped from the exercise, having walked swiftly for a long time, my feet aching in protest. With every step I drew nearer to my home, a feeling of elation drifting through me. I cried out with joy when the treetops of the valley filled my vision, its lush expanse a welcoming sight.

"Yes!"

Continuing on, I passed the heated pool, although I saw it mostly in gloom now, the water looking dark and smelling slightly foul. I longed to have a bath to remove the dirt of travel, but I remained determined to find

Ronan, rounding the bend to climb to the cave. Lifting my chin, I did not see the light of a fire within, wondering if they hunted still. Exhausted and in need of food, I ventured on, my breath labored. As I hurried up the small path past boulders, my lungs ached from the effort, the climb taking me higher.

"Ronan!" Reaching the opening of the cave, I glanced inside. "Ronan?" No one had lit a fire, the cavern empty, although pelts lined the floor. "Where are you?" I left my things in the doorway, approaching the fire pit, feeling the ashes. "Cold." Delving my fingers deeper, I felt nothing other than cold ash. "No one's made a fire in a good while."

Disturbed by that thought, I tossed in a few branches, rubbing wood together to produce a flicker of flame, which I then deposited into the kindling. I added more wood from a large pile someone had left nearby.

"They're looking for me." My shoulders slumped. "Oh, this isn't how I saw this homecoming." The fire added light to the cavern, revealing the pelts on the floor. Several leather bags stood along the wall. I ventured over to them, finding dried meat. "You haven't been gone that long. You left food for me."

Feeling better now, I ate a strip of meat, chewing heartily. I had little choice but to wait for the men to return, deciding to bathe before sleeping, needing the hot water to soothe my throbbing feet and back. I yearned for sleep, but the men might return by morning, and I wished to be clean for them. With that in mind, I ventured from the cave after eating, following the path down the hill in the moonlight, the calls of some bird echoing.

Untying the leather skirt from my waist, I let it fall to the ground. Rocks bordered the edge of the pool mixed with grass and plants, the hum of insects emerging from the surrounding thicket. I waded in, the bottom feeling rocky and slick, the heat of the water delicious. Although it smelled slightly foul, the water soothed and cleaned, a day's worth of dust and grime washing away.

Floating, I held out my arms, staring at the sparkling sky, with the glowing moon suspended overhead. I yearned to be here with Ronan, desiring the feel of his arms. He and Enwan searched for me. They had left meat, knowing I would return. Something scurried in a nearby bush, startling me.

"Ronan?" I had brought a spear, always watchful of trouble. "Who's there?" All remained quiet, some tiny creature having made the noise.

I scrubbed my face and washed my hair, feeling refreshed, yet tired after the bath. After emerging from the pool, I gathered my things and returned to the cave, finding the fire burning still. I added another branch, the flames flickering brightly for a moment. Settling on a pelt, I withdrew a wooden comb from a basket, working it through my hair. Ronan had braided portions of my hair, affixing pretty shells, but the braids felt ragged now, needing to be redone.

Passing the evening in this manner, I groomed myself to exhaustion, eventually tossing aside the comb and snuggling into a soft pelt. The flames flickered off the stone walls, the furthest corners of the cavern in shadow. A wind blew a while later, howling just before the opening, the sound like a low whistle.

"I miss Wolf," I whispered, wishing my pet were with me to keep me company. "You died needlessly." I stared at the ceiling, seeing dark indentations. "But you've been avenged. Those horrible men got what they deserved." A yawn escaped me. "I shall see you in the morning." I referred to Ronan, knowing he and Enwan would come.

They had to.

Eighteen

I slept longer than I wanted, the cave offering shelter and darkness. When I camped in the open, I woke with the sun, the glaring effects prohibiting further sleep. I preferred caves to all other shelters, especially the vastness of this one, the refuge ideal for several families to live comfortably.

When I did finally rouse, I sat staring at the doorway, seeing only the blueness of the sky. I had expected the men to return, the feeling of disappointment acute. Pushing aside that emotion, I drank water from a skin, tossing a few branches into the fire. After eating a portion of meat, I brought out a few pelts to beat them free of dust and bugs. I realized then that the men had been gone longer than I thought. All of the pelts needed beating, everything covered in a layer of dust. I sneezed repeatedly during this process, a frown of dismay emerging on my forehead.

"They've been gone quite some time. That means they should return shortly."

I left the pelts over rocks in the sun and wind, this helping them to smell less of animal hide and sweat. The floor now clear, I swept the cavern of debris, using a sturdy stick with a thatch of firm, dried grass. Sungir taught us how to make these tools, using them to keep his hut tidy. Once I completed the chores, I brought the pelts in again, placing them around the center fire, the flames burning low.

Taking a basket, I set out to forage, bringing the bow and arrows. The last time I foraged in these woods I had been kidnapped. With this in mind, I ventured out as quietly as possible, having tied fur to my feet. Ever mindful of my surroundings, I froze at the slightest noise, a sense of anxious fear gripping me. I did find a bush filled with berries, picking each and every one. On the way back, I stopped often to gaze about, the trees here familiar. I had always felt safe in these woods, never once encountering anyone other than Ronan or Enwan. I knew better now. Even in a paradise such as this, danger lurked.

I ate the berries on the way to the cave, stopping in the doorway to stare into the distance. The valley cut a green swath before the mountains, with a border of forest on every side. The wind howled lowly, the sound portentously barren, as empty as the cavern itself and my life at the moment. A feeling of melancholy rippled through me, the emotion similar to how I had been after my family disappeared. I had spent a season in Sungir's hut alone, alternating between fear and desperation, the loneliness of such an existence hard to bear. I prayed history did not repeat itself.

What if something had happened to Ronan and Enwan? What if they had been attacked by one of those ferocious cats? What if they perished?

"Don't think that way."

But you have to. You might be alone forever, Peta.

"It's far too soon to think the worst."

Can't you feel it in your bones? It's just like the last time.

Tears welled in my eyes, my thoughts hitting their mark with painful precision.

"I pray it isn't so. I shall wait for my man to return. I can wait. I have time."

What will you do if they don't return? You're having a baby soon.

"Not that soon. I've time."

If they don't return, you have to go to Kia. You can't have this baby by yourself.

"I know what to do. Sungir taught us everything."

He taught how to help a woman give birth, but who will help you? What if there's trouble? Women die in childbirth.

"Then that'll be my fate." I frowned deeply, feeling even worse now. "I can manage by myself. I've done it before. I know how to deliver a baby. If I have to deliver my own, then so be it." I lifted my chin, feeling a twinge of stubborn determination. "This will be my test."

Another lousy test ...

With that in mind, I knew I had to begin to prepare. I needed to collect herbs for healing and pain management. I had to plan for the baby. I did not have time to feel sorry for myself. I would not collapse in a heap as I had at the hut. Ronan would return—I knew it. It might not happen as soon as I wished or needed, but it *would* happen.

***

A sense of purpose ushered in many busy days, the tasks at hand keeping worried thoughts at bay, although they returned at night when I lay alone on the pelt before sleep. By morning, I sprang to action, either gathering firewood or herbs or hunting. When it rained, I stayed in the cave and worked hides, scraping away at them until they were ready to be dried. When I felt tired, I slept, my feet oddly swollen. I knew this to be because of the pregnancy, having seen Kia and Hanna in a similar condition.

I collected herbs, hanging them to dry from a stand made of wood, the bundles tied to a center branch, with two similar branches on either side, the legs firmly on the ground. This was how we prepared meat to be dried. I hunted stags every so often, one animal being enough to keep me in an abundance of meat, but I worried about how I would hunt after the baby came. Ara tied her child to her back using strips of leather. I needed to make the same sort of thing, my mind searching for ideas.

After completing the chores of the day, I sat on a rock before the entrance of the cave, staring at the valley below. I oftentimes sat here in darkness, my eyes scanning far and wide, looking for what might be a campfire, but I never saw one. Memories of the past returned as well. I yearned to have the men with me, their presence a comfort. The three of us would sit and chat, the meal always fresh and hot. Then we settled on a pelt and mated, the experience pleasurable.

Despite the many chores that kept me busy during the day, I could not fill every moment with activity, the free times far too quiet. I longed to hear manly banter and the sound of Ronan's laugh. How I missed his humor—his touch. They left to find me, not knowing where I went, or perhaps they had come across a footprint or two, a twig bent over. Leaning against a rock, I sighed with melancholy, hating being alone.

I slept fitfully that night, dark images plaguing what should have been pleasant dreams. I sensed things would not be as I wished them, an inner voice warning me to be strong—not to let go of hope. Each morning I determined to be useful, but by the end of the day, I felt downtrodden again, the quiet nearly driving me mad.

If only Wolf were here, I would have someone to speak to. Cursing Greggor's men, I despised everything they stood for, their behavior disgusting. When I needed a distraction from depressive thoughts, I imagined what I might do if I ever met Greggor. I saw myself lifting the bow and aiming, piercing his chest with an arrow. He deserved no less for destroying the clan on the prairie and killing Kia's love. Those horrible men took me in his honor, wanting to deliver me as a present. They killed my pet. I would exact revenge, if the gods ever saw fit to present me with the opportunity.

***

The days stretched on endlessly, the cave slightly cooler than before, the winter season approaching, or had it already come? I wore a thin pelt around my shoulders to hunt, not needing anything more. The stags weren't as easily found, but one animal kept me in meat for quite a while, my belly always full. As I stood in the middle of the prairie, preparing to shoot, I thought I saw movement by the edge of the wood, my heart suddenly beating harder. Before hunting, I watched the surroundings carefully, always mindful of entering an open field.

Lowering the weapon, I slung the bow over my shoulder, while grasping a spear. With my golden hair and tan pelt, I blended in with the grassland, but my height presented an issue. I bent at the knees, lowering to remain hidden. Then I drew nearer to the woods, a cool breeze lifting the hair from my neck and tossing it about my face. I swore I had seen something—movement at the edge of the forest, but now I doubted myself, unsure if I really had seen anything.

Lingering by a tree, I grasped at the lower branch, hoisting myself upward, where I felt safer than on the ground. No sooner had I done so then I heard the distinct rumbling of a predatory animal, the creature coming to stand beneath me. Sucking in a shocked gasp, I froze, panic constricting my throat, every breath an effort to get in and out. These creatures could climb as easily as the woodland ones with dark fur and long, sharp claws. The cat beneath me sniffed the air, his golden eyes flashing from a face of tan fur. I balanced on a thick branch, affixing the arrow to the bow, ready to kill if it made a move to climb. Perhaps, I should just kill it now anyhow, not relishing the thought of it living nearby.

It made no move to climb the tree, loitering below menacingly, his eyes darting to me every so often. Fully grown, each paw looked to be enormous, far bigger than Wolf's ever were or would be, had he been an adult. I aimed at the creature, having decided to end its life. I could not risk having such things living here, especially after I had the baby. My fingers trembled, my hand shaking far too much. I struggled to calm my nerves, knowing that if I did not shoot now, I would miss the chance.

Letting the arrow fly, it did not hit its mark, embedding into the ground by the cat, which startled the animal. He growled noisily, the sound a loud, angry rumble, which sent a sharp twinge of fear through me. Having missed because of badly shaking hands, I cursed my luck, threading another arrow, but the animal, sensing danger, ran off.

"Blast it all!" I muttered. "Now I've this monster to worry about." Tears filled my eyes. "He knows I'm here. He'll come back. How can I protect the baby with that thing about?"

I sat on a branch wearily, resting my forehead on the tree trunk, tears falling to the wood beneath my thigh. When had paradise turned into a curse? How could I live here now knowing the cats had come? They hadn't been here before. I could not kill them on my own. They could climb easily; the cat could have taken to the tree and killed me where I stood. He could come to the cave and kill me in my sleep.

Sungir had dug deep holes around his hut, placing branches and leaves over them to hide their existence. These caught the woodland creatures easily enough, the animals falling through and injuring themselves. Then Sungir had killed them. I did not have the strength to dig such holes, the task impossible, especially in my condition. I had once fallen into one of his holes, breaking a leg, which Sungir set properly. It healed beautifully, no trace of the break when I walked.

"I miss you, Sungir. You were a gifted healer. You

lived for so many seasons alone, and you thrived." He had been the only father figure I had ever known in my life, thinking of him as my Pappa. "You're with the gods now, watching over me. What do you recommend I do? It's not safe with the cats about."

As I watched the ground below, I searched my mind for a solution, thinking of one idea after another, yet not settling on anything. I knew the cats hated fire, which I already had. Sungir and I had hunted once on the prairie, sleeping out in the open. He had taken branches and sliced the ends at an angle, leaving them sharp. Then he arranged them in a circle, where we sat in the middle with the fire. I could set up these sorts of sharp branches at the entrance of the cave for protection. It wasn't an impossible task.

I waited longer in the tree, watching as the sun began to lower, disappearing over the mountain in the distance. When I felt certain the danger had passed, I climbed down, eyeing my surroundings warily. I threaded the arrow, walking with the weapon ready to shoot, if the need occurred. The shadows of evening approached, the birdcalls few now. Knowing danger lurked in unseen places, I stepped gingerly, making my way home in the gloom, the swaying branches of trees overhead.

Now, even something as simple as picking nuts and berries would not be safe any longer. My thoughts turned even darker, wondering if Ronan and Enwan had fallen prey to the cats at some point. It would explain why they had not returned. I might be alone again …

Nineteen

Living with the threat of dangerous predators, I began the task of fortifying the entranceway of the cave, gathering a particular type of wood, the branches covered in long, sharp thorns that pricked the skin painfully. I arranged these before the doorway, although I cut myself in the process. Leaving a small opening to walk through, I could close it with a door I made from the branches. This project took a great deal of time to complete, with frequent excursions into the forest, where I felt less than safe.

One night, the wind brought the sound of an odd rumble, and I stood by the opening to listen, realizing I heard the cats in the distance. The animals were now hunting the stags I needed to survive, driving the rest of them further away to the safety of the forest. Dismayed, I stared gloomily into the darkness, seeing only speckles of light twinkling in the sky and the moon glowing behind a mass of clouds.

The baby in my belly moved then, the feeling odd, yet comforting. I would have a child of my own soon enough, but I feared not being able to protect it. I needed to be with a clan. I should not be alone like this, especially once the baby came, but what choice did I have? I came back to wait for my man, hoping he had given up the search and returned to the cave, but he hadn't.

"I should return to Kia and my sisters," I murmured to myself. "There's protection with that clan. I know where they are."

I had argued this point endlessly over the last few days, torn between waiting for Ronan and Enwan and knowing I needed to be with a clan for safety. The longer I delayed, the bigger I became, my belly protruding obscenely, large and round. Eyeing the sharp brambles before the door, I doubted the cats would dare to enter, especially with a fire blazing. This offered a measure of defense, but what would happen when I hunted and foraged? They roamed freely in the woods; I had seen the prints of their large paws by the brook and their scat in places. An entire den lurked nearby.

Rubbing my forehead with the tips of my fingers, I felt the beginnings of a headache. I knew what I had to do, but I feared doing it. It was a risk, but, then again, doing nothing presented just as much danger. I had to hunt them before I became the hunted. It was the only way I could continue to live here.

***

Tying my hair back with a length of leather, I wore fur on my feet, with a leather skirt draped around the lower portion of my hips. My belly protruded over the top. I woke early, the sun having just emerged from the top of the mountain, the chill in the air pronounced. Tossing a fur over my shoulders, I picked up the bow and the bag of arrows. Having eaten berries and dried meat, I carried a few strips of meat for later and a bladder of water.

Feeling oddly calm, I opened the thorny partition, passing through it to leave the cavern, my eyes scanning the valley below. The din of birds surrounded me, the creatures searching for worms and insects. The big cats hunted at night, as I had heard the growls often enough in the darkness. Having an idea where they might be, I ventured down the hill, passing boulders on each side, my feet crunching over rocks. Gripping a spear, I glanced at the greyish morning sky, offering up a prayer to the gods, and hoping for good fortune. I planned to hunt the cats today, an idea so outrageous; I could hardly believe I even contemplated it. Yet, here I was, having little choice but to kill first to protect myself and the baby that would come— sooner than later.

I suspected the cats had made a home in the quarry where Ronan and Enwan found the stones they needed for spear tips and tools. I had seen them lounging on the rocks, lying in the sun earlier in the morning before the heat drove them into a shady lair. I planned to stand at a distance, perhaps even climbing a tree. From there, I would take aim, hopefully killing each one.

However, by the time I reached the quarry, I did not see a single cat. Had I misjudged their activities? I ventured onto the rocks to have a better look, seeing evidence of the past, where Enwan had chiseled away stone. I remembered being here with him, watching him work. A feeling of sadness constricted my throat, the memory of that moment so clear—so vivid. I missed him dearly, wondering why he and Ronan had not returned.

Wiping away a tear, I steeled my resolve, knowing I had important work. If I planned to live here, I had to end the lurking danger. I could not reside where the cats were. It was far too dangerous.

"No more tears, Peta," I whispered. "You may cry when it's all over. You've work to do."

Scrambling down the rocky hill, I eyed the forest below, knowing I had to search for the cats, yet hating the chore. For hours I wandered aimlessly here and there, examining the ground for paw prints and scat, finding a print here or there, but it never led to anything. Exhausted, I sat at the base of a tree a while later, chewing on a dried strip of meat, and pondering the situation.

***

The next day, I set out with the same goal in mind, fetching the firewood for later, then searching for the cats, although I failed to find them. Hearing them in the night, I knew they continued to hunt here, discovering several large prints near a water source and a bloody heap of bones near the edges of the grassland, the cats having killed and eaten a stag recently. Running low on meat, I worried about wasting more time on this task, knowing I needed to hunt for my own survival.

Climbing trees proved cumbersome, my belly reducing my agility and balance, my foot nearly slipping off a branch. I chided myself on this, knowing how dangerous it could be if I fell. Not only would the baby die, but I might die as well. If I lived with a clan, I would not have to perform these errands, the men providing food and safety.

As I eyed the forest from a lofty perch, one hand gripping a branch, while I held the other over my eyes, I scanned the area carefully, hoping to see the movement of the beasts, their golden fur mingling with the dried grass, but I saw nothing. Dismayed, I climbed down gingerly, having discarded the fur from my feet. I left the spear and the bladder of water at the base of the tree with the spear, while I carried the bow and arrows, never leaving those where I could not easily reach them.

"Blast you, you stupid animals!" I muttered, arching my aching spine, while supporting my lower back with the palms of my hands. I had spent far too much time on the hunt, needing to kill a stag for dinner, the meat nearly gone. "I can't find them. Where are the stupid things? Where are you hiding?" Frustration and melancholy bubbled to the surface, my eyes welling with tears. Sitting to tie the fur to my feet, I planned to return to the cave, tired of exerting precious energy on this annoying task. I would have to kill the cats when I saw them, not spend all day hunting them down, which yielded nothing other than exhaustion.

Reaching for the spear, a prickle of alarm skimmed down my neck, a brisk wind tossing hair into my face. On instinct, I quickly withdrew an arrow, pulling it taut against the bow, standing with my feet apart, knees slightly bent. No sooner had I done so, then something moved behind the thicket nearby, the footfalls eerily silent. I knew not what it was, and had my instincts not warned me, I never would have taken up the weapon.

Not hesitating, I let the arrow fly. It tore through the thicket, embedding in whatever stood there. I threaded another, pulling it back and releasing it. A low, ferocious growl emerged from the foliage, my chest hammering almost painfully, the fear so intense I worried I might faint. I saw no further movement, although whatever I had hit cried out, the sound resonating.

A loud crashing noise occurred then, something heavy dropping to the ground. I waited by the tree, holding up the bow and scanning the forest for signs of another animal, wondering if I had killed a cat or not. When nothing else occurred, only the birds chirping overhead, I grasped the spear, holding it before me, while gingerly approaching the bushes. A few steps more, and I came upon the target, the golden fur of the animal soaked through with blood, the creature dead.

Relief washed over me, knowing I had dispatched one of the cats, but more remained. The day being long and my hunger pronounced, I made quick work of gutting the creature, tying its legs together with leather and dragging the carcass behind me. I planned to strip its fur free and cook the meat, drying what I could not eat. It might not be as tasty as a stag, but the meat would keep me alive … and the baby I carried.

Dragging the cat to the cave proved exhausting, every muscle in my body aching with the effort. I made a fire, tossing in the thick branches I found in the morning. I cut away strips of meat, marveling at how large its paws were, how long and sharp the claws appeared. I planned to use the claws for either tools or jewelry, perhaps making a necklace. I now had enough meat to see me through, but carving it and drying it would deplete what little energy I had left.

I ate while I worked, tossing strips of meat over the stones in the pit, the meat sizzling on contact. I cut away at the carcass, hanging it over a series of branches to be smoked during the night. The golden hide would make a comfortable pelt, either for wearing or sleeping or both. Once all the parts of the creature had been separated, I ventured down to the heated pool to soak my weary bones, staring glumly at the stars overhead.

"Thank you for the kill today," I murmured, offering up a prayer to the gods. "You warned me of danger. That cat was stalking me. He would've killed me." Tossing water into my face, I sighed, relieved the day had gone so well. "Sungir, you'd be proud. I killed a cat. You taught me so well. You were a good man. I miss you every day, but you weren't young, even then. I'll never be as smart as you, but what I did learn has served me well. I ate tonight. I'll eat tomorrow."

More cats lurked, though. I knew it. I would not expend precious energy hunting them, needing to prepare for the baby, but I planned to be vigilant and prepared, ready to strike the moment the need arose. From the strange fluttering in my belly, an odd feeling of constriction that lasted a few moments and then ceased, I knew it was only a matter of time before labor began. I had a few days left to prepare, or the babe might appear earlier than expected, but much needed to occur before then, time running out.

Twenty

Over the next few days, I observed the odd constriction of my belly, the feeling not painful in the least, but a warning of things to come. I worked diligently, preparing the pelt of the cat I killed, scraping away at it and leaving it to dry in the sun. I bundled the dried meat, filling several leather bags. I braved foraging as well, venturing into the woods to collect nuts and berries, the colder season providing less, but I discovered newer, tastier berries.

Feeling an odd restlessness and a desire to tidy the cavern, I brought out all the pelts for beating, sweeping the floor clean and gathering an enormous bundle of firewood. Various baskets held nuts or tools, a wall lined with them, while pelts surrounded the fire pit. All day I felt the odd contractions in my belly, the occurrences happening with increasing regularity, although I did not feel pain. I ground various herbs, knowing the ones for pain and healing, just as Sungir taught, storing them in small leather pouches. If need be, I could make a healing tea or two.

Sungir warned that if I took the tea for pain, it might delay labor. After witnessing the agony Kia and Hanna endured with child birthing, I vowed not to take the tea, unless I absolutely could not stand it any longer. Expecting to be in labor soon, I sat by the fire and chewed on pieces of meat, staring absently into the flames. A wall of thorny bramble stood before the entrance of the cave, offering a semblance of protection from the cats, although I had not seen them for days.

The contractions in my belly did not worsen as expected, perplexing me. I remembered Kia's becoming more intense with the passing of time, yet mine seemed to stay the same. Surmising the baby would not arrive this night, I prepared for bed, snuggling into the softness of the pelts, the fire warming the cavern. The occasional popping twig startled me, the flames slowly dying. I woke before dawn, feeling as if someone kicked me in the belly, a gasp escaping. Curling into a ball, I gritted my teeth as another wave of pain occurred, labor having finally begun.

Over the course of the day, I spent my time either walking the room or on my hands and knees, moaning from the agony, the pain worsening. The moment of reprieve between the contractions grew smaller and smaller, and it was all I could do to keep myself from making the tea for pain, the contractions wearing on my resolve. The only position that offered any relief seemed to be when I leaned over a rock, my belly hanging beneath me. It took the pressure off my back, but even that did not last for long.

I drank from the bladder, but I did not eat; my hunger had vanished. I thought about what I might do when I had to push, saddened by the fact that I would be alone during this time, wishing to have my family about me or at least another person. Facing the ordeal alone, I tried to remember Sungir's words … hearing him in my mind.

"That's it, girl. You got it. You're ready. You've prepared well. All you need to do is breathe, girl. When you feel the need to push, then hold your breath and push."

In the darkness of the cave, with the fire burning low, I listened to the sound of my breathing. I pretended then that I wasn't alone. I pretended Kia and Ara were there, as well as Ronan, the three of them beside me. I imagined I felt the touch of a hand on my back, Kia smiling with sympathy.

"That's it, girl," said Sungir, his face before mine. Weathered with age, his hair had turned completely white, a sight I had never seen before or since. "Keep breathing, Peta. Keep breathing. The babe comes soon. Do you feel the urge to push?"

"I … don't know," I murmured, shaking my head, and wishing the ordeal to be over. "I just … don't know. I can't stand it any longer! I can't!" Another terrible contraction gripped me, the force of it making me shout. "I can't! Stop it! Just stop it!"

"Squat, girl. Can you squat?"

"I want it to stop, Sungir. Make it stop, please … " I cried, while getting to my knees. "I hate this. I'll never do this again, I swear." Squatting as instructed, I sucked in a breath as another contraction tore through me. "Oooohhh … "

"That's it. You got it."

"I'm never letting another man touch me!" I whimpered in pain.

I wanted to lash out at the voices in the cavern, but I knew it to be futile, because I was the only one there. My helpers were imaginary, the images of Kia and Ronan flickering in and out, as erratic as the flames of a fire. In the end, I could only rely on my own strength and determination, which made me hold my breath and push, feeling how the baby slowly slid lower, pressing against my backbone. I remembered needing to push when the contraction struck, as Kia and Hanna had done with their deliveries. I held my breath and pushed, a gush of wetness rushing down my inner thigh.

Worried it might be blood, I glanced between my legs, seeing nothing other than the glistening wetness of the fluid. When another contraction began, I gritted my teeth and held my breath, pushing, feeling the baby moving lower and lower, until I could not hold my breath any longer, gasping for air. Using the rock before me for balance, my knees pressed into the fur beneath me, offering a buffer to the cold, hard ground. I pushed through another contraction, the spasms not as painful now, but I knew the end drew near, the baby firmly between my thighs, although not out in the least. Exhausted, I yearned to lie down, but I could not.

"I just want it out now! Out!"

Reaching down, I felt the top of the baby's head, a wet, sticky sort of feeling, knowing how close I had come to delivering the infant. I hadn't felt another contraction, finding that odd, so I pushed on my own, although a sharp pain flared.

"Ouch!"

I could feel the head emerge with each push, although it slid inside again just as easily. Annoyed and exhausted, I continued to push, a sharp, horrible pain occurring, as the head finally slid free. I wanted to cry with relief, although I still had more to do, pushing again a moment later, the shoulders emerging, and then the rest of the body sliding free. I reached for the baby, feeling the slickness of its skin, the body coated in some odd substance, but I had seen it before with Kia and Hanna. Remembering what needed to be done, I inserted a finger into its mouth, clearing it of mucus, the baby crying at once.

Relief washed over me, the infant appearing healthy, as I sat back to examine him, realizing I had just given birth to a boy. He was attached to me still. I used a stone tool to cut the cord, tying it closely to his belly. I knew more of the birth matter remained inside of me, and I remembered how we had waited for Kia and Hanna to expel the rest. With that in mind, I picked up the baby, marveling at how perfect he was, how beautiful and pale, just like his father.

Lying upon the pelt, I held him to me, pushing a

nipple into his mouth, hoping he might attach to it. I knew this would help rid whatever remained within me. I felt a tug then, the baby now on the nipple. I nearly cried then, tears filling my eyes, the moment one of pure bliss. It relieved me not to feel the painful contractions anymore. As the baby suckled, I used my free hand to knead my belly, remembering what Sungir taught me. It hurt, but I continued to do so, feeling something slide between my legs a while later, wetting the pelt.

Lifting my head, I saw the afterbirth, the small pile attached to the cord. Tossing it aside, I would deal with it later, desiring to rest for the moment, my body far too weary to do much else. The baby slept now, his mouth around a nipple. My eyes drifted shut … a sense of warmth and peace about me.

During the middle of the night, I woke, tossing the afterbirth into the fire. I took a long drink from a bladder, finding myself parched. Soft leather surrounded the baby, the infant swaddled tightly, as I had seen Kia and Hanna do to their newborns. Chewing on meat, I eyed my son, admiring how small and fragile he appeared, how precious he was. I wished more than anything that Ronan were here to share the moment with me, but it wasn't to be. I thought of what I might name him, knowing that if Ronan were here he would have that honor.

"What will your name be?" The burden fell to me. "How about … Bannon?" I thought that over, the name having some appeal. A man in the clan by the river had been named Bannon, and I had liked the sound of it. "Bannon."

Having chosen the name, I tossed a pelt over my shoulder, intending to sleep. I knew the baby would wake soon enough, although I suspected it to be close to morning anyhow.

"Goodnight, Bannon. Sleep well."

I closed my eyes, offering up a thank you to the gods,

who had seen me through the labor and delivery. I hadn't been alone after all, Kia and Ronan joining me, although only in my thoughts. Even Sungir had helped. I needed them all—their wisdom and support invaluable.

"Thank you," I whispered. "I miss you."

***

At daybreak, I marveled at having slept so well, the baby rousing once to be fed, but he slept afterward. I made a fire, while chewing meat, walking around the cavern to test my legs. Clearly weakened by the experience, moving around helped. Pushing aside the doorway in the thorny brambles, I ventured out to relieve myself, stopping to take a drink of water, the freshness of the fluid dripping from some source above.

"You've a son, Ronan," I murmured, eyeing the valley below, and yearning for the man I loved. "I gave you a son. His hair's as light as yours. He's not Enwan's. You'd be happy about that."

I smiled, feeling gratitude and relief at my accomplishment, grateful I had a relatively easy delivery. It could have gone terribly wrong, if I had been unlucky. Women frequently died in childbirth, more often than not. Hearing Bannon's cries, I returned to the cave, finding him terribly upset, his little face pinched with displeasure.

"Oh, what's the matter, little one? I wasn't even gone very long."

Picking him up, I held him to my breast, where he suckled at once, ceasing all noise. Leaning against a rock, I rested my head upon it, feeling an odd lethargy. I held my baby tightly, overcome by a fierce sense of protectiveness. I knew I would never allow anything to harm my son, the bundle in my arms the most precious thing in the world to me—besides his father and my family.

Twenty-One

Those first few days, I hardly left the cavern, happy and content to care for my new baby, drawn to his perfection and sweetness, even his cries in the middle of the night a wondrous sound. I marveled at how I no longer felt alone or lonely, the baby occupying every moment of my time. When all the strips of leather were soiled and the supply of dried meat low, I knew I had to leave the cave, needing to find food.

Having cut a long piece of leather, I wrapped him in it, affixing it around one shoulder, where he lay against my chest sideways. It went around me and tied at the side. Ara's baby, having been bigger, sat in a leather contraption on her back, but Bannon was too small for that. I had already tied fur to my feet, wearing a leather skirt. My belly had started to shrink, the skin feeling oddly loose here, marked by small purple streaks, where the belly had swollen and stretched. I needed to collect medicinal plants to soothe the skin, remembering the teachings of Sungir.

Leaving the cavern, I gazed at the blueness of the sky, feeling the warmth of the sun upon my face for the first time in days. I carefully scanned the valley for any sign of friend or foe, seeing nothing other than the greenness of the forest. The baby, sleeping against my breast, remained quiet, but I still feared being attacked by the cats, knowing more to be about. Grasping a spear, with the bow and arrows across my back, I held a leather pouch as well and a bladder of water.

Much needed to be done, the cave dusty and the wood for the fire nearly gone. With this in mind, I ventured into the forest, always watchful for danger, finding berries and nuts, the chill in the air warming as the day wore on. When Bannon fussed, wanting to be fed, I climbed a tree, sitting on a lower branch while nursing him, my weapon close at hand. I had not seen large paw prints today or evidence of scat, not knowing where the cats were at the moment.

Wandering around in search of food offered an opportunity to stretch my legs, the exercise tiring, yet it felt good to breathe fresh air, the cavern often smelling heavily of smoke and animal hide. I collected healing herbs and nuts to eat, filling the leather pouch to capacity, having to tie off the end. I did not encounter game, which was disappointing, but I planned to hunt early in the morning, focusing solely on that task and not foraging.

After returning to the cave, I set about beating out a few pelts and collecting firewood, leaving Bannon to sleep in a small basket I made for him, although I hurried to complete these chores, not wanting to leave him alone for long, not knowing what predators might be about. When I arrived with a bundle of firewood, the baby slept still, his tiny hands curled into fists.

My days followed this pattern, the baby and my chores occupying every moment of my time, although I managed to nap when the sun was high, bringing Bannon with me to snuggle on a pelt. I felt stronger each day as well, the muscles in my legs accustomed to the long walks and climbing, when I needed to have a better look at the surroundings. I hunted a stag, killing the creature on the plain, with Bannon strapped to my chest. The baby grew used to being jostled about, sleeping through the entire ordeal.

At night, I sat by the fire scraping away at stone to make sharp tips for arrows. Bannon lay on his back upon a pelt, making noises. I carved pieces of wood for him to play with, although he was too young at the moment to use them. I made an oily type of salve from plants and flowers to apply to the skin, the purple marks on my belly healing slowly. My breasts, heavy with milk, appeared larger than before, the nipples surrounded by a dark patch of pink. I ate more, feeling very hungry, especially after wandering in the forest most of the day.

I stared into the flickering flames, experiencing a moment of sadness. "Your father would be so proud to meet you, Bannon." I spoke often to my son, needing to fill the air with a sound other than the whistling of wind or the crackling of fire. "He's somewhere looking for me. He should've come home by now."

Resting my arms over my knees, I sighed heavily. "I pray nothing bad's happened to him. I worry so. I fear he's gone forever. I know I shouldn't say such things out loud, but … I can't help but wonder at this prolonged absence. He should've returned by now. I hate being alone."

How much longer would I wait for him? I could live here forever, the game plentiful and the berries inexhaustible, but … I longed for contact with others, for conversation … for companionship—mating. I desired to be with a larger group. I missed my family, my mother and sisters.

That evening, as I lay awake staring at the indentations in the rocky ceiling, I thought about what I could do, knowing I had to make a decision soon. When Bannon was a bit older, I planned to return to Kia's clan, needing to see my family again. I despaired that Ronan and Enwan might never return to the cave, something having happened to them. But … I would wait until Bannon grew a little bigger, praying my man arrived before I left.

Where are you, Ronan?

***

Not having been at the cave for a season, I did not know what to expect of the cold, the chill in the air never growing bitterly cold, as it had living with Sungir. It began to rain, some days quite heavily, whereby Bannon and I stayed inside, the sound of water dripping echoing all around us. When the sun emerged, we foraged, finding the bushes bursting with berries and the ground littered with mushrooms.

The stags, having mated during the cold season, now had their babies, the little ones easy kills when it came to hunting, and they weren't as heavy to carry. Bannon traveled on my back, securely bundled in leather that wound around my shoulders, tying at the belly. He knew not to make a noise when I hunted, often being entirely quiet when we left the cavern. I spent a great deal of time training him in this, having learnt how to do it from watching Kia and Hanna.

When he began to crawl, I had to be careful to keep him from the heated rocks around the fire, until he knew better than to touch them. I adored my son, finding his happy babblings a comfort and a barrier to loneliness, although I yearned for Ronan, missing him terribly. I often sat before the cave at sunset, eyeing the distance for any sign of him, wishing he would return to us. He had to know I had the baby by now. It worried me that he and Enwan had not come home. I did not doubt Ronan's affections, knowing how much he loved me. By acknowledging this, it made his absence that much more troubling, thinking the men had encountered misfortune somewhere.

"You have to stay strong, Peta," I whispered, the wind blowing hair into my face, as I stared at the mountains before me. "They're out there somewhere."

I returned to the cave, settling in to sleep next to Bannon, who looked so sweet in repose, his tiny mouth like a pretty pink flower. In the morning, I set about the chores, having woken twice in the night to feed the baby. As Bannon dozed, I grasped my weapon and ventured down to the heated pool, soaking my bones before the sun rose fully, the sound of birdcalls all around.

An odd sense of calm came over me, my decision to leave foremost on my mind. I knew all the things that needed to be done for a trip to Kia's clan, collecting dried meat and leather strips for Bannon, among sharpening the arrows and the spear tip. Washing my face and hair, I firmed my resolve to find my family, knowing in which direction they lived. A two day's walk would bring me to them, the journey complicated now by having a baby, but many women traveled with infants.

"I've waited long enough." Tall reeds grew around the pool, while heated smoke drifted from the water, the smell slightly noxious. "The time has come to go."

I desired the companionship of others so desperately, the emotion far stronger than my fear of cats or other people even. I would risk it all to see my family, not knowing if Ronan or Enwan might ever return to the cave.

Climbing from the water, I headed back up the hill, hearing Bannon's cries. "I'm coming, little one. Don't fuss."

After feeding and changing him, I bundled him into the leather pack on my back, his legs dangling from either side above my hips. Grasping the spear and slinging the sack of arrows around a shoulder, I strode from the cave, intending on hunting one last time—hopefully killing something large enough to sustain me for a while. Having fully recovered from having the baby, I felt stronger and stronger each day, my legs now as muscled and sturdy as before, my stamina the same.

Venturing through the forest, I emerged onto the prairie, although I waited by a tree, watching the grassland carefully—looking for any sign of game or danger. Bannon babbled occasionally, his voice near my ear.

"It's beautiful here," I murmured. "It truly is paradise, but … it's not ideal to be here all alone."

And then I felt doubt again, my fear clouding my judgment, a tiny voice telling me to remain where I was.

You have everything you need here, Peta. Don't go.

I won't be gone long. I only wish to see my family. What if Ronan's with them?

A white man would never be welcome in such a clan; you know that.

But Ronan's not a killer. He's not Greggor or his ilk. He's not a heathen.

It doesn't matter. The dark and the white races don't mix. They never have.

That's not true. I lived with the dark races for a while. Kia and Ara and I lived with a white clan. We were safe there.

But never truly accepted. They only took them in because of you.

Oh, shush!

I hated arguing with myself, but I had no one to speak to, the hours and days so lonely.

"It's time to hunt." I spied a family of stags in the distance, withdrawing an arrow. "Enough arguing. My plans are set. I leave as soon as the meat's dried." I glanced at Bannon, seeing only part of his head over my shoulder. "You're going to meet your kin, boy. It's time I introduce you. It's time we left for a while. Nothing's forever. We shall return."

Lifting the bow, I pulled back on the arrow, letting it fly.

Twenty-Two

Knowing the way, I felt a measure of certainty in the direction I chose, every so often seeing where I had marked a tree, a small X staring down at me. I missed a few here or there, but then I would see another to assure I continued on the correct path. Wearing the golden cloak of the cat I killed, I tossed it over Bannon to keep him warm in the mornings, the baby sleeping peacefully at my back.

The first night, we camped by a large rock covered in a fragrant green mantel, the earth damp here, the area surrounded by enormous trees. Making a small fire, I held my son in my lap, the baby having just fed.

"I know it's dreary being in the sling all day. I'm sorry. Tomorrow evening, we should arrive at my mamma's camp. It's only a bit further." I moved hair from his eyes, the light strands messy. "You've been so good." He rarely complained, sleeping most of the day in the carrier, despite being jostled about by my footfalls. "I've never felt such love. I can't wait for your father to see you. He'd be so proud. You're so like him. I can see him in your eyes. You're going to be a handsome little man."

The snapping of a twig caught my notice, instinct kicking in at once. I left Bannon on the pelt, lifting the bow and arrow, my eyes darting from one corner of the forest to the other, while I listened for the slightest noise. This had already happened once tonight, my senses warning me of danger. Having been careful all day, I had the strangest inkling of being followed, which bothered me greatly.

"Who's there?" I asked in the white man's language, quickly asking, "Who's there?" again, although, this time, in Kia's language. I waited, holding my breath, the baby happily flapping his hands about at my feet, oblivious to the danger. "Show yourself!" I spoke in both languages, not knowing what hid in the shadows, although a twig snapped again.

The sound came straight ahead, the rustling of a bush indicating something approached. Flames from the fire flickered brightly before me, illuminating our small camp and the man that suddenly appeared, although he did not look like any man I had ever seen before. Slightly taller than me, his bowed legs arched like those of Kia's tribe and a pronounced ridge spanned the length of his forehead. Other than those obvious features, his skin appeared fairer than it should, his hair long and tangled, the color of sun dried wood.

Shocked speechless, I stared at him, pointing the arrow directly at his head.

"You may put the weapon down, woman," he uttered gutturally. He spoke the white man's language. "I mean you no harm."

It dawned on me that he had been bred of both races, the combination quite striking, yet disturbing. "Why are you following me?"

"I noted your tracks earlier. I'm ... merely curious."

"I'm flattered," I muttered with sarcasm. "Now, go away."

He eyed the arrow warily, his nostrils flaring. "You know how to use that, don't you?"

"Yes, of course. Why else would I be holding it?"

"I'm Bondo. I'm not from any clan, as you can see. I'm an outcast. I ... lurk about the edges, you could say. I live in the woods, but it's nice to have company."

Bannon began to fuss, wanting to be picked up. Annoyed at the intrusion and not trusting this person in the least, I glared at him. "Go away."

"Can we not share the fire? I've food to cook." He

tugged on leather rope, revealing what hung behind him, a woodland animal of some sort, its claws sharp-looking. "I'd be happy to share with you."

"I'm not mating you." A stark quality entered my tone. "If you make one threat to touch me or my son, I will kill you."

He nodded, his eyes flashing in the firelight, their color indistinguishable in the darkness, but they appeared lighter than brown or black. He tossed down a rolled pelt, the bundle thumping at his feet. Some sort of tool or weapon lay hidden inside.

"I've not given you permission to make yourself comfortable at *my* camp."

"And yet I shall."

Anger rippled through me, but I seemed to have little choice but to subject myself to this man. Bannon cried even louder now. Lowering the weapon, I reached for him, sitting cross-legged on the bedroll, his noises ceasing when he took a nipple into his mouth.

Bondo pointed to the fire. "I'll cook the meat. We can share."

"How long has that creature been dead?"

"Not long."

"I don't wish to eat meat that'll make me sick."

"Nor do I." He bent to the task of slicing open the furry mass, having already gutted it elsewhere. "Why are you traveling alone, woman?"

"That's none of your concern."

"What's your name?"

I sighed, realizing the gods had finally sent me someone to talk to, but I feared him, not knowing his intentions. "Peta."

"That's pretty, Peta. How do you know the dark man's language?"

"My mother is of such a clan. I grew up in both clans."

He brought forth a short stick with a sharp-looking spear tip at the end. Slicing the meat, he held it over the fire with a thick branch, the meat sizzling. My belly rumbled at the smell, the smoke drifting into the air.

"As you can see, I'm of both clans."

"You do look ... odd."

"Yes," he muttered, frowning. "I'm not wanted in either. I don't speak the dark language all that well, but I did understand you. You knew I followed, didn't you?"

"Yes. I guessed something ... trailed me."

"Where are you going? You seem to have a direction."

"I do."

"There are clans about." He pointed. "That way lies a dark one. Further is the white one, which I would avoid." He held out a piece of meat. "Here."

"Thank you." I pulled it from the branch. "Why should I stay away from the white clan?"

"You'd be welcome. I would not."

"Oh." I ate the meat, feeling less apprehensive about my dinner companion. "Do you always follow people?"

"No."

"As you can see, I'm perfectly capable of taking care of myself and my child."

"You are. I won't argue that. I only wish to share a meal."

"Then you'll be on your way?"

"And to sleep for the night."

I knew he would say that. "What if I do not offer that hospitality?"

"You will."

"How do you know that?"

"You're kind. You could've killed me, but you didn't." He reached out the branch, a juicy piece of meat dangling from it. "Here you are."

The food filled my belly, the meat delicious. I hadn't

expected such a fine meal. "I hope I don't live to regret this."

"If I say I won't hurt you, I won't. I tire of fighting. I know I appear hideous to all races, but I'm not a monster."

"I'm not worried about your appearance. It's your behavior or your motives that are of concern. I have to trust you won't hurt me or my babe. It's risky to trust a stranger."

"Indeed."

He had little intention of going away. I held up Bannon, patting his back, as he lay over my shoulder. "I wasn't going to sleep well anyhow." I would have to keep one eye open, a weapon by my side at all times, but I slept that way regardless.

"I'll stay on this side of the fire. I can offer safety. I can help you find the dark clan. You're quite close, only another day of walking."

"I'm aware of that. I know where I'm going. I don't need an escort."

He got to his feet, his eyes on the forest. The leather around his waist hid his manhood. "I've business to attend to. You may help yourself to more food, if you wish."

"What sort of business?" Was he going to signal to other men to come? Alarm raced through me, my hand reaching for the spear.

"Personal business." He noted where my hand had gone. "There's only me. I travel alone."

My fingers slid from the weapon. "I only travel alone as well."

He pointed to the baby. "Not true. What's the child's name?"

"Bannon."

"Where's the father?"

"I'm ... searching for him."

"What man would leave his woman?"

"I was taken by white men a while ago, before the

baby came. I escaped them and found my kin at the dark clan. It's a long story, Bondo. I've been missing. My mate's looking for me. I'm looking for him. I'll find him eventually."

"You look healthy enough. The babe looks hearty. You've done well. I see the claws on your necklace. Did your mate kill that cat?"

I wore the claws with Ronan's stone, the necklaces frivolous adornment, but I liked them. "No. I did."

His eyes widened. "You?"

"Yes." I touched the bow. "With this. It's a fine weapon."

"I've not seen anything like it before. I'd ask you to show me how to make one, but I doubt you'd spare the time."

"I'm sorry." I eyed him, as he stood before me across the fire. "You seem quite capable yourself. You're strong looking."

"I can fend for myself, even alone." He frowned, his bushy brows furrowing. "I'm always alone. I'm not welcome anywhere. I'll never find a woman. It would make me happy to have a mate."

A tingle of alarm rippled through me. "I'm not that woman, Bondo. I'm sorry."

He stared morosely into the woods. "I should do my business. We can talk when I return."

"I'm tired. I plan to sleep as soon as my son's put down." I needed to tidy the pelts and make the bedding comfortable.

"I'm cooking more meat. I'm not ready for bed yet."

I had been prickly to him, deciding to offer a kind word. "Thank you. Thank you for the meal. It was delicious."

"Thank you for not killing me."

I smiled at that. "You're welcome. You'll remain alive, as long as you behave yourself."

Twenty-Three

I needn't have worried about Bondo, the man sleeping on the other side of the fire. Bannon woke twice during the night, the last time right before dawn. Exhausted, I pressed him to my breast, both of us falling asleep in this manner. The noisy squawking of birds woke me a short while later, although I tossed the pelt over my head to avoid the sun. I heard Bondo's movements, the snapping of a twig and his footfalls disappearing into the forest. I assumed he had gone to relieve himself or get firewood.

A short while later, I woke again, hearing the crackling of fire and smelling smoke. Bannon continued to sleep, the baby having turned over on his belly, his bottom hidden by a swath of leather. Throwing off the pelt, I sat up, moving hair from my eyes. The locks had grown impossibly long, reaching past my belly. I cut my own hair, but since falling pregnant, I had let it go, finding the hair useful in the cold morning, keeping my back warm.

Bondo eyed me, his features so strange in the light, his eyes a deep blue. I had suspected them to be so. He sat with his legs open before him, a leather sheath hiding his manhood. Riddled with muscle, his torso sported various scars, one especially jagged near his hip.

"You're even more beautiful in daylight," he murmured. "Such a fair creature."

I had not expected words of flattery, wondering at them. "I come from a white clan, but I don't know where they are. I was separated from my parents when I was very young."

"Then you met up with the darks?"

"My mother found me. It's a long story, Bondo. We lived with a dark clan one season, and I learned their language then. It was easy. I was a child."

"That's useful. You can communicate. You can live with both clans, I suppose."

"I'm ... I don't know." I shrugged, being far too tired for this sort of conversation. "I've been alone too long. I long for my mother and sisters. I waited for my man."

"You said white men took you."

"They did. I was foraging. They stole me away. I killed them and escaped, but I became lost then. I found my kin by accident." A grin emerged. "A happy accident. My man's still looking for me. I pray to be reunited with him. I knew him when I was a child. A great flood separated us, but seasons later, we found one another again. He's my destiny."

Bondo appeared thoughtful. "Have you considered he might ... be dead?"

"I have."

"And what will you do?"

"Survive. I don't know what the gods have in store for me, but survive I must." I glanced at my son, the baby still asleep. "I've Bannon to take care of."

"He doesn't look very old."

"No. I had him in the cold season, but where I live, that season isn't too terrible. I lived in the woods far from here once. White blanketed the ground all season, and it was too cold to be outdoors for long."

"I prefer it warmer. I'm considering traveling elsewhere."

He hadn't forced himself on me, the man keeping his distance. I saw goodness in his eyes, his face kind-looking. In the darkness, I hadn't perceived this, but now I did. I could tell him about the cave. I felt the most ridiculous urge to do so.

"I live above a valley—a fertile valley. We've an abundance of game. There are some cats, but I haven't seen them in a while. I killed one. If Ronan and Enwan return, they'll kill the rest."

He sliced meat, having stored it in a leather bag. It would not keep longer than that, needing to be eaten now.

"There's a cave on a hill. It's quite large, with a fire pit in the center. We've lined it with comfortable pelts. There's a quarry too for spear tips and things. It's not far from the cave."

Holding out a branch, he dangled meat in the flames.

"There's fresh water too. It flows from some source above, near the entrance. I need only stand there and drink it. It's clean. It's never sickened us." The aroma filled the air, making my belly rumble. "There's a heated pool as well. It's at the base of the hill, hidden by rocks and grass. It smells slightly off, but it's perfect for bathing. I adore warm water. It leaves the skin soft and clean. You emerge refreshed."

"You're a born storyteller, Peta."

"It's not a story; it's real. This place exists. It's where I call home." The branch came my way, and I took the meat, the heat of it nearly burning my fingers. "Thank you."

He chewed on a portion, eyeing me thoughtfully. "Why are you telling me this?"

"Because … you might want to seek it out. You say you're looking for a home."

"How many live there?"

"No one now, but I'll return as soon as I've seen my mother and sisters. My mates will return too."

"Mates?"

"Ronan and Enwan."

"White men."

"Yes, but they're kind. They won't kill you on sight, I promise. They can be reasoned with. We want to grow our clan. They'll bring back women, I'm sure of it. The cave's the ideal place for a clan."

A rough sort of laugh escaped him. "And what woman would mate me? I'm a half-breed. I'm loathed by all. I have no home."

"But I'm offering you one, Bondo. You can live there in peace."

"There's no such thing as peace. I've never known it anyhow."

"Then we'll create it. We'll make it."

He grilled another slice of meat, his lips pursed. "You've some odd ideas, woman."

"Perhaps, but … you've been kind to me. I'll tell you how to find the cave. If you're ever in those woods, then you're welcome to come by. I offer you friendship. I offer you a home. If you need a refuge, then the cave will do nicely. I've fortified it with sharp brambles to keep the cats away, but there's a door in."

"I'm listening."

Bannon fussed, the baby waking. "Is there a stream near here?"

"Yes." He pointed. "That way."

I got to my feet. "I'll be back."

I left Bannon on the pelt, trusting that nothing would happen to him in my absence. I hurried into the forest to relieve myself, stopping by the brook to wash my face and hands, the water refreshing. When I returned, I found Bondo where I left him, grilling another strip of meat, while Bannon lay on his back, his eyes wide. I reached for him.

"I've thought about what you said."

The baby suckled a nipple, while I took a long pull from a bladder. "And?"

"It sounds too good to be true."

"It's wonderful," I giggled. "You'll just have to follow the path and find it for yourself. I've marked trees. I can tell you which direction to travel and what to look for. It's only a day away."

"And there's no one there?"

"At the moment, but not for long. The men might've returned."

"Or they might be dead."

That thought bothered me. "I don't wish to think of it that way. They're looking for me."

"You are a prize indeed."

"I'm just a woman. There's nothing special about me."

"I disagree." He appeared thoughtful. "If I live with you, will you teach me that weapon?" He pointed to the bow.

"Yes. I plan to visit with my family, then I'll return shortly. If you encounter two men, one with fair hair, the other dark, you'll know them to be my men. The blond man is Ronan. The other is Enwan. Tell them you've seen me. Tell them I've invited you to live with us. If, for some reason, they don't return, then I'll be there. You can help me kill the cats."

He pinned me with a look. "Will you mate me?"

I sucked in a breath, not having expected the question. Perhaps he would appeal to me more after I grew accustomed to him, but that would take time. "Maybe," I answered honestly. "If you're someone I can trust."

That seemed to satisfy him, his features softening. "All right. I've nothing to lose in this. I can seek the cave out. I'll wait for you there."

"Good." I lifted Bannon over a shoulder. "We must be off soon. I've a great deal of walking yet to reach my kin this evening. I've dallied long enough."

"Have some more meat. It's not going to last. The

rest will be wasted."

"Thank you."

I would tell him how to find the cave, and then I had to be on my way. I hadn't anticipated eating fresh meat or meeting Bondo, but it seemed I had made a friend, and friends were hard to come by in these forests.

***

The heat of the sun beat down upon my shoulders as Bannon and I made our way across a grassy plain, but we soon disappeared into the woods again, the coolness and shade provided by a thick canopy of branches. We had stopped earlier to eat, the baby at my breast, but then I continued on again, hoping to reach the camp before it became dark. Bannon slept in the leather contraption on my back, the baby traveling better than I had anticipated.

Having marked the trees, I spotted the small X I had chiseled onto a trunk, knowing I neared the camp, but not seeing anyone about. Being this late in the day, the women and children had already foraged, returning to their fires to rest and eat. I stopped to listen a short while later, hearing the bark of an animal. It had perceived me, alerting the clan to danger.

Grasping the spear, I braced myself for trouble, hoping they would not kill me on sight. I ventured forth gingerly, smelling the aroma of meat grilling and the sound of voices. A nearby growl resonated, the bushes all around suddenly shaking, darkly skinned men appearing, all of them brandishing spears.

"It's me, Peta! I've come to see my family." I did not recognize any of these men, although I was relieved they had not thrown a spear yet. They seemed stunned I knew their language, their eyes flashing wildly, the white a stark contrast to ebony skin. "I'm a friend of the clan. I've come to see my kin. I'm Kia's daughter. I'm sister to Ara and

Maggi."

They slowly lowered the spears, the aroma of unwashed bodies quite strong. A commotion occurred behind them, the men parting to let someone in, a man I recognized.

I bowed my head slightly, seeing their leader. "Palo."

"This is Kia's daughter," he intoned, waving a hand. "Let the woman pass. She's no trouble."

Relief flooded me, a smile emerging. "Thank you for the welcome, Palo."

He grunted in reply, clearly annoyed the commotion had taken him away from his meal. "She's of no importance." Turning on a heel, he stalked away, the men disbanding.

Twenty-Four

During my absence, the camp had changed a little, Kia's fire no longer where it had been. I strode past families, people staring at me, their mouths falling open. Most had seen me before I had the baby, but a few had not, their expressions almost comical. A dog followed, sniffing at my feet, while Bannon began to fuss, the baby crying, drawing even more attention.

Having arrived in the faded colors of the day, the gloaming of sunset, the camp appeared greyish, the smoke of many fires preventing me from seeing anything clearly, although I heard a voice then.

"Peta?"

Swinging about, I gazed at my sister, Ara, a baby in her arms. "There you are," I exclaimed happily. "I've been looking for you."

"What a wonderful surprise." She approached, hugging me, her eyes watering. "You've had your baby. Is Ronan with you?"

I shook my head. "No. I waited and waited, but I haven't seen him. I had the babe alone."

She gasped. "That's dangerous. You should've returned and had him here."

"I'm fine. It went as smoothly as it could. I managed it."

Kia appeared. "Peta!" She ran to me, her legs bowed just like Bondo's. "My girl!"

I hugged her. "Mamma! Are you well? How's

Maggi?"

"She's making a basket by the fire. She doesn't know it's you that's caused such a commotion. She'll be pleased to see you." She came to stand behind me, lifting Bannon out of the leather holder. "Let me see you, you white, white child. He looks like Ronan, even his hair is light." She held him to her, the baby eyeing her with interest, his cries ceasing. "He looks healthy enough. He's hungry, no doubt."

My breasts felt heavy, milk leaking from a nipple. "Yes, it'll be a relief to feed him. I'm full to bursting."

"Come sit with us," said Ara. "Come rest yourself. You've had a long journey." She took the spear and a leather bag. "Come, Peta. We've supper nearly ready."

A rush of emotion constricted my throat. I had missed being with people—talking to people I cared about. I knew then how badly I needed my family. I followed Ara and Kia to the fire, finding Maggi with a partially finished basket before her, her eyes widening at the sight of me.

"Peta! You've come back!" The little girl jumped to her feet, hugging me. "I missed you."

"I missed you." I held her close, smelling perspiration and campfire on her. "You've grown some more. You're taller. You feel stronger."

Ara's man, Lowe, approached, his hands full of uncooked meat, blood dripping to the ground beneath his feet. He eyed me, a hint of a smile emerging. "You've returned."

"Briefly. I … came this way to see if you've seen two white men. One with dark hair, the other fair. They're my mates. I've yet to find them."

Kia frowned, the ridge above her eyes pronounced. "No, Peta. We haven't seen Ronan or Enwan. I'm sorry."

"Sut and a few men encountered travelers yesterday," said Lowe. "I'll ask them about it."

"What sort of travelers?"

"White men. Friendly men. I'll ask, but take this first. It's fresh from the kill today."

Kia reached for the meat. "I've got it. Peta needs to feed her boy."

Lowe's eyes drifted over me, hunger flaring in his look. I had avoided mating him, but now I faced the same quandary, not finding him remotely appealing, although he was kind. "Yes, Bannon's hungry."

"I like the name," said Ara. "It's good. It's a worthy name for such a fine, healthy little man."

I giggled at that. "I just wish his father could meet him." I sat with Bannon by the fire, the baby hungry, wailing unhappily, until he found my nipple. The cries ceased at once, the infant gulping, nearly choking on the milk, because it sprayed freely. "Oh, that's a relief." I sighed, relaxing.

"I'm sorry you had to have your baby alone," said Kia. "Sungir taught you and Ara well. I can see it's served you. I've been praying for you, my child. I pray every day, often more than once. I do hope you and Ronan will be reunited. I'm shocked he hasn't found you."

"Or I haven't found him. I waited until after the babe came. I've watched for signs, but ... he's elsewhere."

She eyed the new necklace. "Is that your doing?" She fingered the claw, grimacing.

"Yes, I killed a cat."

"The men won't believe it," said Lowe. "I do, though. I know how good she is with her weapon. I've tried to teach them how to use the bow, but they're stupid. They don't want to learn."

That stunned me. "You should all know how to make a bow, Lowe. You need them to protect yourself."

"The men prefer the spears. They're used to them. It's how they've always killed game. They don't want to shoot things at a distance. They want to see the fear in the eyes of their prey. I can't convince them otherwise. It's only Ara and me who hunt in this way."

"Teach your son then, if you can," I said. "It's a worthy weapon. It's saved me countless times. I haven't the strength or the skill to use a spear, although I carry one for protection. It's mostly to ward off the woodland creatures. Arrows are better to kill men, if they mean me harm."

"Such morbid talk," admonished Kia. "Let's not dwell on things of this nature now. It's late, and I wish to relax. Maggi and Ara found nuts and berries. We've meat aplenty. Let's enjoy this reunion, shall we?"

I nodded, weariness seeping into my bones. "I agree. I'm so pleased to see you all again. I'm grateful not to be alone."

Kia touched my hand. "There now, girl. Don't fret. I'm sure you'll find your man again. He's about … somewhere."

***

We snuggled in to sleep, Ara sharing a pelt with Lowe and their baby, while I had Bannon next to me with Maggi on one side and Kia on the other. Being with a clan brought a measure of security, knowing that if a threat presented itself, the men would take care of it. Mangy dogs slept at nearly every fire, ours having one as well, the animal at our feet. I closed my eyes, falling asleep at once, not stirring until morning, even Bannon sleeping through the night.

The sounds of hushed talking roused me, the men preparing to hunt. I had not slept this well in a long time, usually waking often at the slightest sound. I had missed feeling safe and protected, the benefits of a clan quite clear to me. I wanted to ask Lowe if he knew anything else about the white men they had seen, but he left to hunt before I could do so.

Kia slipped from the pelt, squatting before the fire. I joined her a moment later, smiling tiredly into the flames. "I'm so happy to be here."

"You shouldn't be alone. If I had known you'd be alone, I would've made you stay with us."

"I thought I'd see Ronan and Enwan again. I was so sure of it. I don't know what's keeping them."

"You waited a long time. You had a baby all by yourself." A flicker of admiration shone in her eyes. "I don't know if I could've done it. You're lucky you didn't have a bad delivery. I've seen too many women die in that manner—too many."

"It was fine. It hurt, but I managed. I helped you and Hanna have babies. I was lucky. The gods must've taken pity on me. They are benevolent when they please and then they punish me for no reason. I hate being alone. I hate the silence. It's easier now with Bannon, but I yearn for my mate. I miss him so terribly. I ache for him."

"I have every hope you'll see Ronan again. You were separated for many seasons, yet you found one another. It'll happen. Try to be patient. You've done well."

"I wish you and Ara and Maggi could come with me. I know why you won't, but I do wish it. I met an odd sort of traveler on the journey here. He's the product of white and dark parents. He looked so ... strange, but he was kind. We shared a fire and a meal. I told him where I live. He said he was an outcast, not wanted by either race. I felt badly for him."

"I've heard of those sorts before. Most don't live for long. They're considered bad luck."

Then, no wonder he crossed my path, I thought bitterly. "He's just a man who looks different. If he'd behaved poorly, I would've killed him."

"I imagine you would." She smiled slightly.

Yawning, I gazed around, noting that several men lingered, not having joined the hunt. They watched over the women, a few of them staring in our direction. I would have to be careful to venture into the woods alone. I was a curiosity, an oddity, but they wanted to mate me.

"I've thought about what you said," said Kia.

"What was that?" I glanced at her, noting how age had creased the edges of her eyes. Deep lines bordered her mouth.

"I might remain here one more season, then join you. I'm too old to have babies. I ... don't want any of the men here. I could live with you. I'll think on it."

That astounded me, because she had been so adamant about staying with her people. "What about Maggi?"

"She'll come. Ara wants to stay with Lowe."

"I can understand that." It gladdened me that I might soon have family nearby, although it would not happen for a while. "I know where you are. I can always find you."

"It might be impossible if Palo insists we leave, but he says we may stay another season, if not longer."

"Why don't you and Maggi come with me now? Why wait?"

"I haven't decided entirely. I need to think on it more. I need time. If I leave this clan, I won't ever return. These people have been good to us; they accept us. I feel safe here. I know you and Ronan can offer safety as well, but I miss my people. I thought I might find another mate here. It seems no one can compare to Magnon. I loved that man deeply."

Hearing her speak so reminded me of the man responsible for his death. Greggor's men had kidnapped me, ruining the peace of my life, but I vowed to get it back and have my revenge. Anger rippled through me, heating my blood uncomfortably.

"He should be with you. He never should've died the way he did."

She sighed. "I see it now. We were never meant to

stay long with that clan for reasons only the gods know. You and your sister were supposed to learn to hunt. You were supposed to find Ronan again. You have his boy now—a fine, strong little man. I've had my moment of happiness. I have Maggi to remind me of her father. It's all I can ask for."

Tears filled my eyes at her words, our reunions always bittersweet. "Yes. If I look at it like you do, everything is as it should be." I murmured, "For the moment."

Twenty-Five

Foraging with my sisters and my mother brought such joy, the three of us chatting and laughing, the morning air smelling sweetly of some flower that bloomed. I carried Bannon on my back while Bunder tagged along, his sturdy little legs firmly beneath him. He had learned how to walk, although he stumbled often, his mother having to pick him up when he cried.

"These will do," said Kia, glancing into a basket. "We've been blessed this morning with easy pickings." Berries and nuts nearly reached the brim. "We can stop now, if we want. I desire to wash in the creek."

"Then let's do it." Ara set Bunder on his feet, the boy holding a short stick. "He's stinky. He needs a bath."

"We all do," said Kia, crinkling her nose. "Except for Peta. She smells fine."

"I do not," I laughed. "I could use a good soaking in warm water, but I know you haven't any."

We reached the creek a moment later, the water glistening beneath the sunlight that filtered down through the branches. I lifted Bannon from the pouch on my back, letting the baby sit by the water. He promptly closed his fist around wet earth, bringing it to his mouth.

"No!" I took his hand. "That's not to eat." He ignored me, grasping another handful, which I intercepted. Annoyed, I lifted him into my arms. "You can't eat dirt. It'll make you sick."

Kia approached, holding out her hands. "Give him to

me so you can wash. Babies will do that. They'll try to eat almost anything. They learn by tasting things or putting things in their mouths."

"The first of his teeth might be coming in," said Ara. "Bunder was so grumpy when his came. He cried all the time."

"I hadn't thought of that. I should carve a smooth piece of wood for him, something with rounded edges."

"Make it big enough so he doesn't swallow it," said Kia. "At this age, they can choke if things get caught in their throats."

Having this discussion reminded me of the importance of being with my family, of sharing ideas and knowledge. Although Sungir had taught us many things, I knew I had forgotten a great deal. I yearned to have other women to speak to on all matters, as the men had no interest or expertise in this area.

After washing in the brook, we returned to the camp. Several fires burned brightly, the men having returned with meat. I spied Lowe among a group of men, the four of them laughing by the fire, while a man mated with a woman on a nearby pelt. He eyed my approach, interest flaring in his eyes.

"Did you ask about the two traveling men?" I had thought about this all day, hoping someone had seen Ronan or Enwan. "Does anyone know about it?"

A sly grin appeared on his face. "We can discuss it after you mate with me."

I left Bannon with my sister, the babies playing together on a pelt. "That's not why I came this way. I only need information, not … mating."

"We can do both," he offered readily, his smile growing.

"I think not." My hands went to my hips. "I've no desire to mate you, Lowe. I only wish to know about the strangers your men encountered, and where they might be going. If you've nothing more to offer than that, then I'm wasting my time talking to you."

His smile fell, and he muttered, "Stubborn white woman."

The man next to him laughed, "She's ugly anyhow. Why would you want that? You've Ara, who's far more handsome than this … odd thing."

I ignored him, saying, "Does anyone know anything about two white men that might've passed by here?"

"We kill them," muttered one of the men, his dark eyes lingering on me.

"Did you kill them?" I held my breath, truly worried now.

"We did not," said the man by Lowe's side. "I spoke with them, or I tried to. They know a little of the language. They were traveling on to other parts."

"What were their names?"

"I don't know. I didn't ask that. I don't care much." He tossed a bone to a dog, the animal trotting over to get it.

"This is Sut," said Lowe. "He's versed in the white language a bit. You said they were looking for someone."

"Yes, some woman."

I gasped, my heart beating wildly. "What?"

"They were searching for a woman. That's all I know."

"What did the men look like?"

"White," said Sut.

"Did one have dark hair, the other light?"

"I believe so." He shrugged.

"D-do you know what direction they might be traveling?"

He pointed. "That way."

I glanced at the horizon, seeing trees. That had not been the way I came. "When did you see these men?"

"Two days ago, maybe three. I really don't remember.

We had a few words, then they moved on."

"Did they look healthy? Was anyone injured?"

"They'd been traveling for a long time. They were tired, smelly, but not hurt in any way. That's all I know."

"Thank you." I turned, hurrying back to Kia and Ara, the women watching me. "They've seen Ronan and Enwan! The man named Sut encountered them a few days ago. They're going in the wrong direction, though. I have to stop them!"

"Calm down, Peta," said Kia. "Sit, child. Have some food. You can't do anything right this minute."

"But they're not going home. If they're going that way, it means the cave's over there. I have to fetch them. I have to stop them. I want to go home." Tears welled in my eyes. "I have to hurry!"

"You can't set out now, it'll be dark soon. Go at first light. They're not walking now. They're resting themselves by a fire just like we are."

"I have to hurry. I'll need to run." I had a thought. "What if … what if I left Bannon with you? I could hurry and stop them and then come back for the baby."

Ara glanced at my son, who crawled upon the pelt. "I could feed him. I've enough milk, that's for certain. It wouldn't be a hardship. Maggi can help too."

"I'll only be gone a day or two. I'll be back directly."

Kia frowned, her thoughts clearly troubled. "What if something happens, Peta? What if you don't return so soon? Your milk will dry up. You won't have any way of feeding your baby. It's a big risk. You should take him with you or not go at all. Just wait here. They might come back."

"I'm done waiting for things to happen!" I cried fervently. "That's all I've done for so long now. I need to find Ronan. No more dallying about. I'll be back soon enough. I'll still have plenty of milk. If I don't stop them, they'll be so far away. Too far away. They'll meet other women and never return."

"That's not a concern," said Kia. "If you feel you must go after them, then leave Bannon with us. You know I'll love him as my own. Ara can feed him." Her look grew stark. "But, don't linger at this task. Hurry, girl. If you don't find them in two days, then come back to us."

I might finally be reunited with my mate. I wished I could leave right this instant. "Yes, yes, of course. I shall be back before you know it. We all will."

***

I packed my things at first light, kissing Bannon on the forehead, inhaling the sweet fragrance of his soft skin. I would be gone three days at the latest, possibly four, but it could not be helped. Without the baby, I could make haste, covering a greater distance, even running when need be. Bannon hated it when I ran with him on my back, the bouncing making him cry.

Kia stood near, handing me the spear. She looked tired in the first blush of morning, lines etched into her face. "Take care, Peta. I always hate it when you leave. I worry I'll not see you again."

"You will. Have no fear." I grasped the bow, flinging it over my shoulder. "I'm going to move quickly. I've plenty of dried meat and nuts. I shouldn't need to stop very often."

"Be careful. There are other clans about, some not so friendly."

I tapped the bow. "I can manage."

"When you find Ronan, he'll be so happy to see you, my child." She smiled, touching my face.

"I'll be happy too. I've missed him terribly. I've never yearned for anyone like this before."

"That's because he's your true mate. You belong together." She hugged me. "Now, go. You've a great deal of walking ahead of you."

I felt assured that Bannon and my mother and sisters would be well. Many strong, able-bodied men provided for this clan, their snores resonating, as most continued to sleep. A baby cried in the distance, while a haze of smoke lingered from many defunct fires.

"Tell Ara and Maggi I love them."

"I will. I look forward to your arrival."

"Do you think Bannon will miss me?"

"He will, but Ara will mind him carefully. He has a playmate with Bunder. I foresee them being the best of friends."

"I love you, Mamma." Tears fell down my cheeks. "I hate to leave, but I have to find Ronan. He's wandering about in circles looking for me. I'm relieved to know he and Enwan are well. They must be exhausted."

"Then go and get them." She nodded pragmatically. "You're free now to find them. You've tamed a wolf. You killed a cat. You've given birth on your own and survived. Finding two wayward men should be easy enough for you." She chuckled, the sound rough and rumbling. "Go on then. Go find your mate."

Twenty-Six

No sooner had I set foot in the forest than I questioned the decision to leave my son with my mother and sisters. An uncomfortable feeling niggled away at me, mingling with a sense of foreboding. I hadn't gone far when I stopped by a tree, my breath catching in my throat. The impression felt so strong, I nearly turned around and ran back to camp.

"He'll be fine," I whispered, listening to birdcalls in the branches above me. "He's in good hands."

I had waited all this time, hoping Ronan and Enwan would return. Now I knew they were still looking for me, walking about in circles it seemed. According to Sut, they were near, having come this way a few days ago. If I found them, we could all return to camp and retrieve Bannon. But something still bothered me.

"If I don't find them in two days, I'll go back. Two days. That's not a very long time. Bannon will hardly miss me in two days."

I chastised myself then for wasting time debating back and forth, when I could have been searching for my mate, not second-guessing myself.

"Enough! He's fine. I won't be long."

Pushing aside the misgivings, I glanced at the forest carefully, eyeing the ground for prints, which I did see, but they could easily belong to members of Kia's clan. I pressed onward, determined to head in the direction Sut said he saw the white men traveling. I had to find Ronan.

He and Enwan hadn't stopped searching for me, the men exhausted from travel. That thought alone prompted me to continue, the path ending near a stream a short while later. From there, tracks were hard to come by, few people having been here.

By midday, I stopped to rest, my legs aching from running. I felt an urgency I hadn't perceived before, a need to hurry. Having dried meat, I sat at the base of a tree chewing, while I thought of where Ronan might be. After eating, I climbed the tree, seeing nothing other than the forest and a hint of smoke from Kia's clan behind me. I squinted in the sunlight that streamed through the branches, my spirits sagging, but I still had many hours before night, and a great deal of ground to cover.

Upon finding a bush bursting with berries, I stopped to eat, tossing the extras into a leather pouch. I glimpsed what appeared to be a footprint a short while later, the impression of a slender-looking foot, not short and wide like that of the men of Kia's clan. Heartened by this, I soon found another, realizing they belonged to two different men, traveling together.

Hope flared within me, although the prints did not look fresh, having been made a few days ago by the looks of the debris upon them. I managed to follow them, finding what appeared to be a path, although not well used. By evening, the prints could not be seen in the shadows any longer, the need to stop for the night apparent. If I continued on, I might lose them. I made camp near where they were, so I could follow them again at first light.

Settling by the fire, I stared into the flames, feeling a mixture of apprehension and hope, missing my son, yet knowing his father to be in these woods … somewhere.

***

In the morning, I gathered my things, finding a creek to wash in. Spying the prints, I continued to follow them, although they disappeared for a while, but I suspected they would appear again, and they did. I could not travel as quickly, worried I might miss signs of the men, my eyes darting to every tree and bush, some with branches snapped, indicating someone had been this way.

Before stopping to eat, I realized the men had gone in a wide circle, only to break from it now, the prints taking a new direction. I came to what looked like a campfire, where I knelt to feel the ground. Thrusting my hand into the ashes, I felt a slight warmth. This had been used in the last day or two. A short while later, I spotted a distinct X upon a tree trunk, knowing it to be one of my markings. I had to wonder if Ronan and Enwan had seen it, the men having camped here recently, or perhaps, it was someone else.

"They're smart. If they saw the X, they will follow it."

The markings led to the valley where I lived. Excited by this prospect, I decided to return home. I could make quick progress at this, the cave a day away. If I ran, I might even arrive by nightfall, being reunited with Ronan again. This seemed like a sound idea, although running felt painful, my breasts filled with milk, far too full and heavy, and no baby to empty them. As it was, milk dripped from my nipples, the pressure behind them unbearable. Ignoring the discomfort, I darted into the trees, determined to be home by night.

My feet protected by fur, I ran without stopping, sometimes slowing to catch my breath, seeing more of the markings on the trees. I came to a brook a good while later, using a strip of leather to bind my breasts, the flesh here tender to the touch, almost painful. When I ran again, it felt better, although they continued to leak throughout the day, wetting the leather completely. I tried not to think about my son and how desperately I missed him, knowing

I would only be gone two days. This was what I told myself, over and over, to temper increasingly worried thoughts.

As the day wore on and the shadows of evening drew near, I realized I would not find the cave before dark, my spirits plummeting. Forced to stop for the night, I made a fire, staring moodily at the flames and cursing my breasts for slowing my progress. I tried to express the milk on my own, merely touching the nipples to make them squirt, the feeling that of relief. I settled on a pelt, not finding any position comfortable, my body aching from running, every muscle protesting. The overly full and swollen masses of my breasts continued to plague me, although, by morning, they weren't as painful.

Upon rousing, I tied leather to my chest, although the milk had dried now, making the hide stiff. I grasped the bow and spear, slinging the bag of arrows around my shoulder. After setting out, I again found the tracks, but I saw only one set of feet, not two. Perhaps Ronan and Enwan had taken different paths? I knew I wasn't far now from my home, seeing more of my markings on the trees, having placed these where only I knew I could see them, the X's carved beneath the lower branches on tree trunks. The earlier ones were placed on the trunk itself, but I did not want to make it too obvious, as anyone could follow them straight to my home.

I chewed on a piece of dried meat a while later, hoping the valley might be close, waiting for the grassland to appear, which happened shortly. Standing at the edge of the woods, I glimpsed the mountains in the distance, recognizing their white tips. I had not seen any evidence of the dangerous cats, not knowing if they lurked in the golden grass before me. I had little choice but to cross the expanse to reach the cave beyond.

Breaking into a run, I dashed through the prairie, where insects buzzed and fluttered into the air about me.

Watchful for danger, I kept my eye on anything that looked like it moved, seeing a family of stags in the distance. They spied me, fleeing into the forest. Reaching the other side, I stopped to catch my breath, smelling the foul aroma from the heated pool, which lay hidden by greenish fronds and bushes. The path to the cave led through a rocky incline spotted with boulders, although those thinned as I climbed.

Smelling smoke, I knew someone had made a fire, my spirits lifting. Someone was in the cave! Although excited by this prospect, I had to be careful, withdrawing the bow and threading an arrow, holding it before me. I ventured nearer to the entrance warily, seeing an opening in the sharp thorns, the small doorway having been cast aside. I hadn't gone another foot or two when a man appeared holding a spear, his gaze sharp. He had perceived me, despite the silence of my approach. I recognized him at once, although my mood dampened.

"Bondo." Where was Ronan? "Are you alone?" I lowered the bow.

He grinned. "I am. You were right. This cave is rather cozy. I like it."

"Did you encounter two white men on your travels?"

"I did not."

My shoulders slumped. "I see."

"Come inside. I've meat left from last night. I'll cook you something. You look tired."

I wanted to cry, frustrated that I had just run circles around the forest and had not seen Enwan or Ronan, the men elsewhere. "All right."

"Where's your baby?" Concern appeared in his eyes.

"I left him in my sister's care. She has a little one too. He's fine. I'll return shortly to get him."

Upon entering the cave, it looked just as I had left it, the wall lined with baskets and the center filled with pelts, although they would need beating. The fire blazed warmly,

Bondo tossing a few chunks of meat onto a flattened rock. I left my weapons in a heap by the doorway, approaching the burning pit. Lowering to my knees, I wanted to cry.

"You should rest, Peta. You do look terribly tired."

"I ran most of yesterday. I ... was told two white men were in the woods. I thought I found their footprints, but now I don't know."

"Your men will return. Have some faith." He handed me a piece of meat. "Eat. You'll feel better with food in your belly."

I took the offering. "Thank you."

After eating, I collapsed to the fur, my eyes filling with tears. I left my boy with my family to search for my man, and it had yielded nothing other than exhaustion and disappointment. If I had known it would end in such a way, I would never have done this. I slept almost immediately, my body needing rest. When I woke, darkness had descended, the cavern in shadow, but a warm fire blazed. I had slept the day away. Sitting up, my eyes adjusted to the dimness, finding Bondo on a rock picking at his teeth with a stick.

He nodded to me. "Do you feel better?"

"I can't feel worse," I muttered. "I'm fine. I ... just wanted to see Ronan here."

"I'm sorry I'm a disappointment. You said I should seek this place out. It's quite nice. The best cave I've ever seen."

"Have you been to the pool yet?" From the smell of him, I doubted it.

"No. That stinky water? It's best to stay away."

"It's the smoke that stinks, not the water itself. You won't smell like it, I promise." I fully planned to bathe, once I had eaten. "Is there anymore meat?"

"Certainly." He pointed to the rock in the fire, several occupying the pit, the ones further out for warming. "Should still be nice and hot."

"Thank you." My instincts about Bondo had been correct, the man being someone I could trust. "I'm glad you like the cave. I adore it, but I wish my man and my boy were here."

"Why did you leave him?"

"I thought I could travel faster without him. He doesn't like it when I run. I thought ... I thought I'd find his father."

"You will."

He sat with his arms on his knees. The shadows darkened the odd shape of his face, the ridge on his forehead pronounced. Being part dark and white, his skin appeared far paler than Kia's race, although not as white as mine.

"I'm going to wash up. You should come with me."

"To the foul-smelling water?" Humor shone in his eyes.

"Yes, but you won't stink from it. I swear. You'll like it. I thought the same thing, but I know better now. It's truly wondrous."

He considered that, his eyes traveling over the length of me. "Will you let me mate you?"

I did not find him appealing in the least, although he was kind. "No. I'm sorry. I ... not at this time." I knew most men just took what they wanted, often forcing themselves on women. At every clan I had ever lived, the women were obliged to mate, whether they wanted to or not. I eyed him judiciously, looking for any sign that he would not honor my wishes.

"Very well." His lower lip protruded, his shoulders slumping slightly. "I won't force you. I know that's what you're thinking. I want a woman who's willing. I'll never find such a thing, though."

"I disagree."

"I'm too ugly. Women cringe when they see me. Children do as well. I've heard of an outcast clan of men who look like me, but I haven't been able to find them. We're hunted and killed. The dark clans might soon die out."

"I hope not." Worried, I asked, "Is there trouble near? Why can't people live in peace?"

"They consider our race inferior, stupid. We're targeted. We're hunted. It's always been so."

"I've seen it, many seasons ago." I hated this particular conversation, not wishing to dwell on such horrors. "Let's bathe, Bondo. I desire to be clean for once."

"If you insist."

"You'll thank me later."

Twenty-Seven

I gasped, flinging the pelt away, my eyes flying wide. Then I realized I wasn't running in the woods, branches and leaves hitting my face. I stared at the cavern, seeing a lump nearby, Bondo sleeping soundly. A dream woke me, images filled with terror, where I saw Kia's people attacked and murdered, blood soaking the ground. I heard the echoes of screams in my ears …

It's a dream. It's not real.

The feeling that something terrible had happened lingered, gnawing away at me. I put it down to missing my son, my nipples leaking just at the thought of him. I had only wanted to be gone two days, and now I had reached that timeframe. I planned to return to my mother's clan the following morning. I could not bear to be separated from Bannon a moment longer. Then it would be another two days before I reached him.

Bondo suddenly flung back the pelt. "I'm hunting." He eyed me. "I'd like to learn how to use that bow."

"Another time," I said absently, my senses continuing to forewarn me of danger.

"You were right about the bath. I worried I might smell like that water, but I don't. It's refreshing. I shall enjoy it every night, I dare say."

"Yes."

"Is something the matter?"

"I had a bad dream. I saw … carnage. I saw … death."

"That's an unfortunate way to wake to face the day. It promises to be beautiful."

"I have to relieve myself." Getting to my feet, I walked upon pelts to reach the thorny brambles, lifting a piece away. Gazing at the horizon, I glanced from one end to the other, something catching my eye nearby. A man and a woman approached, the man dark-haired. I recognized him at once, my breath coming out in a rush. "Enwan!"

He glanced up, waving. "Hello!"

I raced down the path towards him, my feet pounding into sharp rocks and twigs, yet I did not care in the least. "I knew you'd come back! I knew it!" I flung myself at him, his skin smelling of perspiration. He had been traveling for some time. "Where's Ronan?" The woman beside him eyed me, her hair a dark tangled mess down her back. "Where is he? Does he come?"

He shook his head. "We parted two days ago. He's looking for you still. He's nearly mad with wanting to find you. I told him to return to the cave, that you might be here. He says he will soon enough."

Tears sprang to my eyes. "Oh, thank the gods! Thank each and every one of them!" I hugged him again, delighted beyond words.

Enwan's eyes drifted to the entrance of the cave, a man standing there. "Who's that?"

"His name's Bondo. I invited him to live with us. He's been kind to me. He's an outcast, as you can see." He nodded, his smile returning. I thought him handsome, his face nearly hidden by a bushy beard. "You've been traveling for a long time."

"Too long. We searched for you far and wide. We've some stories to tell. We met other clans."

I stared at the woman, her height a bit shorter than mine. "I see."

"This is Saffron. She's agreed to be my mate. She lost

her family to illness a while ago."

I smiled at her. "Hello. Welcome. We've meat and hot water. We should go up. I want to introduce you to Bondo."

She eyed me, clearly relieved at the kind reception. "You're lovely. You look like Ronan."

We began to walk, Enwan eyeing my belly, which appeared entirely flat again. "What happened to your baby, Peta?"

"Bannon's fine. I left him with Kia. The men of her tribe said they saw two white men passing through, so I thought I might find you myself. I followed tracks and remnants of a fire, but I only ended up walking in a great circle. Then I came home."

We now stood at the entrance of the cave, the sharp brambles blocking the way. Enwan glanced at them. "Why did you do this? Did something happen?"

"We've cats now." I fingered the claw necklace. "I killed one."

A serious gleam flickered in his eyes. "I see. That's grave news indeed, but I'm gladdened the baby's well. I'm stunned to hear you saw Kia again. At least you had help when the time came to deliver him."

"I did not. I was here alone. I had him alone."

His mouth fell open. "Oh, Peta. I'm sorry. I'm so sorry."

"We've a great deal to talk about. Come inside." I motioned for them to enter, Bondo standing just inside the cavern. "This is Bondo. Bondo, this is Enwan and Saffron."

They exchanged pleasantries, Enwan eyeing the man. "Pardon my boldness, but you look like a mixture of races. It's the oddest thing, isn't it, Peta?"

"I find him interesting, yes."

"I was about to hunt."

"I'd join you, but my body aches."

"Please make yourselves comfortable," said Bondo. "Let me hunt for you. I shall bring back something tasty."

"Thank you," I said, waiting for him to leave. Saffron eyed the cavern, her expression startled. "You may sit where you like."

"We could use a bath," said Enwan, dropping several leather pouches and a spear. He carried a bow and arrows as well. "It's good to be home. I never wish to leave again. We came upon several clans that lived perilously out in the open. I can't recommend it."

"There's room here for five other families." Saffron eyed the fire. "Such a fine space."

"The cats worry me." Enwan frowned. "I'll take care of them. I refuse to live where they are."

"I didn't see another one after I killed this one." I pointed to the claws that dangled over my breasts.

"You've done well, Peta. I told Ronan not to worry about you. I told him you were resourceful. He was greatly troubled by your disappearance. We know men found you. We followed their tracks as long as we could."

"I killed them at the first opportunity, then I set out to find Kia's clan. I know where they are."

"I'm glad to hear they're in good health, are they?" A dark eyebrow rose.

"Yes, of course. My sister has a man and a baby. My younger sister's growing by the day. They're as happy as can be expected."

He considered me soberly, his smile faltering. "I can see the sorrow and worry in your eyes. Ronan's coming. You needn't fret about that a moment longer."

"It's not him I'm worried over. I had the worst dream imaginable. I know I shouldn't think too much of dreams, but this one felt real. I never should've left my son with my sister. That was stupid. I have to get him."

"Then I shall go with you."

"No. You're tired. You need to rest." He had traveled

far longer than I had.

"So do you."

"But I've only been traveling two days. That isn't much. I can hurry and reach their clan within two days. Then I'll bring Bannon home to meet his father."

"Bannon?"

"That's the name I chose."

"It's a good one." His smile fell. "Did the men who took you, hurt you, Peta?"

"No. They wanted to bring me to bring to their leader."

"What leader?"

"A horrible man named Greggor. I've seen him before when I was a child, when his men ruthlessly murdered a dark clan. They were taking me to him as some sort of prize. I wouldn't let that happen, though."

"I'm sorry for your misfortune. Ronan and I should've protected you better. It's our fault."

"It's taught me not to be too comfortable in these woods. I thought I was alone, but I wasn't. I'll never make that mistake again."

"Is this Greggor person near here?"

"No, but he's here … somewhere. His men were passing through."

"There are all sorts of clans about," said Saffron. "My clan lived in the woodlands, but sickness took most of us last season."

"I'm glad you found a mate, Enwan. I know you've been wanting a woman of your own."

His eyes drifted over me, interest flashing in their depths. "I've missed you, Peta."

It had been far too long since I had been with a man, my belly tightening pleasurably. "I must tell you that my son is as fair as his father."

He chuckled, "Ah, his seed was stronger. I shall have to try harder next time."

I wondered if Saffron would balk at the idea of sharing her man. "You smell, Enwan. If you wish to mate, you'll have to wash first."

"In good time," he laughed, the timbre of his voice pleasing.

I glanced at Saffron. "I won't touch him, if you don't wish it. I don't want to hurt anyone's feelings about mating. I haven't a clue how things were done at your clan. I've lived with both white and dark clans, the darker ones far more promiscuous. They share women freely."

"You're mistress of this cave. I bow to your will." She lowered her head slightly.

Her behavior stunned me. "I'm ... no one's master. Whoever lives here should be an equal. No one is greater or less than." I glanced at Enwan. "What do you say about it?"

"You've just answered your own question. I like your idea."

"Will anyone mate with Bondo? He's quite hideous, but ... he's a good man."

An odd expression flitted across Enwan's face. "He's not my sort of man. Perhaps, Saffron will agree to it."

I laughed, "I didn't mean you!" The idea of two men mating together struck me as funny, a giggle escaping. He teased me. I had missed his humor, forgetting how silly he could be.

"He's not hairy enough. I prefer my men ... to look more like woodland creatures." A glimmer shone in his eye. "There. Now you know my secret."

Even Saffron laughed, her tired features softening. "Oh, he's always saying strange things to me. Ronan's the same. They've wicked humor, don't they?"

"Yes," I giggled.

"I could mate Bondo, I suppose," said Saffron. "I don't have an objection. The clan I came from was open with mating. Some men preferred their wives only, while others took what they wanted."

"Then it's settled," I said.

"I don't wish to intrude upon your space. I want to be your friend."

"I'm so happy not be alone anymore. I want to be a part of a clan again. I want my son to know other people and make friends. I'd like to be your friend as well, Saffron. This can be our paradise. It's not perfect, but it's truly an ideal spot to raise our little ones. I'm quite eager to see my man again. I hope he comes soon."

"In a few days," said Enwan.

"Then I shall leave first thing to get Bannon."

"You shouldn't go alone."

"I don't like it, but I've learned to live with it. I can manage just fine. You've Saffron to attend to. I've every intention of returning as soon as possible. I'm so happy you're well. I'm just ... so happy."

He touched my face. "All is well, Peta. You know we wouldn't leave you. We were always going to return to the cave, no matter what happened. Ronan's coming soon. You are his world. You're all he talks about. He's been in agony wondering what happened to you and his babe."

"You've given me every reason to hurry. Everything will be back together as it should be."

Twenty-Eight

I had enough dried meat for several days, working my hair into a thick braid down my back, tying it with a strip of leather. I planned to run most of the day, traveling as lightly as I could, taking only a thin pelt, securely wrapped. Bidding Enwan farewell, Saffron and Bondo still sleeping, I stole from the cave before the sun crested the mountain in the distance, determined not to waste one moment of precious time.

Knowing that Ronan would return, I raced through the woods, the braid flying out behind me. Dashing across the open plain, I kept a keen eye on my surroundings, cautious about where the cats might be. Perhaps, they had gone to other hunting grounds. Knowing the path well now, I alternated between running and walking quickly, my body setting a rhythm which sustained me until I stopped to have a meal.

Having spied several of my X's in the trees, I knew the course to be correct, although I would not reach the clan until tomorrow. I hoped to be there earlier, preferably arriving just after sunrise. A leather skirt hung from my hips, while a strip of leather secured my breasts, the nipples leaking often, although not as bad as before. I prayed I had enough milk left to feed my baby still, the body not producing as much without a baby suckling several times a day.

Worried over this and Bannon, I got to my feet, determined to run for as long as my muscles allowed. With nearly silent footfalls, I often jumped over branches and small watery bogs, the ends of branches smacking me in the face. I rested again hours later, catching my breath by a stream, the shadows deepening around me. I needed to make shelter before dark, hearing the rumble of bad weather overhead. When the rain began, I cursed it, seeing it as bad luck, because I now had to look for shelter whether I wished to or not.

I failed to find an outcropping to sit beneath, this part of the forest heavily treed. Slicing several branches with a hand ax, I positioned them to lean against one another, tossing the leather bedding over as a barrier to the rain. I sat on damp earth, the smell filling my senses, as I watched the rain puddle before the opening, dismayed it had slowed me down.

Praying the storm would pass quickly, I chewed on meat, contemplating the success of travel today, guessing I had made good time. An uncomfortable night loomed, especially if it continued to rain, the pelt soaked through, although it kept the water off my head. I would not have a fire tonight, wrapping my arms about my legs and shivering. The rain ceased a short while later, the rumble in the sky moving on.

"There won't be a dry place to sleep," I muttered, crawling out from the shelter. With the dark, nocturnal creatures began to emerge, their sounds filling my ears.

Snatching the thin pelt from the branches I had placed together, I tossed it around my shoulders, picking up the bow and the bag of arrows. Grasping the spear, I continued on, having decided to keep walking, desiring a dryer portion of forest. I might fail in this, but I could not sleep on wet earth, the smell of it deep in my lungs. Glancing at the gloom, the darkness drew closer by the moment, the sun having long since gone down. If the light of the bright orb in the sky appeared big enough, I might be able to see where I went.

Not being able to run, I walked on, determined to find a better place to sleep, my legs protesting each step, my body now feeling the effects of having been active all day. Low hoots echoed, the night animals scampering about. I glimpsed the flare of eyes here and there, little creatures stirring in the bushes. I fought to continue on, my eyes adjusting to the darkness, although it felt like the trees closed in about me, the branches like gnarled fingers tugging at my hair, some of the braid having come loose.

Utter exhaustion forced me to stop a while later, tears of tiredness filling my eyes. I crouched, feeling the ground to see if it was wet here. The fur on my feet felt damp. I should have made a shelter when I had light, despite the rain. It was impossible to find wood for a fire, the darkness like a blanket of black all around me. I could barely see to the end of my hand. For all I knew, I stood near the den of woodland creatures or worse, cats. I heard nothing other than the hum of insects and the hoots from the trees above, but danger lurked.

Crouching near the base of a tree, I drew up my legs before me, resting my forehead on my knees. With the damp pelt around my shoulders, I shivered, unhappy that I might not even sleep this night, needing it so badly.

"One night of poor sleep isn't going to kill me," I whispered, shivering. "I'm close to the clan, I know it. At first light, or even before first light, I'll be off again."

I took a risk walking at night, not being able to see the markings on the trees. I knew the general direction of travel, however, and I remained certain I had continued on it. Now, if only the time would go by faster, if only morning would arrive. I hated sitting here and waiting …

***

Gathering dried leaves, I created a small bed, lying upon it to sleep. I woke several times, mostly to shiver uncontrollably, the night damp and cold. By morning, I had already gathered my things, finding the first of several markings along the way. Stopping at a creek, I washed my hands and face. When I returned to the path, I ate a strip of meat, eyeing the trees. I knew I neared the camp, recognizing a particularly large tree with a distinctive trunk. I desired a hot meal and a fire, but seeing my son remained paramount. I began to run, knowing he wasn't far now.

No women foraged today, the woods eerily quiet. A worn path appeared beneath me, the clan having used it to enter the woods for many seasons. Something in the distance caught my notice, black birds squawking over what looked like a dark lump on the ground. Hearing this sound for a while now, it seemed to echo from all directions. I slowed my steps, approaching what looked like a body—a man of Kia's clan being eaten by the vultures, hungry birds.

The excitement I felt at seeing my son suddenly turned to terror, my instincts warning me of danger. Grasping the bow, I threaded an arrow, standing with the weapon lifted, my eyes darting to every part of the forest. This close to the clan, I should be seeing women and children foraging, their voices drifting, but all remained eerily silent, except for the birds. Glancing at the man at my feet, he sported a lethal wound beneath his chin, his neck having been sliced open.

It took all my will not to succumb to panic, fearing what might have happened to the clan. Continuing on, I held the weapon firmly, working my way towards the clearing where I knew many cooking fires to be from the families that lived there, but the sight that greeted me wasn't warm and welcoming. Instead, it looked exactly as I had seen in my dream; the bloodied bodies of men lay scattered—dead. So many ... had died. The black, horrible birds swooped down to pick away at the flesh, the stench of death lingering in the air. Lowering the bow, I saw nothing alive, besides the vultures. All of the victims appeared to be men. I struggled to hold back tears, arriving at Kia's fire, seeing several pelts on the ground and one of

Bannon's carved wood toys.

I knelt, reaching out to touch the items, while tears blurred my vision. "What happened here? Where are you?"

I never should have left my son. That had been a horrendous mistake. I saw a smooth wood comb and several of Bannon's leather diapers. Sitting on a pelt, I held my face in my hands, as grief washed over me. I had lost my son! Where was my family? Why were the gods so determined to cause me pain? Hadn't I suffered enough already? Weeping noisily, I could not contain my emotions, my body spent from running ceaselessly, only to discover my entire world had been torn apart.

"Hello there," said a voice in the dark man's language.

Shocked, I gulped in a breath of air, jumping to my feet. A woman stood before me, her face haggard. "What?" I had not expected to see anyone here. "Where's my family?"

"The men are dead. The women and children have scattered."

That announcement dried my tears at once. "Scattered?"

"Run off."

"What happened?"

"We were set upon by marauders, the white hunters." She shrugged, her expression bleak. "They killed Palo. They killed our healer. They ... killed my man and my sons. All is lost now." She eyed the surroundings blindly, her look devoid of emotion. "We were here too long. All paths led here. We should've moved camp a season ago."

"I'm sorry this happened. I've seen it before as a child. White heathens came and killed our clan then too. They spared the women and children. We were left to fend for ourselves at the onset of the cold season."

"I remember you." Her eyed drifted over me. "You're Kia's daughter."

"Yes. Do you know where they went?" I planned to

search for them today, but I needed some sort of direction.

"They went that way." She pointed towards where the leader had made his camp. "I saw them there last."

"I have to get my boy."

"The white baby?"

"Yes, that's my son."

"You won't find him with them."

My breath caught in my throat. "W-what ... why?"

"Because the white leader took him."

It felt like someone had kicked my belly, the impact forcing me to my knees. "W-what ... "

"He took him."

I hadn't expected that. "My son!" I cried.

"I don't think he means to harm him. Kia tried to prevent it, but he would not be stopped. He and his men took the boy and left." She waved to the campsite. "After they killed our men. I shall seek another clan, but it won't be easy."

"Have you any idea where the men went?" I whispered, feeling as if I might be ill. "Any direction whatsoever?"

She pointed. "That way. There were many of them. Even with the rain, you should easily be able to follow where they went."

"What's your name?"

"Leenpa."

"I'm Peta."

"I've never met a white woman who could make our talk. I'm sorry for your loss."

"You've lost more. From what you say, my mother and sisters still live. My son's been stolen, but I'll find him. I shall do whatever necessary to get him back." A steely resolve laced my tone, anger replacing the grief. "I won't let that white heathen keep him. He won't grow up to be that sort of evil, not as long as there's breath left in me."

Twenty-Nine

I wandered through the decimated camp, seeing the bodies of men strewn about. What had once been a vibrant clan, now smelled of death, black birds swooping in and tearing chunks of flesh from corpses. A few hungry dogs joined them, the animals having been pets. Saddened by the sight, I kept my head down, treading carefully to avoid stepping on the deceased.

Near the edge of the forest, I saw a white man's body, an arrow protruding from his chest. Stunned by this, I realized Ara must have shot him, or perhaps it had been Lowe. They were the only two people in this clan who knew how to use the weapon. I pulled the arrow free, wiping it on the man's leather skirt. I would add it to my collection. Despite being dead, he looked shockingly large, the muscles in his arms and legs bulging. These people were taller and stronger than the men of Kia's clan. They looked even bigger than Ronan and Enwan, which worried me.

Picking up the path of the marauders was easy, the men so heavy they left deep impressions in the soft earth. From the looks of the bodies, the attack occurred a day or so ago, the corpses still fresh. I planned to walk, not run now, needing to keep a sharp eye on the forest. The men might not have gone far, and I did not want them to see me. As the day progressed, I found more tracks, made up of many footprints. I counted not more than a dozen men, but that had been enough to lay waste to the clan.

A while before sunset, I found evidence of a campfire, with rocks placed in a circle. The rocks still felt warm. They had been here the night before, bones of whatever they had eaten discarded all around. The earth appeared flattened in places where they had slept, crushing blades of grass. I squatted, eyeing the ashes. This would do for the night. All I needed was to gather some wood and settle in, my body exhausted.

With flames flickering, I sat before the fire staring at it absently, my mind digesting everything that had happened recently. I chastised myself over and over for leaving Bannon with my mother and sisters. I should have taken him with me. I had placed my son in grave danger, not knowing that a band of heathens would arrive to murder all the men. The weight of guilt slumped my shoulders, my head hanging.

I cried myself to sleep, waking feeling groggy and tired, the night not having been restorative in the least. My dreams plagued me, images of blood and bodies tormenting what should have been a peaceful interlude.

"I must go soon," I muttered. "I feel dreadful."

After eating dried meat, I ran a wooden tong through my hair, working tangles free. I needed something to do to distract my troubled thoughts. Had Ronan arrived home yet? He would be expecting me, and I would not return. What if I never saw the cave again?

The possibility existed that I might lose my life in this quest. I knew nothing of these heathen men other than the fact that they enjoyed murdering Kia's race. Once I reached their camp, I did not know how I would find my son or take him back. From the looks of the corpse yesterday, the men were strong—far too strong to fight. I did not possess enough arrows to kill them all. I would have to somehow use my wits to find my son and secure his release.

With this in mind, I prepared to go, tossing dirt into the fire to put it out and rolling up the pelt. Encountering a stream, I washed my face and hands, the coldness of the water waking me fully. Picking at my teeth with a stick, I found tracks again, the footprints deeply embedded in places. They veered from the path a short while later, several broken branches on a bush indicating the change. Eyeing the forest, it smelled of some flowering plant, the foliage overhead lush. I marked a tree here, doubting I would remember the place otherwise. I might have to return this way after retrieving Bannon.

Towards the latter part of the day, I felt certain I neared a camp, the prints having led me here. A mangy dog found me then, his teeth baring at the sight of me. I quickly pulled out a piece of meat, holding it up.

"Here you are," I said in a soft voice, not wanting the animal to bark. "Have it." I tossed it to him, which he promptly took. He trotted into the foliage, disappearing.

Inching closer to a small clearing, I glimpsed what looked like some sort of structure, a woman tending a fire before it. Hiding behind a tree, a small community stood before me, the houses similar to the one Sungirl had built, but far smaller. Made of wood and covered in hide, I counted less than a dozen, the clan not big in the least. Besides women and children, a few men appeared, some carrying what looked like stags over their shoulders. Talking and laughter prevailed, the feeling of cooperation strong. I thought of how I might approach them, deciding to be as direct as possible, praying they would not kill me on sight.

Stepping from the shadow of trees, I began to walk towards the first fire I saw, a woman lifting her head to look at me. She blinked, having been startled. Getting to her feet, she eyed my approach. A child sat near her, the girl babbling happily, unaware that a stranger neared. "Good day," I said, trying my best to sound polite.

"Who are you?"

"A traveler. I'm looking for my son."

Several people turned to watch, with a group of men gathering a few huts away.

"I'm looking for an infant. Have you seen him?"

She shook her head, clearly not wanting to speak to me. "You may ask our elder, but I don't know anything."

"Thank you." I braced myself, unsure of what might happen if I approached the men. One of them stood taller than the rest, his shoulders broad. Holding a spear, he stared at me. "Good day. I'm looking for my son. He's an infant. Someone said he might be here."

"Who are you?" He eyed me up and down. "Where did you come from?"

"I'm a traveler. I've walked a good distance."

"We don't have him."

"He was with a dark clan. They were massacred two days ago or so."

He nodded. "That would be Greggor's men."

Those words felt like a spear through my heart, the impact staggering. "G-greggor?"

"Aye. He's leader to all these clans. He's our lord."

People emerged to look at me, some standing in the doorways of their huts. "And … where might I find Greggor?"

"The clan by the water." He pointed behind him. "It's a good walk that way."

"Is it possible to reach it by sundown?"

"Yes, if you're fast."

He had been surprisingly polite, the information helpful. "Thank you."

Another man asked, "You came alone?"

A twinge of unease registered. "I did, but I must be going." Lifting the bow, I grasped it firmly, not letting go of the spear I held. The men eyed the weapon, recognizing it. "Good day to you, men." I wanted to be firm that I would not linger for any reason.

They stood aside to let me pass, one man saying, "She's as fair a woman as I've ever seen. We should keep her. Why let her go?"

"Don't be foolish, Pixen. She'd likely kill you where you stand. We don't need trouble."

I felt eyes on me, the impression troubling. Lowering my head to hide behind my hair, I passed various huts, some with women in the doorway. Slipping into the forest, I found a worn path, the trail winding around towards a mossy ravine, large boulders on either side. Having an inkling that someone followed, I stepped from the track and waited behind a tree, a younger man appearing. He seemed to know I hid, the man glancing about.

I pointed the spear at him, his eyes flying wide. "Why do you shadow me?"

He held up a hand, a smile emerging. "I mean you no harm."

"Then go away!" I stood taller than him, the person no older than a boy, I realized. "Out with you!"

"Who are you?"

"A traveler."

"We don't see women alone."

"I've little choice in the matter at the moment. I'm looking for my son."

"I overheard you. I can show you where the clan is, if you want."

"The path's clear enough."

"What clan are you from?" He eyed me, his expression friendly, yet inquisitive. "You've pretty hair. Your eyes are pretty. You look like you might be the daughter of a god."

Stunned, I had never been flattered so, finding the compliment confusing. "I've lived with several clans. I know the dark language. I have kin among those people. I'm not the daughter of a god." His charm disarmed me, a smile emerging. "What's your name?"

"Kinder. Who are you?"

"Peta."

"I wish you luck on your journey then, Peta. Come

back this way when you leave."

"I'll more than likely have to. Thank you."

I had not expected the heathens to behave in this manner, thinking they might spear me on sight. I passed readily through their community, answering only a few questions. They had given me directions, letting me go. These could not possibly be the people who had murdered the men of my mother's clan.

"Good day."

"Farewell," he said.

He watched me go, the path leading down into a ravine and then up again, stretching out almost into a straight line now. I stopped every so often, wondering if Kinder followed, but I was alone. It wasn't long again when I perceived the evidence of people, hearing voices in the distance. The aroma of something cooking lingered in the air. A dog barked a while later, blue appearing between the branches of the trees ahead.

I stepped from the forest, facing an enormous body of water, the sight surprising me. It stretched on nearly to the horizon, bordered by a small clearing, with the forest on the other side. A series of huts stood near the woods, some having been built beneath the trees. Made from sturdy branches, they opened in the roof to allow fires to be built within, leather hanging in the doorways. Children ran about, laughing and playing, while scruffy-looking dogs lazed by fires, their ears perking at my arrival.

Could this be the home of the heathen Greggor? How could such a monster live with peaceable people? Women turned to look at me, their men staring. I slowed my gait, passing a hut or two, admiring the workmanship of the buildings, wondering what they looked like inside.

I nodded to a woman, saying, "Good day."

She stared at me, saying nothing.

On the other side of another hut, I glimpsed men in the water, sitting on what looked like some sort of wooden contraption, floating upon the surface. During the great flood many seasons ago, my mother and sister and I made a raft from trees, using it to navigate a river to safety. These appeared similar, but different, the men sitting in what looked like the hollowed out portions of large trees.

Two men in conversation stopped talking, their eyes drifting over me. The older-looking one stepped forward. "Who might you be?"

"I'm Peta. I'm looking for my son. He's an infant. He has fair hair and blue eyes. Have you seen him? He was with a clan of dark people." He seemed to know what I spoke of, his eyes flashing with intelligence. "People you murdered, I assume."

"We did find a baby. He's with our lord."

"Your lord ... Greggor?"

"Yes."

I pursed my lips, dreading what might happen next. "Where might I find your ... lord?"

"That house there." He pointed to the furthest structure, a hut far larger than the one Sungir built. A plume of smoke drifted from its center, a woman disappearing into the doorway, a flap of hide closing behind her.

Never in my worst dreams did I ever think I would see the heathen Greggor again, memories of the man clear in my mind. Even after all these seasons, I knew what he looked like, having glimpsed him through the crack of a cave and a rock. The horror of that night could never be forgotten, the course of my life changing dramatically afterward.

"I can take you to him, if you like."

A fire pit stood before the hut in question, several men seated there. "I can manage on my own." I forced myself to keep walking, each step worsening my fear ... but I had to find my son. If it meant facing a monster, then so be it.

Thirty

Sturdy branches threaded together and parts of tree trunks made up the hut, the roof a combination of dried, bundled grass and animal hide. An intricate pattern of bone from some wooly creature outlined the doorway, where a thick pelt hung to keep the chill out. The men, eyeing my approach, got to their feet, the shorter man grasping a spear.

"Who are you?" He stared at the weapon, the bow hanging from my shoulder. "What business do you have with our lord?"

Knowing that whatever we said could be heard inside, I said, "I've come for my son."

He appeared confused, his brows furrowing. The men stood taller than me, each wearing a long skirt of leather, their feet bundled in fur. Being the cold season, the air wasn't as chilled here as in other places, the ground not frozen in the least. The air smelled of smoke and cooking, someone preparing meat inside the hut.

"Your son?"

"The infant you stole at the dark clan," I said a little louder. "The clan you butchered a few days ago."

"This is a matter you must take up with Greggor," said the taller man. "I'll see if he's awake."

Before he took one step, a man appeared in the doorway of the hut, although he had to stoop to pass through, his height formidable. I recognized him at once, never forgetting that face, the man darkly featured, his beard shorn. Wearing a skirt of leather, sewn with decorative beads, his chest remained bare, exposing a wall of muscle laced with old and new scars. Younger than I thought, I guessed him to be nearer to Ronan's age. His eyes remained pinned on me, their look inscrutable, but I felt his annoyance, the man having been interrupted from whatever he was doing, either eating or mating.

I took a step back, not realizing I had done so. I would not be the first to speak, although I yearned to see my son.

"What is this?" he asked, his voice impossibly deep. "Who is this?"

"I'm Peta. You have my son." He seemed to know exactly what I meant, his eyes never once leaving my face. "The infant you stole. I left him in the care of kin—the people you slaughtered."

"She's armed, my lord," said the shorter man.

"I can see that, Owen, but thank you for pointing it out."

People stood at a distance staring our way, wondering at the commotion, no doubt. "My son. I've come for him. I won't bother you for another moment. Give him to me, and I shall be on my way." Although I desired to kill him, my fingers itching to affix an arrow.

You must be careful, Peta! He has Bannon. The only thing that matters now is getting him back. Revenge will have to wait.

As if sensing my thoughts, he said gruffly, "Take her weapons. She may come inside as my guest ... for the moment."

Before I could object, he disappeared into the hut, the leather flap closing behind him. Annoyed with this turn of events, I faced the men, who waited for my bow and arrows. The sound of a baby crying—*my* baby propelled me to thrust the items at the shorter man, whereby I hurried for the doorway, flinging the leather aside to enter. Animal hides covered the ground, some coming from woodland creatures and cats, while a large fire graced the center, the smoke disappearing through an opening in the roof.

A woman sat with a baby, the infant suckling at her breast. "Bannon!" I cried, nearly delirious with happiness, the boy looking healthy. Greggor sat cross-legged on a pelt facing the fire, his expression just as flat as before. "Please give me my son." I would be as polite about this as possible, although I seethed, imagining snatching a rock from the pit and smashing his head in.

Greggor oozed authority, his firm chin lifted slightly. "Shay, this woman claims the baby is hers. Give him to her."

"Yes, my Lord."

I fell to my knees, scrambling over to her, the woman lifting Bannon from her breast, disturbing his meal. He cried at once. I grabbed him, hugging him, as tears fell to my cheeks. For the moment, I set aside all thoughts of murder and hatred, a sense of relief flooding me, the reunion as hopeful and tender as I had dreamed.

"Oh, Bannon," I cried. "I've missed you so. I never should've left you with Kia. Never. If I'd known you'd be set upon by murdering heathens, I would've taken you with me. I would've taken my family too." I glared at Greggor. "Only the gods know where they are now." I sprang to my feet, intending to leave.

Shay fell back abruptly just as Greggor stood, the man incredibly fast, blocking the path to the doorway. "You come here to insult me?" Anger narrowed his gaze. "You take my child. I think not."

I gasped. "He's *my* child! You stole him from his kin. You killed all their men. The women have scattered because of you. Most will die without the protection of their men." Rage laced my tone, the voice not sounding anything like me. I had never been so angry in my life, my jaw grinding painfully.

"It's good you're disarmed." He loomed menacingly. "Sit. It's nearly dark. We shall discuss your grievances in due time. That baby's hungry. I don't wish to stand here listening to his cries. If you're the mother, like you say you are, feed him."

The last thing I wished to do was occupy the same space as this horrible man. "Let me pass. It shall be quiet the moment I leave."

"You've not been dismissed, nor will you be. Sit!" His angry shout filled the air.

I reluctantly did as I was told, although I had every intention of quitting the hut at the first opportunity. Bannon needed to be fed, latching onto a nipple almost immediately, although my milk supply wasn't as robust as before. Perhaps, after he had nursed on each side, it might encourage it to produce more. I felt a distinct lethargy then, my shoulders sagging.

"You may go, Shay. We've no need for you at the moment."

"Yes, my Lord." She bowed her head slightly.

After she left, another woman appeared, her hair not as dark as Greggor's. She blinked when she saw me, not having expected a guest. "I heard a fight."

"This woman claims the infant is hers."

She digested that bit of information. "Oh, I see. That was the disagreement. I know how tired you are. Shall I make her go away?"

"No. I wish to question her, when she's in better spirits." He waved to the fire. "I desire meat, woman. Bring me a meal."

"Yes, my Lord." She turned on a heel, leaving the hut.

"You look tired," he murmured, his attention never once straying from me. "What's your name?"

"Peta."

"It suits you."

"I'll go as soon as he's fed."

"You will not. Sleep here this eve. I've everything you could ask for. The fire will stay lit all night. You may have as many pelts as you like. Food comes shortly."

"I'd rather dine with wolves."

"I somehow expected you'd say that." A tiny measure of a smile appeared, softening his harsh features, making him look almost handsome. A heady, masculine energy radiated about him. I had never encountered such a person before, sensing he would never bow to any woman or man, for that matter.

The woman soon returned with a basket of meat. She set about cooking it, leaving strips on a hot rock, where the venison sizzled. Hungry beyond measure, I licked my lips, debating what I might do next, wondering if I could leave now. Where were my weapons?

"This is my woman, Wildre. Peta will be our guest tonight. See to it that she has whatever she wishes."

I glanced at her. "I'll take my weapons, please. I left them with the men before the hut."

Laughter filled my ears, Greggor's eyes glinting. "She may have everything *but* a weapon. She wishes to end my life, which I find puzzling. Perhaps, I'll ask you about it after I've eaten."

I placed Bannon over a shoulder, the baby nearly asleep. It gladdened me that I still had enough milk to feed him. "You've murdered my mother's people, twice now."

He seemed unconcerned about this, coughing. "Water. Bring me water."

"Are the women here slaves?"

"What?"

"Slaves. This poor woman seems to be your slave. You bark an order, and she runs to do your bidding."

He inhaled sharply, his features hardening. I thought he might say something, but he held his tongue, which must have taken a great deal of effort. Wildre served lightly grilled meat, which tasted delicious, offering a basket full of freshly picked greens and berries. I ate and drank, taking a long pull from an animal bladder. Needing to relieve myself, I gazed at Bannon, the baby sleeping beside me. The affection I felt for my son nearly overwhelmed me, being stronger than I could have imagined. I longed to take care of him, relieved to be with him.

But ... I sat in the chamber of a bear, the animal dangerous, feral. I felt small and insignificant compared to the man across the fire, his very presence making me itch to grab a spear, which I planned to throw in his direction. He chewed meat, his jaw working ... but he continued to stare at me. I could only guess his thoughts.

"I have to ... relieve myself. Is there somewhere to go?"

"Yes, of course. I certainly don't want you doing it in my house. One of the men can tell you where the latrine is." He glanced at Bannon. "You may not leave with the boy. He stays here."

I knew he would say that, scowling as I got to my feet. "Fine!"

"It'll be my pleasure teaching you the meaning of submission ... Peta."

"I won't be here long enough to make it worth your effort." Tossing hair over a shoulder, I turned to look at him, loathing everything about the man. "Don't touch my son while I'm gone." I darted through the doorway before he could respond, finding his men outside.

When I returned, Wildre sat next to Greggor, using some sort of sharpened stick to pick at his fingernails. He stared at me, following my every move. I settled in next to Bannon, the baby fast asleep. Holding my head in the palm of my hand, I gazed into the fire, wishing to be anywhere else, although I had eaten well enough and the hut felt warm and cozy.

"That will be all," he intoned. "You may sleep now."

"Here or with Shay?"

"With Shay. I wish to speak to ... my guest. I don't want to keep you awake. You grow my babe. You need your rest."

She eyed me, a look of displeasure marring her features. "Yes, my Lord." She left without another word.

Greggor untied the fur from his feet, tossing them aside. Then he lifted a beaded necklace over his head, discarding it. I scooted nearer to Bannon, pretending to sleep, although I could not help feeling worried over what might happen next, wishing I had a weapon. Killing Greggor would end my troubles once and for all, the man an enemy of my people, his very presence a scourge upon the land.

I closed my eyes.

"You're still awake. Come here, Peta. I wish to talk."

Thirty-One

I sat up glaring at him. "We've had words. I've nothing else to say."

"You continue to be impertinent."

"I'm not of your clan. You're not *my* master." He did not like that, a hard gleam flaring in his eyes. "I've come for my son. That's all I want." I sat across the fire, needing the flames as a barrier. I had no desire to get any closer.

"You will sit here." He patted the spot next to him.

I lifted my chin. "I prefer here better, if my son needs me."

"He's asleep. He's fed. I want to talk to you."

"We're speaking now."

"Come here!" he growled.

I shuddered, gritting my teeth. "As you wish," I spat.

"I do. You need to temper your tone with me." Getting to my feet, I approached him, kneeling on a pelt as far from him as I could. He patted the fur beside him. "Here."

Moving slightly, I sat cross-legged, satisfied at the distance. He reached out, clamping thick, punishing fingers around my arm, and dragging me to him. I flailed wildly, reacting out of instinct, a fingernail connecting with his cheek, drawing blood. Stunned, he froze, his chest rising and falling. I had not meant to injure him, his actions provoking the response.

"You're hurting me."

"You must be taught manners. You're as wild as a

damn animal."

"You're in no position to judge me, *murderer*. You ruin lives. You've made orphans out of many, many children." The fingers around my arm fell free, although I now sat far too close to him. I feared moving, not wanting him to touch me again. "You're the nightmare of all my dreams, Greggor. Ever since I was a child, when I think of evil, it's your face I see." Was that pain that flickered in his eyes, or had I imagined it, the emotion passing quickly.

"This is why I wished to talk."

"What could you possibly say to atone for your behavior? How would anyone make amends for such atrocities?"

"You may be quiet now," he grumbled. "I don't know how you came to be with the dark people. I suspect you were orphaned."

I nodded, honoring his request that I remain silent.

"I hardly need explain myself, but my father and his father and every other man I've ever known have killed the inferior race. You cannot breed them. They're useless."

I had to bite my tongue, but keeping silent tested me sorely. I sat sullenly, staring at the wound I had inflicted, a tiny trickle of blood falling down his cheek. If only I had my bow.

"Our healer, Ripa, has given his blessing in the matter, just like the healer before him. It's how we've always dealt with the inferiors." He eyed me sideways. "I can see you disagree. I wish I could offer you some proof regarding their weakness, but ... I don't have it at the moment. A woman from my clan was bred by a dark-skinned man once. She gave birth to a hideous creature, the baby deformed. It died within the hour. She died as well."

How would that explain Bondo? He was of mixed race. He could speak. He was intelligent. Everything he said was a lie.

"I've spared women and children, because I'll not kill innocents."

It doesn't matter what you say. You're a monster.

"Speak then. I can see you're fair to bursting to voice your opinion." He touched his cheek, redness appearing on a finger. "You've drawn first blood. You've already flayed me with words. I know more are to come."

"I am an orphan. I don't remember my family, but my mother found me wandering around. She took me in. She found my sister, Ara, as well. We both needed a family. My sister's dark-skinned. My mother's dark-skinned. She's a wise, smart woman. I love her dearly."

I gazed at the fire, choosing my words carefully.

"We lived with different clans, even the white clans taking us in. They didn't murder my mother on sight. After the great flood, we joined a dark clan, the men kind and providing. My mother fell in love with Magnon, the leader of this clan. He was the love of her life. They had a child named Maggi. She's my sister. We lived in the middle of an open plain on a small hill in a cave. It was the perfect shelter for the cold season. One morning, a group of men approached. You were among them."

"I vaguely recall such a cave."

"The children hid in a small chamber, a rock placed before the opening. I saw you then, you and your horrible men. You murdered each and every man, taking my mother's lover away from her. She's grieved her whole life for that man. You stole her happiness. I saw you murder a man. I won't ever forget it. You're the monster of my nightmares."

He swallowed, the nob in his neck moving.

"The attack was unprovoked. The dark clan wouldn't have done a thing to you. They might've invited you in for meat and a warm fire. You killed them all. Then you took the white women. If you'd seen me, you would've taken me as well."

"All the bastards bred died, Peta. They don't survive."

"I know a man, his name's Bondo. He's of mixed race. He's just like any other man, although his appearance is a bit odd. He's just fine."

"There are rare exceptions."

"I don't wish to argue the issue. I told you what I know. I've nothing else to say."

"It grieves me to hear I'm the monster in your dreams. Such a thing sits ill with me."

"Imagine what it was like to be a child, to see it happen through the eyes of a child. There are things I'll never forget."

"I behaved with honor. I did as my healer directed. My father did the same. It's always been so."

I said coldly, "Then you're all murdering fiends. Each and every one of you."

"Every other white clan I've ever known has done the same."

"You and your clans are not gods, yet you pass judgment as if you were. It's not your right to kill those not of your race. It's wrong. You don't even realize it's wrong. That's why speaking to you is a waste of effort. You're the stupid one. You're incapable of seeing another perspective. You won't ever learn or change."

"We'll have to disagree for the moment." He frowned. "I have to think about this. You're wrong on many issues as well, Peta. I can't convince you of anything. I can see you're stubborn. You'll just have to stay a while and see things for yourself."

"I've seen plenty." I yawned, desiring to sleep. The pelts did look comfortable. Fully submerged in the world of dreams, Bannon's little chest rose and fell with each breath.

"You may sleep beside me."

"I don't wish it. No. I'm sleeping with my son." I got to my feet before he could grab me, hurrying to Bannon's pelt. Greggor glared my way, his mouth a thin line. I lifted the pelt over my head, closing my eyes.

***

Sleeping little, I dozed on and off, feeding Bannon a short while later, because he fussed. My mind far too active, I devised a plan of escape, waiting until Greggor's deep snores filled the hut. I tied fur to my feet, snatching Bannon in my arms, even before the birds woke, although most would soon squawk with the coming dawn. Needing to find my weapons, I stole from the hut soundlessly, standing before it in the chill of morning.

Not knowing where my things might be, I paused to strap Bannon to my back, having brought a bundle of leather for this purpose. Once he was secure, I peeked inside a nearby hut, seeing the sleeping forms of women, Greggor's wife and Bannon's wet nurse, with a baby by her side. My bow stood just inside the shelter with the spear. Grasping them, I ran from the hut, silently passing others along the way. A dog barked in the distance, startling me. If I were seen, the men would alert their leader.

I dashed into the woods at the first opportunity, Bannon bouncing on my back, the baby unhappy about this, fussing. He hated to be jostled so, but it could not be helped. I had to reach a safe distance before I could walk. The darkness of the forest proved dank and eerie, although I saw the path, it being quite wide this close to camp. I thought to step from it soon enough, not wanting anyone to see my footprints.

A shout rang out behind me, a man's angry voice booming. I did not hear what was said, far too focused on escaping. I dashed into the foliage, the leaves slapping my face. I felt a measure of security in this, knowing I might be hidden now. Bursting from the bushes on the other side, I gasped, finding Greggor there, standing before me with a spear. A look of rage twisted his face, his mouth a grim line.

"I knew you'd do this." A hint of a smile appeared, unnerving me. "I expected no less."

"My man waits for me. I must go."

Despite the gloom, I saw him clearly, the smile vanishing. "Your man?"

"Bannon's father; the man I love. I belong to him."

"No woman's ever run from me." I moved to lift the bow, but he knocked it from my hands with the flick of a wrist. "Remind me to hide that better."

"I don't belong here!" I said fiercely, angry at having been caught. Bannon cried in earnest now. "I'm expected elsewhere."

"I weary of this argument. You shall stay as long as I decree." He picked up the bow, examining it. The first rays of light fell down upon us. "A fine weapon. I've one myself, although I don't often use it. It's a newish sort of tool. Not many people know of these, although a woman at the dark clan was proficient enough. She killed one of my men."

"That would be my sister." A measure of pride drifted through me, Ara having done the deed to protect those she loved. Then I worried he might have killed her. "Does she live still?" I held my breath.

He sighed. "We didn't touch her. Go on. We return to the hut now."

If only he hadn't taken the bow. I wasn't nearly as good with the spear, knowing he could easily best me. Annoyed that the escape hadn't succeeded, I vowed to find another way out.

"Walk," he barked. "You've angered me enough for one morning. I should take you over my knee. Punishment would do you good."

I gritted my teeth, moving past him, finding the path a moment later. I felt him behind me, his energy like a thick wall of thorny bramble. If I did not walk fast enough, I imagined it might tear holes in me.

"Did you sleep at all?"

His question surprised me. "Not much."

"You need your sleep, Peta. The baby needs milk for feeding."

Bannon's cries echoed, his distress evident.

"Do not run from me again," he said darkly. "I won't allow it."

I chewed on my lip, my mind spinning with thoughts of escape. He had no say over my thoughts. They were my only allies at the moment—my only hope of freedom.

Thirty-Two

Sleeping on and off, I listened to men speaking a while later, my face hidden beneath a pelt. Bannon slept beside me, his body soft and warm.

"I don't trust her," said Greggor. "Someone has to watch over the little scamp. She's liable to run again."

"She's fair to be sure, but no woman's worth such effort. She insults you by running away. You're leader to all the clans in the region. You're owed due respect, my Lord. I don't know why you'd tolerate this."

"She's wild. She's without a clan. She knows not how to respect her elders. I shall take great delight in teaching her, Owen."

Laughter rang out, a man chuckling. "Indeed. I don't doubt that. If I had one such as her, you'd not see me in a good while. I'd bed her soundly. How is she in this manner? Does her anger transform to passion?"

Flinging back the pelt, I glared at the men across the fire, disgusted at having to listen to this conversation. They stood by the doorway dressed for hunting, Owen holding a spear.

"Ah," he said, smiling. "She's awake after all."

Greggor's eyes drifted over me, something indefinable in that look. Despite having to chase me through the woods before dawn, he did not appear angry. "I shall have to tell you once I've had her, Owen." He nodded at me, a hint of a grin appearing. "You've heard every word, I'm certain."

"I thought it a nightmare," I muttered. "The raving of

idiots. I wish it were a dream."

"And she insults you again. A good beating would set her right, my Lord."

"There are other ways to deal with women. I'd not want to mar that perfect skin, although ... I can think of a few ways to punish her without leaving a mark."

"Ouf!" I flung myself beneath the pelt, hiding from their sight.

Laughter filled the hut, Greggor's tone discernable. "I see this as a pleasurable challenge. I look forward to every moment. You mustn't be overly concerned, Owen. It's well in hand."

"Indeed," he chortled. "I'm beginning to understand, my Lord."

"Take the men east. You won't have trouble finding game. I'll join you in a few days. I can't trust she won't try to run away again; I know she will."

He would be in the hut the entire day, the idea of it alarming and irritating. I hoped all the men might hunt, giving me the opportunity for escape, but that was not to be. I could not sleep any longer, feeling angry over the situation.

"Travel safe," said Greggor.

"Yes, my Lord."

I did not need to peek from the hide to know I was watched, feeling the eyes of my enemy from across the fire. Needing to relieve myself, I sat up, brushing hair from my face. "Go away."

Amusement flickered in his eyes. "This is my hut, Peta. This is my clan. I can hardly ... go away."

"Might I stay with Shay and Wildre? I'd prefer to be with other women."

"They'll be here soon enough to see to my needs."

I did not even want to know what those were. "I have to ... use the latrine."

"I shall escort you." He got to his feet, his head

nearly touching the wood of the ceiling.

Finding that idea appalling, I grimaced. "Ugh."

I tied fur to my feet, wearing a leather skirt. My hair fell in such a way it offered warmth, the strands hanging down my back and chest. I stomped past him, slipping from the hut to squint in the sunlight, the air smelling fresh, with a hint of smoke from the fires. Glancing over my shoulder, Greggor stood behind me with a spear, his expression bland, but I could feel his interest, his presence overpowering. Ignoring him, I strode towards the opening in the forest, several men turning to look at us.

"My Lord," called a man. "Good day."

"Aye," he intoned. "Travel well; hunt well."

"We will indeed."

Women stopped to stare, some holding infants. I offered a smile to them, having no quarrel with the women. It was the man behind me I objected to, his presence an irritation. Escaping now would be impossible. I had to think of a new way of accomplishing this task, my mind suddenly darting from one idea to the next. He waited for me to urinate, standing by the path. I would hardly escape now, especially without Bannon. He knew that, of course. He knew I would never leave without my son—ever. I made that mistake once before, but not again.

***

While nursing Bannon, I had little choice but to watch what occurred across the fire, Wildre cooking meat for Greggor, even feeding it to him with her fingers. She appeared heavily pregnant, her belly protruding above a fine skirt, the leather adorned with small wooden beads in a pattern. She fussed over the man, combing his hair, which hung past his shoulders. When he tired of her attentions, he grunted, pushing her away gently. She left the hut a moment later. Shay appeared then, bringing a baby with her, the infant about the same age as Bannon.

She sat next to me, her smile filled with kindness. "Have you eaten today?"

I held Bannon over a shoulder, patting his back. "I have. I'm fine, thank you." She had been the one who took care of my child after the heathens had kidnapped him. "Thank you for feeding my son in my absence."

"They were stunned to find the boy with the dark clan. They never expected it. The dark ones take in orphans, I've heard, but it's still unusual."

"My mother is dark. I'm an orphan."

She nodded. "That's what I've heard. You speak their language."

"I do. They're not an inferior race, as you all think. They're a gracious, kind people. They would never attack anyone without provocation. They would never kill indiscriminately. Only the whites do things like that." I glared across the fire, knowing Greggor heard every word.

"Our lord has his reasons. He follows the directions of the healer. He's an old and wise man."

"Old, yes, wise, no."

"You mustn't speak that too loudly. He's earned our respect."

"I'm not of your clan, nor will I ever be. I belong elsewhere. I've a husband and a home. He's looking for me now. I came to get my son, that is all." I longed to drive a spear through Greggor's heart as well, but I might have to settle for a quick escape with Bannon instead. Perhaps, one day, we would meet again under different circumstances.

Shay smiled slightly. "You're going to be difficult to sway, aren't you? You've your mind set on things."

"I do. You're wasting your breath on me."

"Then we should speak of something else."

"Indeed." I would be forever grateful to her for taking care of Bannon, the baby babbling happily, crawling around on a pelt with her son. "What's his name?"

"Luka."

"Does he belong to Greggor?" I whispered.

"No. I've a husband. He's the man named Trent. He's hunting at the moment."

"Oh, I see."

"Our lord's wife is Wildre. She's the daughter of a neighboring clan." A look of concern passed over her face. "I'm worried for her."

"Because of Greggor? Does he beat her?"

"No, it's not that. She's lost two babies before, the last nearly killing her. I pray it doesn't happen again. No woman's been able to give him a baby yet. His wife before passed away during childbirth."

I digested that bit of information, stealing a glance at Greggor, who stared gloomily at us, having overheard the conversation. Despite not being someone I liked in the least, I did feel a small measure of sympathy for him.

"He took Asprey's death hard, the poor man. She was a lovely young woman, the healer's daughter. It happened many seasons ago. He vowed not to take another wife, but a pact with another clan changed all of that."

"Pact?"

"There was a fight over this land. Greggor came with his men and took it. He ousted Wildre's people."

"Why does that not surprise me?" I muttered.

"And to stop the bloodshed, he agreed to take Wildre as his wife. She's a good and kind woman."

"I agree. Her only fault is her choice of mate."

"Enough!" bellowed Greggor. "I'll not sit here and listen to this." He pointed at Shay. "You'll not gossip in this manner; do you hear me?"

"Yes, my Lord. I'm sorry. I only wished to tell Peta our history."

"I shall do it."

"I'm sure your version of events would vary greatly

from how things really happened," I murmured, smiling at my own joke, and how well Bannon and Luka played together, the babies crawling around on the pelt and babbling happily.

"If you'll excuse us for a moment, Shay. I wish to have a word with Peta."

"Yes, my Lord." She reached for her son, holding him in her arms. Then she hurried from the hut.

"Come here, Peta."

"I must watch my son. He's liable to touch the stones. They're hot." The fire pit stood before us, although the flames flickered lowly.

"Bring him with you."

Annoyed at having been singled out, I picked up Bannon, slowly moving to where Greggor sat. "You've been fed. Your woman's combed your hair. Perhaps you require I pick your teeth?" I taunted him, wondering how far I could push the man, testing the waters of his tolerance. I let Bannon down on a soft fur, the baby reaching for a necklace of big, round beads.

"You say things to annoy me, to stir my anger," he murmured, his eyes darkly colored, lingering on my face. "You know exactly what you do, Peta."

"You're right. I … am rebellious by nature. I shall cause you endless grief, my … Lord." The last word stuck in my throat before I forced it out. "I'm always going to behave like this. I'll be a thorn in your side, until you let me go." Then I added, "You'll curse me. You'll wish you never set eyes on me."

"Aye, I shall rue the day, I know this, but it changes nothing. No one has ever intrigued me in this manner. I look forward to taming you. I wish to be there the moment your anger turns to passion. Your tone will soften. Only words of love will fall from your mouth."

Trapped by the weight of his stare, I shuddered, the feeling worrisome. I whispered, "Never."

Thirty-Three

Having been awake before dawn, I yawned repeatedly, while Wildre and I beat pelts in the sun, Shay watching the babies. Greggor disappeared into the woods, leaving us alone. I thought about taking his spear and Bannon and running, but he would find me soon enough. Exhausted, I returned to the hut, resting with my son by my side, the baby asleep. My eyelids grew too heavy to keep open ...

Waking some time later, I turned to see Bannon asleep, the baby so sweet-looking, his mouth full and pink. A prickle of awareness drifted through me, where I looked the other way, realizing Greggor sat near, his attention fixed on us.

"Have you rested enough?"

How long had he been watching me? "I'm ... I believe so."

"I've delayed eating, because I didn't want to wake you."

Sitting up, I tossed hair over a shoulder, slightly stunned by this admission. "You didn't have to bother. You can make all the noise you want. I would've slept through it."

"You need your rest. You shouldn't be up in the middle of the night, racing through the forest."

"I wouldn't have to, if I hadn't been kidnapped and held against my will."

He sighed. "You're beautiful when you're quiet,

Peta."

Did I see a hint of humor, or had I imagined it? "Then you'll have to bind my mouth, my Lord. It's the only way I'll stay silent."

"There's another way."

He reached out, grasping the back of my neck, the force of the motion drawing me near. I gasped, only a fraction away from him, the heat of his breath fanning over my face. His lips crashed down upon mine, a tongue darting into my mouth. The connection set off a flurry of varying emotions from shock to repulsion, although that soon drifted away, the kiss far more compelling than I imagined. He thoroughly seduced my mouth, his lips soft and coaxing, a tongue exploring and retreating, gently encouraging mine to meet it and engage.

I pushed him away then, a moment of sanity reminding me that he was not someone I wished to do this with. "You've had enough," I spat. "No more!"

I got to my feet, feeling slightly unsteady, my body oddly heated from within. He considered me lazily, a hint of a smile appearing. I wanted to slap the smug look from his face, my fingers curling into tight balls by my side. I could only imagine what he thought, knowing he had caught me off guard. Picking Bannon up, I cradled him securely, needing distance from my captor, the man eyeing me with a knowing smirk.

Wildre returned with a basket. She cast a glance at me, her look questioning. "I've brought you berries, my Lord." Greggor said nothing, continuing to stare my way. "Here you are."

"Might I go out to have some air?"

"You may, but stay near the hut." He nodded at Wildre. "Watch over her."

"Yes, my Lord."

"If she goes too far, shout loudly. I shall come."

"Yes, my Lord."

I slipped from the doorway, standing outside with Bannon, the sun nearly blinding me. Women performed various duties during the day, beating out pelts or minding children, the sound of them playing resonating. A man sat in one of the wooden boats in the water, catching fish, while others brought in firewood.

Wildre approached. "You may sit with me, if you wish." She tossed down a pelt. "Some sun would do us good." She smiled slightly, gazing at Bannon. "Your babe's handsome. He's a good boy."

I had just kissed her husband, although not by choice. Her kindness felt like an uncomfortable weight upon my chest. "Thank you." I sat on the pelt, Bannon crawling around, pulling at blades of grass. "If you eat that, you'll be sick." He ignored me, driving a fistful of grass into his mouth, his face grimacing. "I told you. It's not good, is it?" I had to laugh, finding him entertaining.

"Shay said she spoke with you. She told you our history."

"That your husband's a barbarian? Yes. I know that all too well."

"I doubt she'd call him such a name. None of us would dare, and he's not what you say he is."

"I disagree. I've seen what he's capable of. It's one of my keenest childhood memories, unfortunately."

"It's not my position to defend my husband, nor will I. He acts as he sees fit. He does what's best for the protection of our clan. I merely wish to offer you friendship. He ... seems to have developed a fixation on you."

"Which I don't want."

"I'm aware. You've a husband somewhere."

"Indeed. I plan to be reunited with him shortly."

"Does he have warriors? Will they attack?" Such a thought bothered her, her eyes wary. "Should we expect it?"

"No. He's only one man, but I love him. I've loved him my whole life. He's a good, kind man. He's searching for me as we speak." I suspected he had returned to the cave, only to discover I had disappeared yet again.

"You don't believe Greggor to be good and kind, do you?" She patted her belly, making a face.

"Are you all right?"

"I ... haven't had much luck with children. I hope this one is different."

"Are you in pain?" Despite being Greggor's wife, I would not judge her for her choice of husband, knowing she hadn't had a choice. Her father had given her over to the man.

"I'm not certain." She forced a smile. "I'm fine. I shall have a child soon enough."

That was a lie, I could tell. "Is the baby moving?"

"Yes, of course."

"When was the last time you felt it move?"

"A while ago."

"How long is that?"

"It's really none of your concern. I've spoken to the healer about it."

The more I heard about this healer, the less I liked him. "Has the baby moved today?"

"I believe so."

I touched her arm. "Wildre. You must tell me. I've some experience with childbirth. I spent many seasons with a man of great knowledge. He taught my sister and me many things. I had Bannon on my own, without anyone's help. I would not wish that on any woman, but I had little choice."

"Alone?" She eyed me. "That's ... terrifying."

"Has the baby moved today?"

She swallowed noticeably. "I ... don't believe so."

"Might I examine you?"

"How would you do that?"

"Touch your belly. See if you've opened … down there."

She pointed between her legs. "There?"

"Yes."

"You're not touching me there."

I refrained from rolling my eyes. "Now's not the time to be shy. I only wish to know if your body is preparing to have this baby. By inserting a few fingers, I can tell if the opening has widened. I had to do it to myself before I had Bannon. That was how I knew I could push."

"Greggor would never allow it. He trusts only our healer."

"What if I examined you in private? In your hut?"

She thought that over, biting her lip. "All right."

"It won't take long. I should see what's happening. I might be able to help you."

"Or make things worse."

"No."

***

Wildre let me examine her, the woman skittish about having me touch her between the thighs, but I felt her opening, realizing she wasn't in labor. I pressed fingers gently onto her belly as well, moving the baby slightly, but I felt no motion within. Concerned the baby had died already, I held my ear to her stomach, listening and waiting to feel movement, which I did not.

"What's the matter?"

"I fear … I don't feel the baby moving. I feel nothing at all."

She pushed me away, frowning. "Then we're done," she snapped. "I don't need you poking and prodding me. I've had enough."

"Something isn't right, Wildre. I have to speak the truth, no matter how painful it is to you."

Greggor suddenly appeared in the doorway, having come to find me. "What are you doing?"

"Nothing, my Lord," said Wildre quickly. "Nothing."

"She's in trouble. I suspect the babe's ... deceased within her. It's not moving."

A host of emotions passed over his face, the last being anger, which he directed at me. "You'll not play your games with my wife, Peta! I know you delight in attacking me by saying hurtful things, but this is going too far."

"I do not say this to be hurtful, my Lord. I say it because I'm worried about her. I've some experience in helping women with childbirth. A gifted healer taught me. He trained me in this respect and others. I only wish to—" He grabbed me, hauling me to my feet, his face lingering over mine.

"Enough," he intoned, his nostrils flaring. "Don't cause my wife more grief than she's already had."

"That wasn't my aim."

He let me go, where I stumbled backwards, nearly falling into the fire. Bannon played with a furry toy, someone having sewn a piece of hide to a small, round basket. It could be thrown as well, the design simple, yet ingenious.

"Leave her be!"

"I truly only wish to help."

"You wish to help?" He appeared incredulous.

"Yes."

"Then I want you naked and waiting for me in my hut. Leave the baby here. That's where I most need your ... help."

I gasped. "I will not."

"Then you're useless. I don't know why I stayed here while my men hunted. I'm confronted by your disobedience at every turn."

"That was your choice. If you wish to watch women tend to babies and domestic tasks," I shrugged, "I can hardly stop you."

"And you run your mouth again." He glanced at Wildre. "How fare you?"

"I'm well."

"The truth!" he thundered. "Don't placate me with words you think I wish to hear."

"I ... something isn't right, my Lord."

"Blasted! I shall get the healer."

Thirty-Four

We waited in Greggor's hut, the only sound being the crackling of the fire and Bannon's baby talk. He cooed and chortled, testing the strength of his voice. I watched over him, while casting wary glances towards Greggor. Shay left to summon the healer. Sullen, Greggor sat across the fire, his expression morose. Wildre worked a basket, although she too noted her lord's displeasure, keeping her eyes downcast.

"Bring the boy to me," he demanded.

"What?"

"You heard what I said, Peta."

Grasping Bannon, I held him in my arms, venturing to where he sat. "Here you are."

He took him from me, holding him up, Bannon kicking his arms and legs, a peal of delight leaving his lips.

"You're a fine boy. I could wish for no finer. I've waited for my own child these long seasons."

I cast a glance towards Wildre, wondering what she thought of this, but she kept her eyes lowered.

"Asprey died birthing my babe, who then died directly after. Wildre's lost two babies already, one being very early in the pregnancy, the other nearly at this time." He set Bannon on his lap, the boy flailing his arms and babbling. "I thought it unwise to try again, but Ripa said she could bare it. He said she's strong enough."

Having examined Wildre, I found no evidence of illness, but that hardly explained why some women could not bring a pregnancy to term. There were things clearly amiss with her. "It might be … " I eyed him, "if you want my opinion, my Lord. I'm only a woman after all. You've made it clear my worth is solely reserved for your baser needs." His gaze narrowed, a small tick jumping in his cheek. *Oh, my!* I had angered him. I should have kept my mouth shut.

He was about to say something when the figure of a man filled the doorway, Shay following him in. The healer stood shorter than Greggor, with long, dark hair. His face appeared thin, his eyes too close together. He glanced my way, dismissing me with a look. "How can I help you, my Lord?"

"Examine my wife. She says the baby has ceased moving."

He knelt beside Wildre, his hand on her shoulder. "Is this true?"

An odd expression passed over her features, a mixture of fear and doubt. "I … I believe so, but I can't be certain. I hope it moves. I … don't know."

Chewing on a nail, I watched them, feeling apprehensive and worried. Bannon seemed happy in Greggor's lap, the boy eyeing the fire. Ripa felt Wildre's belly, pushing gently here and there. At one point, he placed his ear to the distended bump. A puzzled look appeared on his face.

"It's premature to tell, my Lord."

"Is the babe alive?"

"Yes, of course, my Lord. All is well." He smiled thinly. "You need only some rest, my dear. No more running around. No foraging until after you give birth." He clearly only wished to tell Greggor what he wanted to hear. "No need for concern."

"Thank you, Ripa. You may go."

"Yes, my Lord." He quit the hut a moment later.

Wildre smiled, but her lips fell, as she glanced at me.

"I never should've listened to you. You're wrong."

I knew I wasn't wrong, but I did not wish to upset her. Time would prove me right. "I wish you the best, Wildre. I pray for your health and the health of your baby."

She frowned. "I'll see about supper, my Lord."

"You mustn't tax yourself. Rest easy, wife. Let Shay and some of the other women assist you."

A sour expression appeared. "What about Peta? She's done very little to help with the chores, my Lord. Will she assist with the dinner preparations?"

"Not tonight. You may go."

I felt badly for the woman, knowing the impending tragedy that lurked within her and her husband's indifference. She resented me, I could tell. I would be equally as hurt if Ronan cast me aside in this manner.

"Yes, my Lord."

After she left, I eyed Greggor, seeing his face in profile, his attention on Bannon. He touched my son's face, a finger tracing his smooth cheek.

"You've made a beautiful child," he murmured.

"Thank you."

"You're ... one of the fairest women I've ever seen. You've a tongue on you, but when you're quiet, you're perfect."

I hated him with a passion, but those words struck me as funny. He was the most annoying, dangerous man I had ever met—my sworn enemy, yet, here I was trapped with him against my will. Now, I laughed hysterically. I giggled for a long moment, perplexed by the situation, knowing that all was not well here by any means. He must have felt it too.

"I've never seen you smile before."

Bannon squirmed in his lap, the baby crawling to the pelt, where he ventured over to me. Holding his hands, I brought him to his feet, where he toddled awkwardly, losing his balance a moment later.

"It won't be long before he walks."

Grasping my hair, I gathered it, undoing a knot, and then leaving it hanging, where it fell to my belly. I did not know what to say now, feeling awkward speaking like this with him.

"You've many opinions, don't you?"

"You prefer me quiet."

"And yet I ask what you think."

"Are you asking now?"

"Speak."

"You confound me, Greggor. You say one thing and want another. Which is it?"

"Your thoughts on Wildre."

"You don't wish to hear that. It's not good."

"You still maintain the baby's dead."

"I'd prepare for that eventuality, my Lord. I'm sorry."

He clenched his jaw. "Fine."

I touched his arm, wanting to offer solace. "I truly am sorry. I know you've desired a babe of your own. Poor Wildre will need your sympathy, your comfort."

"Of course, when the time comes. We shall wait and see."

"Her body will expel the babe in due time. We'll know sooner than later."

He glanced at where my hand was. "I desire you offer me comfort, Peta."

I snatched my hand away. "I shall bring you food."

"It's not food I want, woman," he growled, reaching for me.

Within an instant I found myself beneath him, his manhood alarmingly erect. Shocked, I pushed against his chest, feeling the heat of the skin there. The taut planes of his muscles rippled under my fingertips. A dark, angry face loomed over mine, hair falling into his eyes.

"This is exactly what I want."

"No!" I fought him, pushing at his chest, while I struck him in the face, scratching him with a nail. It drew blood, a line appearing just above his beard.

He stilled, touching the wound, a look of surprise in his eyes. "You little hellion."

Lifting a knee, I threatened to kick his groin. "You must cease this," I warned.

He pushed the knee away easily, his lips upon mine. I turned my head to avoid him, his mouth hot against my neck, biting gently at the sensitive skin there. A hand trailed a path from my hip to my belly, and then up to cup a breast, trapping a hardened nipple between two fingers. I gasped, squirming beneath him, his mouth upon my lips, although this time, I did not turn my head. I felt the fight leaving me, as a tongue entered my mouth. Bannon, having gotten to his feet, braced himself on Greggor's back, the baby making babbling noises. He noted this, laughter escaping him, the sound rumbling in his chest. He ceased attempting to mate me, reaching out to grab my child.

"I'm trying to breed your mother! What's this about?"

I gazed at the man I had wounded, a trickle of blood seeping from the scratch on his face. That was the second time I had done so. He held my son up, the boy squealing with delight. Greggor chuckled, placing Bannon on my belly, the baby sliding off to play with a toy.

He leaned over me, although the smile flattened. "Now, where were we?"

I lifted a knee. "I was about to dampen your ardor."

"It'll take a great deal more than your knee, my love."

When he teased like this, smiling and laughing, it confused me, the feeling worrying. I pushed against him, sitting up, my hair a riot about my shoulders. "Your supper comes." I heard women at the door, silently thanking them for the intrusion.

"I can send them all away and instruct them to take

Bannon." The tips of his fingers drifted down my arm, the sensation producing a tingling feeling. "I'd rather make a meal of you."

The rich timbre of his voice washed over me. "I think not." I moved to get away from him, eyeing him cautiously from the edge of the pelt.

As the women arrived to cook the meal, I struggled to make sense out of these troubling emotions, finding the playful nature of Greggor a revelation. The way he treated my son—the look of affection in his eyes for a boy that was not his own—everything about that worried me. If I did not find a way to escape, Bannon would think the man to be his father. He would come to trust him. I could not let that happen.

Thirty-Five

The next morning, Greggor allowed me to forage with the women, although he kept Bannon with him to assure I did not escape. While they searched for nuts and berries, I picked healing plants, one among them for pain. I had an inkling Wildre might need it. They frowned upon the things I filled my basket with, Shay appearing confused.

"What is that for?"

"It's an herb for pain."

"Are you needing it?"

"No. It's not for me."

We ventured to a creek, stopping to bathe, although it felt cold. I shivered, washing up, my hair floating in the crystal-clear water. We stood near a small waterfall, the water rushing over the rocks and collecting in a deep basin. I did not wish to linger here long, finishing as quickly as I was able. Scrambling up the embankment, I grasped my hair, wringing it out. Sensing eyes upon me, I faced the foliage, spying a pair of manly legs, the feet encased in leather. Greggor stepped from the bushes, holding Bannon in his arms. Stunned, I gaped at him, wondering if he had followed us all along.

Shay nodded. "My Lord."

"I thought you might be here." He glanced at Wildre. "How are you? You're supposed to be resting."

"I'm perfectly fine, my Lord." She smiled brightly, although I wondered if this was just for show. "I feel very well indeed."

He remained unconvinced, drawing near. "But you were ordered to rest."

I tied the leather skirt at my waist, reaching for my son. "I'll take him."

"I thought some air would do him good."

Bannon's eyes lit with interest, his countenance happy. "I forage with him often when I'm home, but you won't let me."

"Perhaps one day I'll trust you, but not yet. I don't wish to hunt you down in the forest and drag you back."

Wildre picked up the basket. "We're finished now. We didn't need to go far."

"Let me hold that." He took the basket. "I'll escort you home. You really shouldn't be out wandering around in your condition."

"Everyone's worry is for naught, my Lord. I'm perfectly well."

"I pray it to be so," he murmured, his look stern.

Wildre and Shay led the way, while Greggor and I walked together, the path wide here. I glanced covertly at my companion, the man beside me in his prime, his physique towering and strong. I did not worry in the least about being attacked by woodland creatures or vicious cats. He held a spear firmly, knowing how to use it expertly. I longed to hunt, wondering where he had hidden my bow.

"What are you thinking?"

"I like the peace of the woods. I miss hunting."

"What sort of hunting?" He pointed to my necklace. "Cats?"

"No. I prefer stags."

He thought about that. "Perhaps I can accompany you in the morning, if you like."

He would never let me venture out with the bow alone. "I suppose."

"Do I have to worry about an arrow through my neck?"

That would be one way to secure my freedom. "No."

"You took too long to answer."

"I should kill you." We neared the clan, the smell of smoke in the air.

"Be careful about voicing empty threats."

It had been so easy to kill his men, but ... they had been different. They were vile. I chided myself for these thoughts, angry that I seemed to be weakening where Greggor was concerned. He might not be ugly and smelly, but he had committed unspeakable atrocities.

"What are you thinking now?"

"I'm remembering what started all of this."

"Started what?"

"Your stupid men kidnapped me. I was pregnant with Bannon then. They took me from my home."

"What men?"

"Someone named Zendi."

Shay stopped walking, staring at me. "Zendi? Do you know where he is? My sister's half mad wondering what happened to him."

Greggor waved her away, saying, "You go on. Leave it to me to question Peta. Take Wildre back to the hut. I shall join you in a moment." She looked like she might object, her mouth open, but then she turned, striding away, Wildre following. Greggor glared at me, his expression forbidding. "What do you know of Zendi? He's been missing too long."

"I wouldn't expect him anytime soon."

"And why would that be?"

"He met his end at the tip of an arrow."

His look revealed disbelief. "There were two men with him."

I searched my memory, vaguely recalling the names. "Pondo and Kunchin, I believe." He blinked. The fact that

I knew the names of his men lent some credence to my claim.

"They're all missing."

"Indeed. You'll never see them again."

"Explain to me once more how you know these names? Did you overhear the women speaking about it? Is this some game you play, Peta?"

"Not at all." I transferred Bannon to my other hip. "I was foraging one day in the woods near where I live with my husband. Three heathens came and took me. The man named Zendi said I'd be a fine prize for his master, whose name is Greggor. I realized then that he spoke of you. He said you were angry with him over some misdeed or something. He wished to present me to you as some sort of recompense."

Everything I said struck true, his eyes never once leaving my face.

"I managed to get my weapon back. I climbed a tree, and then I picked them off, one by one." I shrugged. "They were rather unprepared for such a thing. That was the beginning of all my misfortune. I returned home to find my man and his friend gone—to search for me. Then I went to look for them, finding my mother and sisters. I went home again to have the baby—alone. I was alone for quite a while." I muttered, "I hate being alone."

The blood drained from his face.

"All my misfortunes of late are because of you. I returned to my mother and sister and gave them Bannon, so I could look for Ronan. Someone had seen two white men nearby. I thought I could find them quickly, but I could not. I went back to get my son only to discover you had taken him. It's because of *you* that I've been separated this long from my man. You've torn my life apart."

"Your list of grievances against me is rather long."

"Yes, it spans seasons upon seasons. When you killed the dark men of the clan in the cave, we were left without protection. None of the women hunted. We had to fend for ourselves during the cold season. While crossing the plains, cats attacked, killing my friend Bena. She was only a child. That was how I came to live in the woods, finding an old wise man there who taught me how to use the bow."

He sighed, his shoulders lowering fractionally. "You really did kill my men?"

"I had to defend myself and my unborn child, yes."

"They have wives. Shay's sister is—was Zendi's wife. I'd not mention this to her if I were you."

"Why were you angry with Zendi?"

"He tried to replace me. I was gone more than a season, and he took over. He took my wife as well, even though he had one of his own. He thought I'd not come back. Well, I did return." He appeared thoughtful. "At least now I know what happened to them."

"And what shall you do about me?" I asked boldly.

"The fact that you murdered three of my men?"

"Yes."

He considered it for a long moment. "We could declare our little war finished."

"What do you mean?"

"You admonish me on my conduct regarding the dark-skinned people. You've killed three of my men. Are we even?"

That stunned me. "Are we even?" My voice had risen. "I can only guess at how many people you've murdered in cold blood. I kill three in self-defense, while you murder scores for sport or whatever your reasoning is. We will *never* be even."

"You stubborn, irritating woman," he muttered, anger flickering in his eyes. "I should assemble the clan. I should tell them what you've done. Do you know what they'd do to you?"

I shook my head. "You wouldn't do it." He bluffed

so poorly. I saw straight through him.

He knew it, fuming. "Let's not speak of this again!"

"What of your threat to expose me to your clan?"

"They'd rip you limb from limb."

"I'm prepared to face my fate," I blustered, wondering how he would react to that.

A rough sort of laugh escaped him. "We shall hunt in the morning. I want to see this with my own eyes. If you can kill a stag with one arrow, then you might've killed my men. I know so little about you. I can't tell if you lie. You might say anything to rattle me. You're trying to get under my skin. I don't like it."

"I would never lie about killing someone. I didn't want to do it. I hated it, but I had no choice."

He took my arm, pulling me forward. "Let's go. Enough of this talk."

At the dwelling a short while later, greyish smoke plumed from the opening at the top, the aroma of something delicious roasting. I ducked into the leather doorway, finding Shay and Wildre there, with Luka on a pelt. Sitting down with Bannon, I waited for Greggor to appear, the man filling the doorway. He cast an indifferent glance about the room, his eyes softening when they fell on Bannon.

"Here you are, my Lord," said Shay. She held out a basket filled with meat, which sat upon a bed of green edibles and mushrooms.

Another man appeared a moment later, the healer, Ripa. "We've a disagreement between men, my Lord. It could resort to violence if someone doesn't step in soon. I'm sorry to bother you."

Greggor took a deep, steadying breath, clearly irritated. "I'm at supper, Ripa. Can't it wait?"

"I am terribly sorry."

I thought he might throw the basket across the room, but he got to his feet, reaching for a spear. "Very well. This better resolve quickly." He glanced at Shay. "The meal looks delicious."

"Thank you, my Lord."

"How do you feel, Wildre?"

"You've asked the same not that long ago. I'm still fine, my Lord."

"Good." Before he took his leave, he glanced at me.

"Don't you want to know if I'm well?" I provoked him, knowing I shouldn't.

"When I return," he murmured. "I'll take you over a knee and spank you like an misbehaved child. You deserve no less." He disappeared then, leaving everyone stunned speechless.

Thirty-Six

I feigned sleep after supper, listening to Greggor speak with Owen, the men discussing clan issues. I did worry he might follow through on his threat, but he kept his distance, sleeping across the fire. Bannon woke twice during the night to be fed. By morning, I felt groggy and exhausted, hearing someone moving about the space.

"Get up, Peta," barked Greggor. "We hunt."

I flung back the pelt staring at him. He towered over me, wearing a newish looking leather skirt, his feet encased in fur. "It's so early."

He frowned slightly, displeased by something. "Why must you look so beautiful with sleep in your eyes? You look so sweet and innocent."

How would I respond to that unexpected praise? "Um … "

"Get up. We hunt soon. I wish to see this prowess of yours."

Sitting, I gazed into the fire. "It's still dark outside."

"We leave soon."

Bannon continued to sleep. "Who will take care of my son?"

"Shay. We'll bring him to her. Now, let's go."

Goodness, he seemed grumpy today. "Fine!" I hurried to affix leather to my feet, tying my hair back. "I'll need my bow."

"You'll have it. It's in Shay's hut."

His wife and her friend did not sleep with us, the

women having been banished by Greggor. "I'm ready, but I have to … urinate."

"We go then."

I lifted Bannon from the bedding, the baby feeling like a warm lump in my arms. After depositing him with Shay and her baby, Luka, Greggor handed me the bow and the leather sack of arrows. It felt good to have my weapon, flinging it over my shoulder. It was like being reunited with an old, trusted friend. We set out then, the camp beginning to stir, men gathering to hunt. They grouped together, all of them holding spears. Only a few had bows, and they appeared slightly different than mine, far bulkier. My bow, long and sleek, was made of strong, yet supple wood. Greggor carried a spear and a bow as well.

We followed a path, my feet crunching over dried leaves. The cold season having come and gone, flowers of various colors grew, their sensual, spicy fragrance filling the air. Speaking little, Greggor seemed to have a spot in mind, his strides far wider than mine. I had to hurry to keep up, my breath catching in my throat.

"Stags and things are about," he murmured.

"Do cats live here?"

"No, of course not. We've killed them all."

That did not surprise me. "I don't like cats."

"They're dangerous, to be sure."

The ground damp, my feet felt chilled. "And you've lived here all your life?"

"No. This is a new settlement, only a few seasons old. We were north before, where the cold season was especially harsh. My father, on his death bed, made me promise to move the clan elsewhere. We'd exhausted the hunting as well."

"Where's your mother?"

"Dead. They're all dead, including my younger brother, Geon."

"Oh."

"None of my sisters survived either."

"Despite your efforts at removing the dark-skinned people from this world, my sisters and mother are still alive."

We should have perished after the attack on the clan in the cave, leaving us without men to feed or protect us. Sheer providence or luck allowed us to live ... but I had no clue where my family was now. Greggor was responsible for many of the troubles I had experienced in my life, only the flood not being his fault.

He stopped walking, reaching into a leather bag for a dried piece of meat. He handed one to me. "Let's sit a moment."

We hadn't gone far enough to need rest. "I'm not tired."

"Nor am I, but I wish to speak to you."

"We can walk and talk."

"Which will scare away the game. Sit," he ordered.

I dropped before a tree, leaning against the trunk. Chewing the meat, I eyed him, as he sat only a few feet away, leaning against another tree. "And what do you want to talk about?"

"You resent me."

"I should, yes. You've had a hand in ruining my life several times now."

"It ... pains me to know you think me your worst nightmare. I shouldn't let it bother me, but it does."

"Perhaps you have a conscience after all."

That statement sat uncomfortably with him, his features pinching. "No people talk to me the way I let you talk to me, Peta. I'm leader of this clan. I provide and care for my people. I've done as the wise healer has said, following his direction most of my life, as my father before. You do not agree with some of my actions, that much is clear."

"No."

"I imagine you as a small, frightened child, hiding in the wall and watching me … go about my business."

"Ruthless murder."

"Yes," he muttered. Taking a deep breath, he stared into the foliage, his eyes unfocused. "I can't take any of it back. It's over and done with."

"You might improve in my estimation, if you promise never to kill the dark ones again. Leave them be. They mean you no harm. They wish only to live and care for their families."

He pondered that, his attention returning to me. "I shall consider it." Something else seemed to bother him. "Can you forgive me?"

"Does it really matter if I do?"

"It shouldn't, but it does. I wish to right those wrongs, but I know I cannot. You're only a woman. Your feelings don't even matter, but I can't help wishing you saw me in a better light."

"If you can refrain from killing innocents, perhaps."

He sighed, still irritated by the looks of it. "That's a start, I suppose." He got to his feet. "Let's find some game then. I'm eager to see if you really can shoot that fragile looking thing."

"I can." Standing, I waited for him to lead the way, his eyes drifting over me. "My Lord?"

"Nothing," he muttered, walking.

We came to a creek a short while later, stopping to wash our face and hands, the water icy. I picked up a rock that looked pretty, noting how smooth it felt. Greggor sat watching me.

"You're a handsome woman," he murmured. "I plan to keep you as my wife."

Stunned, I glanced at him over my shoulder. "You have a wife."

"She's unable to give me children. I suspect she'll lose the one she carries now, if it's not lost already. We've had no luck when it comes to breeding. I often wonder if I'm not cursed."

My thoughts ran along the same lines at times. "I don't know."

"I'm going to keep you and make Bannon my son."

That was alarming. "I've a man waiting for me."

"He can find another. He was foolish to let you go."

"Foolish?" Anger flared within me. "Your boorish men kidnapped me and took me from my home. That was hardly my husband's fault."

"It's the fate of the gods. They brought you to me."

We had mostly declared a truce this morning. If I were to voice my thoughts, letting my anger fly, then it would ruin the hunt. "Let's speak about this at another time. I wish to kill game." I climbed from the rocks along the water's edge, picking up the bow. "Shall we?"

He joined me, the two of us leaving the path now, walking as quietly as possible. In a small clearing up ahead, I spied a mature stag, the creature sporting broad antlers. Greggor nodded to me, threading his arrow, and pulling back on it. It flew through the air, missing its mark and embedding into the ground.

"Damn!"

The stag, realizing danger lurked, bounded into the forest, but not before I lifted my bow, the arrow slicing through the air and striking its hind leg, wounding the animal. I could have hit it in the neck, but stags in motion proved challenging.

"It's hurt," I said. "We'll have to follow it and finish it off."

The fact that I had been the one to hit it bothered him, his eyes on the bow in his hand. "I don't have as much practice with this weapon. Like I said, I prefer the spear, but I would've needed to be closer."

Leaving the bow at my feet, I took a hold of his, having a look at it. The wood he used wasn't as strong or supple as it needed to be, the wood not having enough spring. Taking one of his arrows, I pulled back on the weapon, finding a spot on a tree I wished to hit, and letting it fly. It missed its mark, the arrow disappearing into foliage.

"It's the weapon. It's not made well."

"Let me see yours." He tried it, releasing an arrow. "It's far smoother, isn't it? It's so fragile-looking, but I have to agree. It's far superior. Will you show me how to make one such as this?"

I could not help feeling a measure of pride that he asked me. "Yes."

"What sort of wood do you use?"

"I'll show you which trees are best. There are a few I prefer more than others."

"Let's find the stag, shall we?"

"We'll follow the trail of blood."

He stepped before me, leading the way. We came upon the wounded animal a short while later, my arrow protruding from his hindquarters. Greggor speared it through the skull, killing it instantly.

"Thank you for your sacrifice," he murmured. Then he proceeded to gut the creature, the entrails falling from the belly in a bloody mass, soaking the ground.

I retrieved my arrow, wiping it on new grass, the smell of damp earth and blood lingering. Hoisting the stag upon his shoulders, we returned to the path a short while later. Greggor did not seem to mind the blood that dripped down his back, the animal's wounds seeping. We spoke little, arriving at the encampment a while later, Greggor depositing the animal before a hut, where a woman emerged.

"Here you are, Gerta. Something for the meal tonight."

"Yes, my Lord."

He turned to me. "I need a swim."

Glancing at the water, I did not envy him, the bath promising to be frigid. "I'll get Bannon. He'll want to be fed."

"You proved to be a good shot, Peta. I suspected as much anyhow."

Hunting with him had been enjoyable. I liked his company, which bothered me. "You'd do better with a better weapon, my Lord."

"I want you to show me everything you know about it."

By doing so, the entire clan would soon learn from him, everyone improving their hunting skills—their ability to kill anything. I shouldn't help him, the man being my enemy. I shouldn't have agreed to earlier. "I'll … think on it."

"Do that."

A woman ran to us, Shay approaching, her expression frazzled. "My Lord! Your wife's in labor. Do come!"

"I shall clean up first. Labor's last a great deal of time. I won't dally." He strode to the water's edge, leaving his things in a pile at his feet. Then he dove into its grey depths, disappearing from sight.

I glanced at Shay. "How is she?"

"I know something's the matter. I've called for the healer."

"She's not felt the baby move in quite a while. Yes," I said bleakly. "Something is indeed wrong."

Thirty-Seven

We gathered in Shay's house, the interior spacious and warm. Wildre had been in labor all day. The healer shooed us from the hut before supper, Greggor having already returned to his. I found him with Bannon, my son playing with a furry round toy. Seeing them like this, the easy manner in which they interacted, they did appear like father and son. I had to force myself to remember all of Greggor's misdeeds, my feelings towards him softening far too much.

"She should've had the babe by now," he murmured, gently touching Bannon's blond head, the boy babbling happily.

"Or it could go on longer. Mine lasted all day and night, from what I recall."

"And you had Bannon all alone?"

I fell to my knees, sitting next to him. "Yes."

"Weren't you frightened?"

"I was, but there was little I could do about it. I know enough about childbirth to deliver a child, but if I had any sort of complication, it might've gone differently. Bannon was easy. He wasn't breach. The cord wasn't around his neck. I was lucky."

Shay appeared, carrying a basket. "Here's your supper, my Lord."

"How's my wife?"

"The same. The healer's doing everything he can."

I had offered her a tea for the pain, but Ripa had

forbidden it. He did not want me interfering with his work, the man fully in control of the situation. Wildre was his master's wife, and he knew best how to care for her. I would not argue with him, knowing how sad the outcome might be. The baby had died days ago, if not longer.

We ate the meat, Bannon nursing a while later. I put him to bed on a soft pelt, touching his sweet face. His father had yet to meet him, which made me long for Ronan. It felt like an eternity since I had seen my husband.

Greggor watched me, his expression bland. "You think of the boy's father, don't you?"

"Yes." How had he guessed that?

"This Ronan person."

I nodded, wondering where this conversation headed.

"I've never been jealous of any man before in my life."

Feeling a chill, I draped a pelt over my shoulders, the wind outside having picked up.

"I pray I never meet him."

"Because you'll run him through with a spear?" He remained quiet, confirming my fear. "Then I pray you never meet him. He doesn't deserve to die at your hands."

"Come here."

The stark tenor in his tone worried me. "Why?"

"Because I command it."

I crawled over to him, worried over his dark mood. Things would get worse soon enough, the announcement I had been dreading—the death of Wildre's babe, or perhaps, Wildre herself. I had to brace myself for this eventuality. Greggor drew me onto his lap, an arm draped over my belly. I resisted the closeness, stiffening.

His mouth brushed my ear. "I need a small measure of comfort from you, Peta. I know you don't wish to give it, but I'll take it all the same."

"I've little choice."

"I won't kill your man. I long to, but I won't. I've

you. He's lost you."

That statement alarmed me, the idea something I had fretted over for a while now. What if I was meant to live here instead of with Ronan? I had to wonder at the turn of things, if the gods had led me here for a purpose. All sorts of thoughts had been drifting through my mind recently, my emotions a jumble of conflicting feelings.

"I'd never hurt you," he whispered. "I'd give you fine sons and daughters. I've never wanted a woman more than I want you."

I resisted the urge to look at him, to touch him, my fingers itching to do so. He squeezed me tightly, his breath in my ear. "I've needed this. I need you."

Shay burst into the hut, her eyes wide. "My Lord!"

"What is it?"

"The babe's come, my Lord."

"And?"

"Oh, my Lord. I'm so sorry."

He got to his feet, depositing me on mine. "Is my wife well?"

"Yes, but … the babe's not breathing. Ripa's doing what he can, but … I dare say he's gone."

"It was a boy?"

"Yes, my Lord."

"I shall see my wife then." He stalked from the hut.

I glanced at Shay. "Is there anything I can do?"

"We're managing, Peta. It's a sad day for everyone, but we did suspect it, didn't we?"

"Yes, sadly, yes."

"That poor woman. She'll never have a baby. I don't think she should try again. She's losing a great deal of blood too."

My mouth fell open. "Then I should help. She could die, if that's not taken care of. I've herbs I could give her to stem the blood."

"You may try, but Ripa might have other ideas. He's

healer to our people. He has Greggor's blessing. His wishes come first in all things."

I frowned at that, realizing I had far more power at the cave, Ronan and Enwan turning to me for guidance relating to bites and scratches, often asking me to make a poultice for one thing or another. I cured headaches and toothaches quite easily. At this clan, they would never listen to me, thinking their healer omnipotent.

***

By some miracle, Wildre stopped bleeding, tired and weak, her skin greyish. Greggor and I sat by her side during the night, the people of the clan arriving in the morning to condole with us. Most brought offerings, whether it was a soft piece of leather or a beaded necklace or nuts and berries, they spoke of their sadness at his loss. People came all morning, but I had to leave to see to Bannon, the baby awake and wanting to be fed.

Exhausted from not sleeping, I gave him to Shay, the woman bringing him to her hut. They would bury the baby later in the day, a hole having been dug already. Barely being able to keep my eyes open, I slipped between two soft pelts, listening to the sounds of people speaking before the dwelling, more arriving to offer condolences to their lord. I slept almost instantly, but movement woke me a short while later, a man having joined me. A steely arm draped across my belly, the heat of Greggor's body pressed to mine.

"I'm sorry I woke you," he said, yawning. "Sleep. Wildre's asleep. Bannon's with Shay and her babe. All is quiet for the moment."

I closed my eyes, not hearing anything else he said, succumbing to sleep. When I woke later, I lay in Greggor's arms, the man snoring lightly. I saw him clearly in the firelight, someone having added more wood. A dark beard mantled his chin and cheeks, his nose slightly crooked from having been broken a time or two. The pelt came to his chest, exposing some of his scars, the whitish raised skin indicating many past injuries.

Slipping from beneath the pelt, I left the hut soundlessly, hearing a baby crying in the next one. Bannon fussed, having been left alone with Luka. I wondered where Wildre had gone, her pelt empty. Tossing several sticks into the fire, I held Bannon to my breast, the boy feeding at once. I gazed at my weapon against the wall, knowing I could take it and my son and run. No one would think twice about it, being distracted by the stillbirth and the impending funeral.

I failed to move to put these thoughts into action, Shay appearing a while later. "Oh, there you are," she said.

"Where's Wildre?"

"She desired to bathe in the creek. I didn't want her to, but she insisted. Some other women are watching over her. I'm dreadfully tired."

"I can manage the babies. You sleep. You needn't worry over them. I can feed Luka."

"Thank you."

Greggor appeared in the doorway, his look angered. "Peta. I didn't give you permission to leave. Come at once."

"I'm watching the babies."

"Bring them."

I gathered Bannon and Luka in my arms, the boys nearly the same age. "Yes, my Lord." I found it odd how I jumped to do his bidding now.

He held open the leather in the doorway. "When I woke alone I thought the worst. I thought you might've run off."

"I didn't, as you can see." But, that had been on my mind.

"This is where you stay. I wish you only in this hut."

"All right."

"Where's Wildre?"

"Shay said she's bathing at the creek."

"It's too cold for that. She'll catch her death."

I shrugged. "I don't know. It was her decision. She's with several women. She's not alone."

"After she lost the last babe, she was despondent."

"I can imagine."

"She tried to hurt herself. I'd best go check on her. She shouldn't be alone."

"Then you should keep her with you at all times."

His look betrayed him, the idea not appealing for some reason. "She's with Shay at the moment. If she cannot be trusted alone, then she'll have to stay here."

"She slept here before, didn't she?"

"Yes."

"Before I arrived."

"Yes."

"What's changed?"

He contemplated that, his look furtive and slightly guilty. "I ... my feelings towards Wildre have changed. I shall always take care of her, but I won't try for another child with her. It's too dangerous. I've spoken to Ripa about it, and he agrees. There's something not right with her womb. She's unable to carry a baby to term. I don't wish to kill her."

I wondered at what else he might say, waiting.

"I want you to be my wife. I desire only you, Peta. I could love you. I can make you happy—if only you'd let me."

Thirty-Eight

We stood around the small hole in the ground, the body of Wildre's baby wrapped in leather with flowers and beads strewn around. A wet, cold wind blew, worsening the experience for everyone, Wildre standing with a fur around her shoulders, her eyes downcast. I hadn't been with this clan for very long, but I knew they cared about one another, everyone from the community having come to lend support.

Ripa spoke words of condolence, blessing the babe and wishing it a safe journey to the land of the gods. I held Bannon and listened, while Greggor stood with Owen and Shay, Wildre on his other side. He escorted her to the hut afterwards, staying with her for supper. I cooked my own meat over the fire, enjoying being alone for once, this giving me some time to mull over Greggor's earlier words.

I chided myself for even considering his offer, a part of me wondering if perhaps this was where I now belonged. If I did not find some way of escaping soon, I might never leave. Enwan had found a woman, and so would Ronan, the men capable and self-sufficient. I had to consider this possibility, that my life had been thrown off course for a reason.

Bannon slept soundly, the baby having been fed. I tossed another branch into the fire, as Greggor stepped into the hut, a fur around his shoulders. The rain came through the opening in the center of the hut, making the fire spit and hiss, smoke lingering in the air. I sat on a soft pelt, reluctant to look at Greggor, because he seemed to know my thoughts too well. With all the sadness of the day, I felt a measure of sympathy for him, wanting to offer solace.

"She's sleeping."

"Wildre?"

"Yes. I've not told her my plans, not wishing to upset her further today, but I will eventually." He sat next to me, untying the fur from his feet.

"What plans?"

"To make you my wife."

"I doubt she'll like that."

"It's my future I must consider. I wish to have children. I want strong sons to hunt with. It's necessary I continue the family line."

"There are other women who would readily be your wife." I had seen the way the younger girls looked at him, the open yearning in their eyes, even at a funeral. He would not have trouble finding another mate.

"That may be, but I've only the desire for one."

Those words bothered me, especially after everything that had happened today. "I'm tired. I'm sleeping." I dove into the pelt, drawing it over me.

"I as well. I could sleep for days." He slid in next to me, an arm going around me. "You're cold."

"I was wet through earlier." The delicious heat of his chest pressed to my back.

"I'll warm you."

My eyes drifted shut, exhaustion numbing my mind. "If … you must."

***

In the morning, I woke alone to the sound of Bannon's cries. After feeding him, I ventured from the hut in search of Greggor, but I suspected he hunted with the men, although he left one by my door, presumably to make sure I did not escape. This man followed me into the woods, waiting by a tree while I relieved myself. He then followed me to Shay's hut, where he stood just outside the door.

"Who is that?" I asked after entering, feeling annoyed.

Shay worked a basket, her fingers dexterous. "Frendo. He's a hunter."

"Then why isn't he hunting?" I set Bannon down to play with Luka.

"My husband's man is watching over you." Wildre appeared tired, her skin still alarmingly grey.

"How do you feel?"

"Terrible." She clutched at a fur, bringing it to her throat. "Greggor won't ever get a baby on me again. I know it."

"It's dangerous," said Shay. "You've got to regain your health."

"I don't care. I only wish to give him the son he deserves." She cast a glance my way. "I suppose he's chosen you to fulfill that task now. He won't sleep with me anymore. I've been banished to the servant's hut."

"We only sleep. He's not touched me in that manner."

"Not yet." She frowned deeply, staring at the fire. "I've failed. I've not been the wife he needs."

"Please don't be so hard on yourself," said Shay. "Let me make you a tea."

"I've plants for a restorative drink. I can grind the leaves. They're dry now."

"The healer says I'm only to have what he makes."

"What if my tea helps you?"

"I'm not to drink anything from anyone else."

"A gifted healer once taught me all he knows. I can make you feel better."

"You've nothing to lose," said Shay. "She can't hurt you."

"No, of course not," she said bitterly. "Greggor's the one who cast me aside, but only after he laid eyes on her. He's smitten. He's blinded by her beauty. She's another man's wife, but he doesn't care. She'll run at the first opportunity, but all he thinks about is bedding her. I'm useless to him." She hung her head.

I wanted to console her, but I thought it unwise. She blamed me for her problems, and I did feel a measure of guilt over it. Her words did ring true, unfortunately.

"Shall I make that tea?"

"Do what you must," she muttered.

I ground the leaves, steeping them in hot water until the fluid became ready to drink. I handed the warm bladder to Wildre, who took a sip. She grimaced. "It tastes disgusting. Are you trying to poison me?" Then her look sobered. "Do you have a tea for … death?"

My mouth fell open. "I do not." But Sungir had taught my sister and I how to make one from certain mushrooms. "Just drink it. It's not delicious, but it'll make you feel better. It'll help with the healing."

"If I'm no longer the leader's wife, what am I? What man in the clan will want me now? They all know my womb's polluted. They know I'm useless."

"Please don't make yourself uneasy," said Shay, casting a glance my way. "Don't trouble yourself with these thoughts, Wildre. They aren't helpful." She touched my hand. "Why don't we get some air?"

I got to my feet. "All right." We stood at a short distance from the hut, Frendo watching us. "The boys play well together."

"I worry over her terribly. She's in foul spirits."

"Women can be emotional after birth. She lost her child. She's grieving."

"You've some influence over Greggor. Can you speak

to him about Wildre?"

"Yes."

"She's weak and despondent. If he makes her leave, if he banishes her somewhere, she'll kill herself. I know it."

"He wouldn't do that."

"She can't give him a son. She can't breed again or she might die. He has no need for her."

"I'll speak to him, but he has his own mind about things."

"You'll be our lady soon enough." She bowed her head slightly. "I can only ask if you'll help. I can't make you do it."

Stunned, I stared at her. "Your lady?"

"When he makes you his wife. It's only a matter of time. Everyone's talking about it. We all agree you're a good choice, even if you're an outsider."

I was far more of an interest to these people than I thought.

"He listens to you. Although he's vexed with you, he's not lifted a hand against you or your boy. Anyone can see he adores him. He adores you."

I bit my lip, feeling uncomfortable with this discussion. "I have a husband elsewhere."

"Why would you want to leave? You've a strong, virile man who can provide for you."

"Ronan can do that just as well."

"Yes, but Greggor's leader to many clans, not just this one. He's respected far and wide. He's greatly reduced the dark-skinned ones, culling them effectively. They'll soon die out altogether, given enough time."

Those words horrified me.

"I know you accept the dark ones, but they've never been useful. They're too stupid to teach anything. You can't breed them, because the babies are born deformed. It's a sad affair, but it's the way it's always been."

"My mother and sisters are dark. They're not stupid

people. They're more my people than the whites. I love them, and I always will." I lifted my chin defiantly, finding this discussion abhorrent.

"I've angered you."

"If I were to be mistress at Greggor's side, I'd make sure everyone thought differently about the dark people. You're all wrong about them. They're just like you and me. They love their children as deeply as we love ours. They're only trying to make their way in the world and survive. They've been targeted indiscriminately for no reason other than pure ignorance. Shame on you all for thinking so poorly of them."

"I'm sorry for upsetting you."

"The only thing that upsets me is *your* simple mind. You all believe yourselves the superior race, but you wouldn't know it by your actions. You judge those you know nothing of. My mother took me in when I was very little, having found me alone. She fed me and loved me. I know nothing other than love from that woman. She taught me the dark man's language. She's always been a strong, capable person. She's smart too. Her advice never fails to be correct."

Shay stared at the ground.

"If I'm to be the leader's wife, there will be some changes." I had never realized it before, but I had the opportunity to alter the thinking of these people, and possibly all the other clans. Did the gods have this in mind?

Thirty-Nine

Having shone Greggor what tree to choose, we sat in the hut and worked our new bows, flattening any bumps and making grooves where leather twine belonged. I had not spoken to him about Wildre yet, the woman still living in the hut with Shay. I did not see a reason why she had to leave.

Owen ducked his head in, coming to stand before us. "My Lord. We're about to hunt. Most of the men are participating."

Greggor used a rough rock to smooth the wood. "The ambush hunt?"

"Yes." He glanced at me. "How long must she be watched over?"

"She's a damn sight better than some smelly mammoth," he chortled.

"I only ask because the men wish to know when you plan to return."

Greggor pursed his lips. "When I feel like it, that's when. You can manage it."

That answer did not sit well with him, a frown emerging. "Yes, my Lord."

"I'll join the hunt soon enough. I want to finish this bow first. Peta says ours aren't made of the right wood. That would explain why they're so difficult to use. She's demonstrated how effective hers is. It's a fine tool for killing animals at a distance. It might save us from having to drive herds over cliffs."

"Yes, my Lord."

"Is there any other business you have here, Owen?"

"No."

"Then go hunt."

He nodded. "Good day to you."

"Good luck and safe travels."

"Thank you." He turned on a heel, leaving the hut.

Greggor stared after him. "Can I leave you alone without you running away?"

"Yes." But, was that true? Over the last few days, the thought of escape seemed further from my mind. It wasn't the first thing I thought of when I woke in the morning anymore. I felt his attention, my skin prickling with the awareness.

"I'm not so certain. I've yet to bed you. Once I've done so, you'll not wish to leave."

"And your prowess in this area is ... *that* good, my Lord?" I shouldn't goad him, but I could not help myself.

A rumble of laughter filled the hut, his eyes shining with mirth. "I suppose, although I've had some ... er ... disappointing experiences. It helps to have a passionate woman. I feed off that passion and give in equal measure."

"I've had two lovers. They are both good."

"Two?" An eyebrow lifted.

"I live with two men. One is my mate, the other is his friend, who is more like a brother."

"That's an interesting arrangement."

Heat rose to my cheeks at the look he gave me, his mind working out what such ... encounters might look like. "They are the only ones I've been with."

"They pleasure you at the same time?" Sitting cross-legged, his leather skirt tented now, such talk clearly affecting him.

I put the bow aside, getting to my feet. Although the fire had died down, it felt decidedly warm now. "I should see to Bannon. He might wish to be fed." Moving by

Greggor, a hand shot out, fingers closing around my wrist, the grip firm.

"I'd like to hear more about how you enjoy being pleasured, Peta."

"My son needs me." I pulled at my hand, but he would not let go.

"*I* need *you*." He drew me onto his lap, his manhood rigid beneath me. "Tell me more about this ... interesting relationship."

"You can imagine it yourself."

"Oh, indeed," he murmured, his eyes flickering warmly in the firelight. "I can imagine quite a few things."

"I really should feed my son."

"Shay will do it. He's in good hands."

I had denied him several times before, although I suspected I would submit today, his ardor like a swift, raging river, stoked to new heights. He grasped my face, kissing me, his lips soft, yet insistent. My palms flattened to his chest, feeling the firmness of the muscle here, the skin as heated as my own.

"You always taste sweet," he whispered.

"You've rarely kissed me."

"I've done so twice before. I've a good memory."

A tingle of pleasure drifted through me, my body responding to his touch. I had not been with a man in a long time, and every womanly instinct I possessed desired to be held and pleasured. His tongue slipped into my mouth, seeking and tasting, then retreating just as quickly. I did the same to him, boldly exploring. We fought this battle over and over, whatever resistance I might have had melting.

I leaned into him, my arms snaking around his neck. He smelled of sun and wind, with a hint of a clean, natural scent. My fingers delved into thick, dark hair, the strands soft. He grasped me at the waist, the leather skirt suddenly loose. It fell away a moment later. Then he cupped a breast, the fullness of it filling his palm. Capturing a nipple, he toyed with me, squeezing gently. A flood of arousal pooled between my thighs, propelling me to kiss him harder, rubbing myself against him, my body speaking words I would never dare say out loud.

He noted this at once, shifting so I lay on my back. Tossing aside his clothing, he gazed at me, longing and heat flaring in his eyes, while hair fell around his face. When had he grown so handsome? I grasped his neck, bringing him to me, my mouth demanding he kiss me.

"You're everything I imagined," he whispered. "And more."

"We needn't talk," I uttered, sounding breathless.

A low chuckle escaped him. "Indeed. No more talk then."

Reaching between us, I felt his manhood, my fingers curling around the breadth of him, the size an unexpected surprise. I played here for a moment, which brought forth wetness. He did not remain idle, a hand having landed on my belly, but it did not stay there, drifting lower. A finger stroked me, adding kindling to desire already out of control.

"Oh, Greggor … you mustn't wait. Please … " I grasped at his buttocks, the globes firm in my hands. "Please!" I did not have to beg again, the man above me obliging, thrusting deeply with one push. "Oh … yes!"

I gasped at the feel of him, the intrusion staggering. Not having engaged in this sort of activity since before Bannon's birth, I trembled, my body opening for him, yet sheathing him in silken wetness.

"By the gods," he murmured hoarsely near my ear. "You were meant for me." Whatever else he might have said made little sense, the words garbled by a moan.

My fingers dug into his buttocks, feeling the muscles move, a rhythmic dance occurring. I lifted my hips, rubbing sensitive, heated flesh against him. I shuddered, the edges of release like an approaching storm gathering faster than anticipated.

"Yes, Greggor!" And then I shattered, gasping from the pleasure.

He drove deeply, seating himself to the hilt, while moaning in my ear. Feeling wetness, I clung to him, wrapping my legs around his hips, while clutching at his neck. Exhausted from lovemaking, I took a deep, steadying breath, Greggor falling to his side, but he drew me near, his mouth on my neck.

"We shall do that again soon."

Did I feel regret now? There would be no going back. "But … I should feed my son," I whispered weakly.

"I shall drink from your breast."

"No," I giggled, that idea odd.

His hand splayed over my belly, the fingers impossibly big. "You're perfect."

"I am not. No one's perfect."

"You're perfect for me. I've been waiting for you my entire life."

He appeared tired, yet happy, a smile lingering around his mouth. It was so easy to forget our history—every horrible thing that had ever happened, far too easy.

"This is a new beginning."

I could not agree to that, knowing Ronan waited for me, the man not having met his son yet.

"I sense your hesitation still. I don't mind. Winning you over completely shall be my life's quest. I relish the challenge." His hand slid upwards to touch my breast. "If I must seduce you to this end, then it'll be my pleasure to do so."

"I had a life before you. It had only just begun. I can't forget all those memories just because … just because of … lust."

"It's not just lust, Peta. I want you by my side as wife. You're a strong woman. You're not afraid of me."

What happened to my resolve? Why could I not resist him? Even now, after everything that had happened, I craved his touch. "Let's not talk about this. It's best we don't speak at all."

I fought to push the guilt aside. I would chastise my weakness later, but even that would solve nothing. My predicament remained the same. I was no closer to Ronan now than before Bannon was born, my life in the hands of the gods, who seemed to have a plan. I could not guess it either, their machinations odd and mysterious, but they had led me here … to this man of great power and influence, who ruled from a chamber of bears.

The animal hide over the doorway kept the hut dark, although some light came in from the hole in the roof. Touching Greggor's face, I felt the roughness of his beard, this hair having scratched my neck earlier.

"What are your thoughts, my love?"

"They … are conflicted," I said with honesty. "I can't make sense of them at the moment."

"I didn't hurt you, did I? I don't think so."

"No. I'm fine." His hand stroked my back, the feeling comforting. "You didn't cause physical pain."

"Can you see a life with me?"

"But then Bannon won't ever know his father."

"I'm his father."

When I did not return, Ronan would find another woman. He would have children with her. Enwan had already brought a woman home. They would go on and live their lives.

"What can I do to persuade you? Is there something you want? All you have to do is ask."

"Will you promise not to hurt the dark-skinned people?"

"Done."

"Truly?"

"Yes. What else do you want?"

"I … my mother and sisters are missing. Your attack scattered them. I worry over their welfare."

"I shall find them for you."

"No! That would terrify my mother. You mustn't do that. If she ever knew I … was with you, she'd be horrified. I should be horrified. I never should've let you seduce me." It was difficult to keep the guilt away when it seemed determined to ruin my happiness. "I don't know. Let's not speak. When we talk, it just … makes things worse."

"These matters will resolve in time, Peta. I understand your worries. I can see how you struggle. I'm sorry I've been the source of fear for you. I'm sorry."

I eyed him, seeing a look of remorse, a glimmer of regret in his eyes.

"I can't undo what's happened. I had my reasons. You've made me consider things differently. I realize I could've … refrained from some actions. I am leader, but I follow the wisdom of the healer and the healer before him. I won't blame them for my deeds, but it's always been our way."

"You're right. Nothing will change this night."

"You're wrong. A great deal has changed. Can you not feel it?"

I swallowed, my throat oddly constricted. "I don't want to … feel anything for you. I don't want it. I shouldn't."

He smiled slightly, the expression making him look youthful. "Aye, but you do. There's nothing more I need to say. Time will take care of the rest. Time can be an enemy. It can also be a friend." He pulled me near. "Now, kiss me. I wish to love you again, my beauty. I shall never get enough of wanting you."

Forty

They planned a great feast after the mammoth hunt, the men killing several animals, their size impressive. Remembering the clan by the river, all those seasons ago, they hunted the big beasts as well, but they only ever retrieved one at a time. A deep hole filled with burning embers cooked the meat, large portions of it wrapped in leather. It took all day to prepare for the event, everyone helping.

Upon returning from foraging with Shay and Wildre, I entered the hut to see Bannon in Greggor's hands, the baby lifted high. Stunned at the sight, I wondered what this was about. He lowered him to blow noisily on his belly, Bannon screeching with delight.

I set the basket down. "What are you doing?"

"I'm making him laugh." He tossed him in the air again, Bannon giggling. Then he blew on his belly, making an odd sound. My son was in hysterics, laughing and screaming, flailing his arms up and down, even kicking his legs. This went on for some time, the two of them enjoying the play. He eventually set him down, Bannon crawling over to him and pushing at his chest.

"Da da … pa … pa … "

I had never heard him speak before, my mouth falling open.

Greggor lifted him onto his lap. "He knows who his father is."

A host of conflicting emotions drifted through me.

Chewing on a fingernail, I contemplated this …, knowing there was no easy answer. Shay interrupted us then, slipping into the hut.

"Everything is nearly ready, my Lord." She smiled at me. "We shall have a wonderful feast. I can smell the meat everywhere I go."

"I look forward to it." The entire clan had gathered, a celebration occurring.

"And thus we usher in the warm season," said Greggor. "The gods have been generous, haven't they?"

I could not entirely agree, having lived through turbulent times and worrying over my family. Bedding Greggor had been a mistake. I never should have let him seduce me. I could not stop thinking about … him.

Shay eyed us, standing awkwardly by the doorway. "Come out when you're ready then. People are gathering, my Lord."

"We will. Give us a moment, will you?"

"Of course." She ducked out of the hut.

Greggor touched my face. "I don't pretend to know your thoughts, but I hope you can make peace with whatever troubles you, Peta. I can offer you a good life. I desire you like no other. I've only had a small taste of you, yet I want so much more." He pulled the finger from my mouth. "Stop that. You'll bite the nails down to nothing."

I hardly knew what to say to him, distracted by his lips. I lowered my gaze to avoid them. He held my face, forcing me to look at him, kissing me. Not having the will or the strength to refuse him, I wrapped my arms around his neck, returning the kiss.

"We shall never make it to the feast like this," he murmured, chuckling. "You were gone foraging for what felt like an eternity."

"It wasn't that long."

Bannon pulled himself up on his leg, the boy babbling and making screeching noises.

"He's more and more vocal." Greggor ruffled his blond hair. "I think he'll walk soon enough. He's strong."

The leather in the doorway flew inward, Owen appearing. "My Lord, we eat soon."

"Why can't a man be with his family and not be interrupted?" grumbled Greggor. "For the love of peace, man."

"I'm sorry. I thought you'd like to know." He eyed us, a look of concern on his face.

"Aye, now I know."

I slid from his lap, getting to my feet. "I'm hungry. I could eat." I reached for Bannon, but Greggor took him.

"I've got the little one. Let's see about a meal, shall we?"

Owen nodded, casting a glance my way. "Is she to be your wife then?"

"She already is."

The shock of that settled upon me. I hardly knew what to make of it.

"Will there be some sort of ceremony, my Lord?"

"I suppose. I'm not overly concerned about it at this very moment, Owen." He nodded at me. "Come along, Peta. The clan awaits. They'll want to get a better look at their new mistress."

***

Families gathered by the pit where meat cooked, the aroma caught by the breeze. I held Bannon, the boy's eyes wide as he stared at all the people, a sea of faces around us. Torches flickered with evening setting in, a cool wind arriving from the lake. I brought a pelt, having tossed it around my shoulders and over Bannon. I followed Greggor by a step or two, as he cut a path through the crowd, people bowing in reverence. Holding his head high, he stood taller than most, his shoulders impossibly broad.

Wearing a short leather skirt about his hips, his torso bare, he exuded masculine strength, the women eyeing him with interest. I realized then that he could have any woman he wanted in this clan or any other, the idea sitting ill with me.

"My people," he intoned, his voice booming. "I congratulate you on an excellent hunt. The gods have blessed us with this meat. They've watched over the hunters. No one was killed or injured. We've much to be grateful for."

A baby cried in the crowd, while a low murmur rose, everyone looking in our direction. I spied Shay and Wildre standing near the healer. Wildre appeared forlorn, her fingers clutching at a leather blanket around her shoulders.

"These have been trying times, as you all know. I thank you for your condolences and your prayers. The gods haven't been kind to me or Wildre." He glanced in her direction. "It's best my wife not attempt another pregnancy. This has left me with little choice but to choose another wife."

A low rumble drifted through the throng, people looking at me. I lowered my head, embarrassed by the attention.

"I wish to introduce a fine young woman by the name of Peta. She has a son named Bannon, who will now be my son." He turned to me, a hint of a smile upon his face. Then he took Bannon from my arms, the boy kicking his legs. "This is my son." He held him high, while a murmur rumbled through the crowd. "This is my son, and this is my wife, your new lady." He pointed to me. "Please welcome her with kindness."

I swallowed the lump in my throat, my mouth suddenly dry. Everyone stared at me, their expressions hopeful. I worried they would not accept me being an outsider, but no one shouted an insult, the crowd opening to surround us.

"You've made a fine choice," said a man. "She's

proven she can breed, and she's easy on the eyes."

"Congratulations!" someone shouted.

"The gods have blessed you now, my Lord," a woman said.

Greggor laughed, the sound rumbling. "Indeed." He faced the crowd, holding Bannon in his arms. "The time for grief has passed. We must look towards the future. I've waited too long for a family such as this, despairing it might never happen. I wish to share my good-fortune with you all." He shouted, "Praise be to the clan! Praise for all of you, my good people!" He grinned. "Let us eat this fine food!"

***

My son slept almost immediately, his small fists having rubbed at his eyes, the boy exhausted. I had eaten far too much at the feast earlier, clansmen bringing over the choicest portions of meat. My belly looked as if I carried another child, but I did not regret the meal, having enjoyed myself immensely. The only moment that dampened the pleasure of the evening had been seeing the downcast nature of Wildre, the woman sitting with several of her friends and Shay. Once being esteemed as the leader's wife, she was now unmarried and unwanted, her role in the clan diminished.

"Come here, wife," said Greggor. He sat waiting for me, the flames of the fire reflected in his eyes. "I've waited all evening for this."

I crawled over to him. "To sleep?"

"I'll love you first, then we sleep."

Sweet anticipation drifted through me. "I thought you might be too tired, my Lord."

"To mate you? Never." He drew me to him, his lips against my cheek. "You and Bannon have changed my life for the good. I never knew how bleak things really were before you boldly ventured into my clan. I'll never forget the first time I saw you. You were a wild thing from the woods with an angry gleam in your eye. None of us intimidated you, least of all me."

I settled in his lap. "I came to kill you, if you must know. I wanted revenge."

"I read it in your eyes. I know."

"And you weren't worried I might follow through? Kill you in your sleep?"

He touched his chest. "You slay me in other ways."

I met his gaze.

"If I lost you, death would be my only comfort. I know not if I can fully trust you yet, but time will reveal all. One day, I'll have to hunt again or else lose the respect of my men. Only the old or the infirm remain at camp with the women and children."

"You are neither." I eyed his mouth, craving the touch of those soft, full lips.

His fingers tightened about my midsection. "What do you wish, Peta? Do you still desire to return to Ronan?"

I hadn't thought of him all day, feeling a twinge of guilt. "I … I haven't fully decided."

"Then I must redouble my efforts to convince you, to sway you. I need you on my side." He touched my face. "I wish to erase all your bad memories of me. I'd make you forget everything other than what we have now."

If I remained with him, Bannon would see him as his father, never knowing Ronan. I struggled with my conscience on this issue, thinking of reasons to stay and reasons to go, the latter list growing shorter and shorter with each passing day.

"We can discuss this later, can't we?" I wrapped my arms around his neck, his arms tightening about me.

"Or you can speak to me with your lips."

I adored him like this, his eyes half-closed with passion, his manhood growing harder beneath me by the moment. Kissing him, I took all he offered and more, being the aggressor at first, until he pressed me to the pelt, a hand landing on my belly. My fingers threaded through his hair, and I waited breathlessly for what might happen next.

"Tonight," he murmured. "I shall pleasure you with my tongue."

I shivered at the thought. "If you must, my Lord."

A chuckle rumbled in his chest. "Then I'll give you my seed. You're strong enough to take it. You've surrendered to me, but I demand full compliance."

"And that is?"

"My babe in your belly." He gently kissed my stomach, the flesh distended from the full meal. "Only then will I know I've conquered you completely."

Forty-One

I watched Greggor pull back on the arrow, aiming for a hanging basket in the distance, covered in leather, the wind blowing it from side to side. He stood with his legs apart, the muscles in his back bulging with the movement, the arrow suddenly vaulting into the air, arching and embedding into the leather.

A smile stole across my face. "Well done." This had been his first attempt with the new bow, having only just completed it today.

He eyed it. "I never thought something this delicate to be so accurate. I'm in awe of the weapon. I can see the possibilities."

"I find it useful. I've killed countless game with it," I shrugged, "and a few people." He knew of what I spoke … and I would not regret it.

"I'm trying again. It might've been luck." He threaded a new arrow, letting it fly a moment later.

"Not luck." The arrow tore through the leather with such force, the target fell to the ground. "You don't need more practice, Greggor. You've mastered it already." I thought back to how long it had taken me to learn, embarrassed that it might have been a full season. He was a skilled hunter, no matter what weapon he used.

Greggor slung the sack of arrows over a shoulder. "I'll get them. I don't wish to waste them. They took long enough to make."

I thought we would be gone longer. "I'm happy to

see Bannon."

"I won't be a moment."

I watched him, waiting for him. The sunlight fell upon his shoulders, streaming through the branches, while muscled legs trod soundlessly. No longer concerned with using the new bow, his attention lingered on me.

"That came so easily to you."

"I've used a spear since I was a child. This weapon is rather simple. I fear it'll make my men lazy after I show them how to make it with better wood." He dropped the bag on the ground, resting the bow upon it. "They're wondering if I shall ever hunt with them again."

"You will."

"They think I've grown weak."

"Weak?"

His eyes drifted over me. "That I've fallen under some sort of spell."

"They do not," I giggled.

"Indeed." He reached for me. "I'm entirely distracted by you, my golden-haired witch."

"I don't keep you from hunting. You can't blame me."

"Oh, I can. I do blame you. I'd rather bed my wife than chase after stags." His lips brushed my cheek. He smelled of the sweet citrus of pine. He took my hand, leading me to a small field, the wind blowing gently through the tall grass. "We needn't rush back just yet."

"What do you propose to do now?" I hardly had to ask, knowing exactly what he intended by the heated look in his eyes. He untied my leather skirt, the garment falling to my feet. "My Lord?"

Bending at the knee, he drew me down with him, the grass surrounding us on all sides, hiding us from view. "Pleasure you beyond measure, Peta. That's what I intend." His hand drifted between my thighs, encountering wetness.

He need only look at me a certain way to send my body into fits and tingles, the anticipation of mating a force too strong to resist. I often attacked him, grasping at his broad shoulders, while wrapping my legs around him, my mouth ravaging his. I tried to do so now, but he expected it, chuckling gruffly, and turning me in his arms.

"My Lord ... " I sounded winded.

"Much work remains to be done."

"What do you mean?"

"To tame you."

"Would you prefer me more docile?"

"Not at all. I like you like this. No woman's ever been as aggressive. You lose all control at times. I like that very much." His teeth nipped at the skin on my throat.

A hand delved between my thighs, a finger stroking intimately. Being as tightly strung as I was, I feared reaching my pleasure far too soon, his touch accurate and persistent. I longed to have him inside of me. Getting to my hands and knees, I waited for him to take me, feeling the moist earth at my fingertips. When nothing happened, I glanced over my shoulder.

"Greggor?"

He beamed, a naughty gleam in his eye. "Yes, my love?"

"Why do you hesitate?"

"Because I find your rounded backside beautiful."

I backed into him, desiring something other than flowery words. "Don't wait any longer."

"Yes, mistress." Humor laced his tone. Holding my hips, he drove deep with one easy push.

His size and firmness never failed to astonish me. "Yes! Oh, please!"

"My duties never end. I've an insatiable wife."

I bit my lip, trying not to cry out, but failing. "I'll do anything—anything—just don't stop."

All humor lost now, we uttered something, but

nothing coherent emerging in the least. The fierceness of the passion brought a swift end, my body shuddering from pleasure, while he groaned raggedly, the sound carrying.

"Peta!"

Then he collapsed upon me, a weight I could not withstand, my cheek pressed to the grass. He fell to his side, scooting near. A hand gently touched my back.

"I don't know what happened," I murmured, trembling from tiny aftereffects.

"I'm going to take you again in a moment. I want to try to draw it out for once, not ... not this animal sort of mating."

I glanced at him, laughing, "Oh, my. Is it possible to make it last longer?"

He snorted. "Not with you."

"Again, you blame me for something I can't control." The warmth of the sun caressed our bodies, an insect buzzing annoyingly.

"I shall endeavor to go slowly."

"That would be ... wonderful." I leaned over him, my hand on his chest. The black lashes around his eyes appeared impossibly thick.

"Perhaps we should nap a little." He yawned.

I sighed, feeling happy for the first time since having been separated from Ronan. Resting my head against his chest, the sound of his heart lulled me to sleep.

***

We sat around the fire that night, Bannon playing with a toy, while I worked a piece of leather, scraping it repeatedly. Greggor filed the tip of a spear, the sound like rocks grinding together. In the evenings, after supper and before bed, we sat and worked like this, until Bannon needed to be fed.

"I've agreed to hunt tomorrow with Owen and the

men."

"I see."

"It's time. As much as I'd like to stay and … love my wife, I must attend to clan matters. It's important to let the men see me lead. I could use the exercise as well. I've grown soft."

I eyed him. "I disagree, my Lord."

He chuckled, "Oh, I know you do. There are some hard parts of me you enjoy quite a bit."

Lowering my gaze, I smiled at the leather in my hands.

He reached out to ruffle Bannon's hair. "You're a good boy tonight. He's not fussed too badly today."

"Shay said he had a long nap. He might be awake half the night."

"I've gotten used to sleeping half the day. Getting up with the dawn will be a challenge."

I found I preferred him with me, enjoying his company. "If you hunt with the bow, it shouldn't take all day."

"The men are used to their spears. It'll take time to make new bows. I'll have to show them which wood to use." He moved stone against stone. "There's something about hunting an animal and spearing it that brings men together. It requires everyone's participation, even those that are weak or young. They all play a part. Some kill, while others distract the animal."

"But we've enough meat from the other day."

"Most of that's gone. What could be smoked was, but the meat won't keep."

"I lived once in a hut in the woods, and we had a hole in the ground that kept things frozen. It was ingenious."

He nodded. "Yes, I've done that, but it's not cold enough here."

"I prefer it warmer."

"So do I, but that means more hunting."

"Ma … ma … mama … "

I reached for Bannon, holding him to my breast. "It's time for supper."

"Shay will bring it."

"I want to ask you about Wildre. I've been wondering about it."

"About what?"

"She's so dreadfully unhappy. You've cast her aside. I feel … a measure of guilt over this. It's my fault."

"Don't. I've every right to choose another wife. I need children of my own to rule the clan after my demise. It's a necessity." His eyes drifted over me. "But, I do want you. You're my necessity."

I thought about the evening to come. "Maybe you won't be too tired, my Lord," I murmured, feeling drawn to him—wanting him.

He set the spear aside. "I suppose *something* could be done about that."

"Thank you, my Lord."

Forty-Two

A rustling in the hut woke me, Greggor tying fur to his feet. "Go back to sleep," he whispered, his hand touching my head. "I'm sorry I woke you."

"Um … "

He stole from the shelter a short while later, the sound of men speaking outside, but … sleep soon took that away. Thinking he had returned for some reason, I felt a rough shake on my shoulder.

"Peta!"

"W-what?" I turned to see Wildre standing there. For a moment, I worried she meant harm, knowing how upset she was that I now lived with Greggor. "What is it?"

"I've come to free you."

"What?" I sat up, glancing at Bannon, the baby sleeping.

"Shay and I have packed your things. Everything's ready for you. I've dried meat and bits of leather for Bannon's diapers. There's leather for your back, to carry the baby."

Her words drifted over me, sinking in slowly.

"Everything's been arranged. Frendo's agreed to look the other way."

"You want me to … "

"It's your opportunity to escape, Peta. The men will be gone all day. They're hunting further south than before. The younger men wish to impress Greggor. He's been absent from the hunt for some time." She pursed her lips.

"You really should get up now."

"I walk away."

"Yes, like you've long expressed a desire to do. You've a man waiting for you. You've spoken often enough about Ronan. He's the baby's father after all. Now's your chance to be free. I've your weapons ready and several pelts rolled. All you need do is tie fur to your feet and leave."

I knew why she desired me gone, but my feelings were a puzzle, an odd reluctance preventing me from leaving the bed. Shay appeared in the doorway.

"What's taking so long? I've been waiting. She must put distance between them. They have to lose her tracks. She has to go now."

A knowing gleam flickered in Wildre's eyes. "The feelings you have for him will soon go away. Once you're back with your man, you won't think of us ever again. Greggor will recover from your disappearance quickly enough. He didn't hesitate to throw me away. He won't weep for you, Peta. He'll find another woman to mate with."

I frowned at that. "I ... can't leave like this."

"There's no other way," said Shay. "He won't let you go, you know that. Your family waits for you. If you stay here, you'll never see Ronan again. You'll never find your mother and sisters. If you do not wish to be reunited with your family, then, by all means, just sit there. We're giving you the chance to return to them."

Chewing on my lip, my mind spun. I had not thought of escape in a while, the desire for it oddly waning.

"You love the man who gave you that necklace," said Wildre. "That pretty rock around your neck. You never take it off. You've given the cat claws to your son to play with, but you won't give him the rock. It means something to you. This Ronan person is special. He's never met his son. If you stay here, he won't meet him—ever. Greggor will never allow it."

"Greggor will never forgive me for running away." Tears suddenly filled my eyes. "He'd be terribly angry."

"For a short while," said Wildre. "Then he'll realize you're not worth the effort of hunting down. He'll turn elsewhere for comfort."

"That's not true! He would *indeed* hunt me. He'd never stop looking until he found me. It would ruin him."

"He's not known you long enough to feel the depth of those sorts of emotions." A cold, bland expression appeared on her face. "He's already growing tired of you, if you can't see it. He's left you to hunt. The thrill of the conquest has played out. Now, he'll be with the men mostly. It's the way of things, I'm afraid."

Why did her words strike me as untrue? "I'll ... I need to think on this. He'll hunt again tomorrow morning. Let me think of—"

"But he'll sense your emotions. You're far too transparent, Peta. You wear your feeling for all to see. If you're thinking of leaving him—he'll know it. You've the benefit of surprise now. He's not suspecting it at all. He trusts you."

"Which makes this all so much worse. I'll betray him terribly. He'll be so hurt. If he finds me, he'll likely kill me rather than bring me back."

"Then it's best you go at once," said Shay. "You've the better part of the day to put distance in. By evening, when they return, you'll be far, far away."

"That boy will never know his father."

"His father's Greggor," I whispered, feeling torn and miserable.

"But you know that's not true." Wildre knelt before me, her eyes alight with sympathy. "I can see how you struggle, but can you really trust your emotions? Do you really believe you love him? These feelings stem from the newness of the relationship. It's thrilling to be with a man so virile, so compelling. He knows the effect he has on women—he knows. For him, the thrill is the hunt. You presented a challenge for a while, but you succumbed like all the rest. Your judgment is clouded at the moment. Once you've gone home to your man, you'll realize the error of your ways."

She seemed to know exactly what to say to confuse me even more, to make me question everything. I would never see Ronan or my family again if I stayed; I knew that.

"Your man's waiting for you." Shay glanced at Wildre, the women silently agreeing to something.

"Yes, he's a three day's walk from here, I believe," said Wildre. "That's far, but not too terribly far. If, for some reason, you can't find him, you know the way back. You can always return."

"To a very angry Greggor."

"He'll have found another wife by then," said Shay, shrugging.

I ran fingers through my hair, conflicted by confusion and warring thoughts. "I don't know."

"Why don't you tie fur to your feet," said Wildre. "Prepare to leave. Once you've traveled a ways, you can think on it. If this doesn't feel right, you can turn around and come back."

Shay frowned at that. "She should just go. We've wasted enough time talking to her. I thought she'd take the opportunity eagerly. There might not be another. Perhaps she doesn't love this Ronan person as she says she does. She's willing to give him up rather easily. She's not even been here that long."

Annoyed by those words, I got to my feet. "I'll go," I muttered, feeling wretched and worried, but knowing in my heart I had to leave. "I'll go."

Wildre suppressed a smile. "We've everything ready for you. I even sharpened your spear last night. All you need do is prepare yourself and the baby."

Although blinded by tears, I tied the fur to my feet, reaching for Bannon, who slept. "Will you help me get him on my back?"

"Yes, of course," said Wildre.

They made a sturdy-looking carrier, far better than the one I had. Bannon, still asleep, rested his forehead between my shoulder blades. The women escorted me from the hut, where Frendo stood outside, his attention on the lake. He did not look at me once, seemingly unaware of what happened, although I knew he knew.

"Here you are." Shay gave me the bow and the sack of arrows.

"Thank you."

I eyed the hut, a host of emotions drifting through me, the feeling of remorse so strong I nearly ran back into the shelter. I would never see it again, or Greggor. I had never felt so torn …

"Shall we escort you to the woods?" asked Shay.

"No. I can m-manage. If I … if I can't do it, you'll see me soon enough." Then another thought presented itself. What if someone waited to kill me? This seemed like a coordinated ploy to get rid of me. Could I risk such a thing?

"Goodbye, Peta," murmured Wildre. "Safe travels."

Shay smiled kindly. "May the gods be at your back. May they protect and guide you."

"Thank … you."

I began to walk, my feet so heavy, feeling like rocks had been strapped to them. Several women stared our way, although they quickly set about whatever they were doing, ignoring us. The early morning chill lingered, a cold breeze drifting over the lake. Grasping the spear, I turned for the woods, a path parting the trees.

Glancing over my shoulder, Shay and Wildre stood by the hut watching my departure, their expressions neutral.

The things they said bothered me, but some of it rang true to one degree or another. Perhaps, it *was* best to leave now before I grew even more attached to Greggor. If I stayed any longer, I would fall pregnant. There could be no doubt about that. Stepping into the trees, I gazed about warily, worried someone might try to kill me. Keeping a sharp eye out, I listened to birdcalls overhead, waiting to hear the snapping of twigs.

I walked far too slowly, every instinct within me desiring I turn around.

"If I don't leave now, I never will," I whispered. "He'll be so angry. I can't even imagine how he'll act when he returns from the hunt and finds me gone." I shuddered to imagine it. "If I go back, he'll never know I tried to escape."

But, if you don't leave now, you'll never go. You know it. You love him. It didn't take very long either. Can you imagine how you'll feel when you're pregnant? You'll never see Ronan again or your family. That man will never know his own child. You have to go, Peta.

I argued with myself, one opinion reasoning why I should stay, the other declaring the need to go. If I truly meant to escape, I had to walk faster, careful not to leave a single footprint. But, I loitered at times, deliberately breaking off a branch or scraping my foot over moist soil. By the time I stopped to feed Bannon, I knew I hadn't gone very far at all.

While the baby suckled at my breast, tears fell, dripping to his blond head. He cried then, not liking this.

"I'm sorry," I sobbed. "So sorry. What do I do? I have to decide now. If I don't walk faster, he'll find me and kill me. If I run, I might escape. I've never felt so terrible about anything."

After changing Bannon and securing him in the leather carrier, I began to walk, chewing on a piece of dried meat. My strides lengthened slowly, my arms swinging at my sides. I no longer heard the sounds of camp now, the only noise coming from woodland creatures, the forest thick and green around me. Veering from the path, I walked briskly in the direction I remembered coming, from where the dark clan had lived—where Kia and my sister had been. With any luck, I might reach it before nightfall.

Forty-Three

What began as a slow, hesitant escape soon evolved into a brisk walk, my muscles adapting to the exercise readily, but I knew I would be sore in the morning. I veered here and there, not walking a straight line, in the event someone tried to follow. Careful not to disturb the earth, I trod upon packed leaves mostly, Bannon sometimes sleeping and at other times babbling, the baby bouncing on my back.

The shadows lengthened as the day wore on, although it remained light still. After stopping to feed Bannon, we ventured out again a short while later, the smell of something foul in the air. I knew we neared Kia's camp, where the men had been slaughtered. The bodies had been left out in the open to rot, and from the smell of it, they could not be far.

Bannon slept as I approached the edge of the wood, the clearing before me where the clan had been. I pressed a piece of leather to my mouth and nose, not wanting to breathe too deeply. The corpses could not be recognized anymore, the skin having been eaten away by animals and bugs, flies buzzing everywhere, the sound resonating. I did not wish to linger, careful of where I stepped.

Seeing the carnage reminded me of the man who created it, Greggor having come through, slaughtering everyone, scattering the women and children. It was hard to imagine the man I loved committing such an atrocity, but he had. The senseless murder of so many ...

Averting my eyes, I passed the camp, hurrying into the woods to escape the smell. When Bannon woke, I searched for a place to make a fire, feeling exhausted from having walked all day, with evening rapidly approaching. I sat on the other side of a large rock, making a small fire. Bannon crawled around on a pelt, playing with the only toy I brought, my cat claw necklace.

"Here you are." I took his little hand, helping him to his feet where he wobbled, trying to balance. "You've got it."

"Ba ... ba ... ba ... " he spoke in his baby language.

I listened to the sounds of night, expecting men to crash through the foliage at any moment, Greggor arriving furious with me, ready to murder me. But this did not happen, hearing only the resonance of insects and nighttime creatures hooting in a branch somewhere. Settling in to sleep, I held Bannon close, while I cried again, the tears like an endless flood, leaving tracks down my cheeks and wetting the pelt. I wanted to make the fire bigger, so anyone passing could see it, but I hadn't done so, hiding from sight behind a large rock.

"And now we sleep," I whispered, my hand upon Bannon's back, rubbing gently. He would not be awake for much longer. "You're such a good boy. You travel well." I closed my eyes ... drifting ...

The call of some noisy bird woke me, my senses suddenly alert to danger. Sitting up, I eyed the forest keenly, seeing nothing out of the ordinary. Affixing fur to my feet, I placed Bannon into the leather pack, sliding the straps over my shoulders. Bundling the bedding, I withdrew several pieces of meat to eat on the way, having a sip of water from a bladder. Kicking dirt into the fire, I ventured from the relative safety of the boulder, my feet crunching over rocks and dried leaves.

My heart still heavy, I did feel a little better today about the decision to leave, knowing Wildre and Shay had been right. I had the element of surprise on my side, Greggor not having anticipated it. He could read me far too well, and, if I planned to escape, he would know it, preventing it. As I walked, I relived every moment we spent together, and by the time I stopped to feed Bannon, I doubted everything all over again. Later in the day, after seeing the first of the markings on the trees, I began to feel stronger, knowing I traveled in the right direction.

Resting that night, I stared at the twinkling of the sky through the branches of the trees, listening to a wolf howl in the distance. I kept the bow near me at all times, my senses aware of all noises. The howls soon drifted away, the animal moving on to hunt prey elsewhere. Closing my eyes, I slept fitfully, waking at the slightest sound. Before dawn, I gave up on sleep, bundling Bannon and setting out again, eager to be home by evening, perhaps earlier.

My thoughts kept me company, but they often brought sorrow, centering on a feeling of disappointment that Greggor hadn't come to find me. With his strength and stamina, he should have reached me by now. I should have been less careful with my footfalls … but then I chastised myself for those thoughts, because, hopefully, Ronan waited. He had never seen his son. I had to remember all the things I adored about Ronan, the man having been a part of my life since I was a child.

After feeding Bannon, we set out again, the markings leading the way. I knew where to look for them, sometimes having made them beneath branches to hide them. I stopped a while later to wash my face and hands, changing Bannon by a creek. He splashed around in the water, giggling happily.

"I know you're tired of travel. I am too. We should reach the clearing soon enough."

With that in mind, I slid him into the carrier, positioning him on my back. He fussed for a moment, not wanting to be trapped so for hours, but it could not be helped.

"Just a bit further, little one."

I glanced at the branches overhead, trying to judge the hour, thinking it to be early afternoon. Setting out, I thought of the first time I had been in these woods, being followed by an orphaned wolf. I missed Wolf, the animal meeting its end at the hands of Greggor's men. I had forgotten about that. Why was it so easy to forget his faults? He had been responsible for so many of the atrocities I had lived through, yet, I cried when I thought of him.

"Time will make it better." I had to believe that, or I would have to live with this horrible feeling of having made a dreadful mistake. "Ronan's not a mistake." As I walked, I chanted this over and over. "Ronan's not a mistake!"

By the time I reached the clearing, I felt torn between anticipation and grief. Eyeing the golden grass, I searched for any sign of cats or other predators, not desiring to encounter trouble. Bannon prattled on in his baby speak, the boy having woken from a nap. The mountains in the distance filled my vision, the cave a short walk away.

"I'm home."

It looked exactly as I remembered, a gentle wind blowing over the tall stalks, while an insect with colorful wings fluttered by. I need only cross this to reach my destination. Setting aside any misgivings—it being too late to turn around now—I stepped forward ... venturing into the future.

***

Rounding the bend past the heated pool, I smelt smoke, someone indeed occupying the cave. I had not seen anyone yet, the path leading up the side of the hill. The barking of an animal echoed then, my arrival having been noted. A man appeared at the entrance of the cavern, standing tall beneath the sunlight, his hair the color of dried grass. I felt a jolt of recognition, seeing Ronan. I swallowed the lump in my throat, a riot of emotions drifting through me. He held a spear, his eyes finding me.

"Peta?"

The dog bounded down the path, racing towards us. I worried he might attack, the animal exuberant, his tail wagging from side to side. Ronan took off then, running after him, although the animal reached us first, sniffing my feet.

"Hello there," I said gently, praying he did not sink his teeth into my ankle. I held a spear, prepared to poke him with it, if needed.

Ronan rounded a bend, emerging at once, while a man and a woman came to see the commotion, standing at the entrance of the cave. I recognized Enwan, but I had never seen the other woman before. Enwan brought a mate back with him, but this woman wasn't the same person.

"Peta?"

Tears filled my eyes. "Ronan."

"Where have you been? I've searched high and wide for you." He tossed the spear down, drawing me into his arms. "I never thought I'd see you again." Then he stiffened, having felt Bannon. "Is this my son?"

"Yes," I breathed.

A look of shock and happiness drifted over his handsome face, his blue eyes sparkling, glistening with tears. "My son."

I nodded, hardly trusting my voice. I withdrew an arm from the leather strap, pulling the baby forward. "This is Bannon."

Ronan took him, holding him awkwardly, clearly never having held a child so small before. Bannon fussed then, not recognizing who held him, his eyes filling with tears.

"He doesn't know you. He'll have to get used to you."

"My son." The cries did not bother Ronan in the least, as he held him close, his hands trembling with emotion. "I was so worried about you. I can't tell you how worried I was. I found evidence that you'd been taken. I found the bodies of three men, but you were gone."

"I killed them."

Enwan appeared, a smile on his face. "I told him you'd be back." He petted the dog. "This is Putty. He's friendly enough, but far too loud."

"My son." Ronan kissed Bannon's face, hugging him. "I've a son."

"I was forced to deliver him on my own." I wondered who the woman was, as she approached.

"This is Leota," said Enwan.

"Where's Saffron?"

"Sleeping. She's heavy with child and tired."

"You've two women now?" I giggled, happiness drifting over me in waves. Seeing Ronan thus enraptured warmed my heart.

"No, she's Ronan's."

My smile fell. "Oh."

Ronan drew me into his arms, crushing Bannon between us. "I've missed you so dreadfully, Peta. Come inside. You look like you've been walking for ages. We've much to speak about."

I nodded, inhaling the scent of him, leather and musk, his hair smelling a little of smoke. "I've missed you too."

***

Relaxing before the fire, a jubilant feeling lifted my spirits, Saffron and Enwan sitting together, while Leota sat next to them. Ronan found her while searching for me, the woman fair-haired and blue-eyed. Bondo appeared, having been hunting, carrying a small stag over his shoulders.

"Thank you, Bondo," said Ronan. "We shall eat well tonight. Enwan and I caught fish."

"That's what I smell," he said, noting my arrival. He stared at me. "Peta. You've returned." He nodded, smiling. "I'm glad. You were missed."

"I'm happy to be back." I held Bannon in my lap, having fed him. "He's ready for sleep." Ronan joined me, as the others spoke, Bondo carving up the stag to eat.

"He's perfect."

"He looks like you." I placed my son on a soft pelt, the boy clutching a furry toy. "He's tired of walking."

Ronan drew me away, taking me in his arms. "I never thought I'd see you again, Peta. You disappeared ... from the face of the land."

"I've much to tell you." We sat in the shadows of the cave, the flames flickering off the walls. "I left Bannon with Kia's clan to search for you. Some men said they saw two white men in the woods."

"You found your mother and sisters?"

"Yes, I did. I looked for you, but didn't find you. I came back to the cave and Enwan was here. He said you'd return shortly. I then hurried to Kia to get Bannon, only heathens had attacked them. They took my son!"

"By the gods," he murmured, appearing horrified. A hand fell to my shoulder, gently caressing my skin. "What happened then?"

"I went after them. I ... found Bannon in the clutches of ... Greggor."

He frowned. "That name sounds familiar."

"Yes, it should. He attacked our clan when I was a child. He's someone I hate."

"And he took our son?"

"Yes, he took him for his own."

"And you've been there all this time?"

"For a while. I … was there." I hesitated, not knowing how to proceed. "He … he wanted me to stay. He wanted me to be his wife."

"This Greggor person?"

"Yes."

"I see." He sighed deeply, eyeing me. "What's the matter? Are you worried he'll come?"

I nodded. "Yes."

"We're well hidden here."

"Not well enough."

"Were you careful to hide your tracks?"

"Yes."

He drew me near. "I care nothing for any of that. I only want you. We have to trust the gods will protect us. You've come home. It's all I've ever wanted. I thought I'd go mad missing you."

I glanced at him. "You've your own story to tell. Who's Leota?"

"I found her in my travels. I … didn't know if I'd see you again. We always said we wanted a larger clan. She's with child."

So many things had changed while I had been gone. "I see."

He kissed my cheek. "I love you, Peta. You're all I think about. I desire only you in my arms. I never wish to be parted again. We've been separated far too often as it is. I care not for the games the gods wish to play with our lives. It's not amusing in the least."

"No, it's a cruel trick mostly."

"We've won for the moment. I have you back where you belong."

"Yes," I breathed.

Epilogue

Ronan and I slept on a pelt, with Bannon nearby. I woke in the middle of the night to the sounds of mating, Enwan and Saffron moaning softly. When I drifted to sleep again, I experienced a series of dreams ... only the last one remaining in my memory, because I gasped, sitting upright, a sense of terror drifting through me. It took a moment to get my bearings, realizing I was home. I was safe. Gazing around the chamber, I saw the forms of people sleeping, hearing snores.

Sliding from the bedding, I padded over to the entrance, a wall of thorny bramble offering a barrier to the outside. Putty joined me then, the dog having perceived my motions. I ventured to the rocky ledge, the giant orb in the sky illuminating a small portion of the valley below.

Sitting here, I scanned the area, searching for the flickering of a fire or the light of men holding torches. A feeling of unease clung to me, the dream from moments before fresh in my mind. I had seen Greggor ... the man as angry as a raging god, his mouth pressed in a grim line, while fury hardened his eyes. He was somewhere in the woods with a handful of men. They searched for me ... *they came.* The instinct to run left me agitated and uneasy.

"What's the matter?" said a voice at my back.

I jumped. "Enwan," I whispered. "Go to bed. You should be sleeping."

"Why do you sit here like this?"

"I can't sleep."

"Something's troubling you." He settled in next to me, having brought a pelt with him. He draped it over our shoulders. "What's wrong?"

"The man I was with."

"Greggor?"

"I fear he comes."

"How do you know?"

"I just know. He ... he's very angry I escaped."

"Then, when he arrives, we shall kill him."

I sighed. "I ... he's not ... entirely bad."

"But he slaughters innocents."

"Men. He kills men."

"You defend him now?"

"I don't want to," I whispered miserably, tears glistening in my eyes. "I wish I didn't ... didn't feel this way."

"What are you talking about?"

"Ronan and Bannon and I must leave. We can't stay here. He'll come and ... and I don't know what he'll do."

"Ronan won't want to leave. This is his home."

"It's not safe at the moment. It's better if I'm not here when Greggor arrives. I can't imagine what he might do."

"You'll feel differently at dawn, Peta. You're tired and distraught. Anyone can see you're troubled." He put an arm around me. "You can rest easy now. You're safe here."

"But none of us are safe. I have to leave come morning. Ronan and I can't stay."

He sighed. "You've only just returned."

I feared for my friends, not wishing to bring destruction to them, although I could not be sure how Greggor would react. "I wish it wasn't so, but I'll speak to Ronan at first light. Perhaps we might only be gone a few days. We could travel across the valley and watch the cave from there. If Greggor arrives, you can tell him I've gone on. Or you can tell him you haven't seen me."

He stared into the darkness, his look inscrutable. "If you feel you must."

"Or we should all leave."

"Saffron's due to give birth soon, Peta. She's in no condition to travel."

"Bannon and I can go alone."

"Ronan wouldn't allow it."

"Then we must depart together." I shivered, feeling a chill in the air. "It's the only solution."

"Has this man ever harmed you?"

"He's killed people I know. He's stolen my son from me."

"Has he ever harmed you? Has he ever struck you or Bannon?"

"No."

"Does he have a violent nature?"

I had never seen such a thing from him, although I had observed him in battle before, his strength great. "I don't know. No. But, he's ruthless. He's trained with the spear. I ... taught him how to make a bow. He had one already, but it was poorly designed."

"I see."

"He ... took me as wife," I whispered.

"Was he cruel? Did he force you?"

I knew what he asked. "No. He was ... kind and gentle."

"Then he sounds like a reasonable man."

"He's going to be very mad. I ... hurt him. He cares for me. He wants me. He thinks of Bannon as his own."

"That's concerning."

"It's why I worry. If he finds me, he'll take me back. I don't want to see him kill Ronan or you or anyone else I love." Tears flooded. "Don't you understand that?"

"I do." His arm tightened about me. "You're in love with him."

I gasped. "No."

"You've grown attached to the man at least. You were, as you say, his wife. It took courage for you to leave. You're a strong woman, Peta. You care for those around you. Even though you hate this man, you care for him. I'd be surprised if you didn't."

"No."

He ignored that, saying, "You should speak to Ronan then. If you still feel strongly about leaving, then go. We can manage here well. Bondo's a help, and I've two women to mind, with a babe on the way. We shall wait for your return. You mustn't fear, Peta. All will be well." He squeezed me. "Yes, all will be well."

Also by Avery Kloss

Caveman
Caveman 2
Caveman 3

Clan of the Wolf
Chamber of Bears

Made in the USA
Monee, IL
22 July 2022

10160311R00177